Witness Protection

Holly Copella

To Linda Weiss

ACKNOWLEDGMENTS

Copella Books: First Paperback Edition 2015
Cover Artist: Island
SelfPubBookCovers.com/Island
Printed by CreateSpace, An Amazon.com Company

PUBLISHER'S NOTE

Chapter One

The four-passenger, Bell helicopter flew high above the city, which looked almost peaceful in the late afternoon. It was a beautiful sunny day and the flight had been smooth and tranquil. An attractive woman in her mid-twenties, Jackie Remus, piloted the small commercial helicopter. She was at home behind the stick, giving an innocent impression much like a child on her bike. Flying had been her life since before she could walk. From the time she had been legal to fly, her professional life had been perfect. Flying allowed her to escape back to a time when her father spent his free days sitting alongside her high above the world. Her memories were precious. Sadly, memories were all she had anymore. A fairly handsome man in his early forties, Governor Lyle Kempton, sat in the co-pilot's seat and enjoyed the view both inside and out. He spent almost as much time gazing at his attractive air taxi pilot as he did the panoramic view of the city below.

The second passenger, seated in the back, was a sturdy and unemotional man. Jackie didn't know what to make of Dexter Smyth. He hadn't said a word since she'd picked up the pair back at the private airfield where she worked. Lyle, or Governor, as he liked to be called, was unusually chatty and perhaps a bit too friendly. She wasn't sure if he was just enjoying the flight or stolen peeks at her cleavage.

"Tell me, Jackie," Lyle announced cheerfully. "What prompts a young woman to become a pilot?"

"What prompts anyone to become a pilot?" she replied with a look of humor.

He hid his embarrassed smile and gave her a timid look. "Was that a little sexist?"

"A little, perhaps," she replied and brushed it off without care.

Jackie had grown used to the harmless flirting of male passengers over the two years she'd worked for Titan Air. Being a military brat her entire childhood, she'd heard and seen it all. She became one of the boys at an early age, and the men in her father's platoon knew it. You didn't mess with the commander's daughter. On the other hand, being tormented mercilessly came with the territory. Jackie could take it and dish it out with the best of them.

"I didn't mean to offend you."

"I'm not offended," she replied and concentrated on her flying. "My father raised me by himself. Well, him and the rest of his platoon. So I suppose it was only natural that I chose a profession worthy of a Navy SEAL's daughter."

"That's fascinating--and a little intimidating," Lyle remarked and held back his nervous laugh. "I guess your father's a bit of a bad ass, huh?"

"He was," she announced then hesitated while shifting uncomfortably in her seat. "He, uh, died during a covert mission a few years ago."

"I'm sorry."

"Don't be. He died a hero, which is the way he always wanted to go," she said then gave a nod to the tall building roof in the near distance. "That's our building just up ahead." She was glad they'd almost reached their destination to avoid further conversation about her father's death.

The helicopter gently set down on the roof's landing pad and shut down. As expected, there was an entourage of people collected on the roof awaiting the governor's arrival. Several people from the media approached the helicopter as the governor and his assistant got out. Jackie turned on her seat in the open doorway and started her paperwork for the first half of her journey. Lyle approached her from around the front of the helicopter before the awaiting press had time to reach him. Dexter was quick to intercede and keep them back so that the governor could speak freely to his attractive pilot. The governor laid on the charm while casually standing before her where she was seated within the helicopter.

"Why don't you join us for the fundraiser at the old library?" he asked cheerfully. "We can have cocktails and get to know each other better." He extended a card with the details.

With the way he'd been ogling her the entire flight, she shouldn't have been surprised by the invite, yet somehow she was. She hid her humor to the notion of someone like her at a swanky fundraiser. She hadn't met a man yet who could get her into a dress. She was a little too proud of the fact that she hadn't been caught dead in a dress since she was five years old.

"I'm not dressed for a fundraiser," Jackie teased.

"You'll be the most beautiful woman there, I guarantee it," Lyle announced with amazing sincerity.

His charm fascinated her, but she still didn't care for the idea of some soirée with a bunch of rich and pampered elites. It wasn't the sort of place she'd fit in.

"Thanks, but I think I'll pass," Jackie said.

"Of course," he suddenly announced then grinned boyishly. "Fundraisers are boring."

Jackie smiled knowingly but didn't comment.

"Why don't you meet me at the library afterwards around nine," he suggested while maintaining his enthusiasm. "We'll grab a bite before heading back."

She wasn't sure why she considered his suggestion, but she'd have to eat at some point anyway. He was an undeniably handsome man and seemed gentlemanly. She suddenly didn't see the harm. It might even be fun.

She returned the smile and nodded. "Okay, I'll meet you at the library at nine for a late dinner."

"Great. I look forward to seeing you tonight, Jackie," Lyle announced, now beaming with delight.

As Lyle turned and left, Dexter gave her a quick once over. He grinned almost slyly, which didn't settle well with her. She suspected she wouldn't care for the man had she gotten to know him, but that look reinforced her suspicions. Something about him set her on edge, and that wasn't easy to do. Dexter joined the governor as he approached the awaiting crowd of reporters, party planners, and the mayor himself. Once the crowd was swept away and down the roof stairs, Jackie eyed the card in her hand. She smiled and nodded her approval.

"Dinner with the governor?" Jackie remarked softly aloud to herself and placed the card in her pocket. "Definitely an improvement over my last dinner date."

Her last dinner date, which she fondly referred to as 'the date from hell', was nearly four months ago with a dashingly handsome man she'd flown across several states. It was a fun afternoon of casual conversation and mild flirting. He boasted endlessly about his acting career, which didn't impress her, but it wasn't a total turnoff either. Over dinner, she discovered that his 'acting' career was actually the beginning of a promising porn film career. His biggest selling point was offering her a role in an upcoming shoot. She wasn't sure what vibe she had been transmitting prior to his announcement, but she knew what vibe she'd sent directly afterwards. She graciously declined his offer and smiled her way through dessert, but the experience was enough to swear her off men for the last four months. Dinner with the governor had to be an improvement. He was, after all, a career politician, so he had a certain image to maintain. It'd be nice to have dinner with someone respectable for a change.

Chapter Two

The slightly beat-up, yellow taxi pulled up to what was once an old mansion converted into an impressive library. There was little surrounding the stately library except a few new homes that appeared recently built and considerably dark both inside and out. It was a little before eight-thirty that evening. Jackie got out of the taxi, knowing she'd arrived too early, and took a moment to admire the structure. The building had to be over one hundred years old with detailed stone exterior and glass sunrooms added to each end in recent decades. With the painstaking restoration to the outside, she could only imagine some of the original mansion remained on the inside as well. The small parking lot and curbs were void of vehicles, announcing the fundraiser had ended some time earlier. She wasn't sad that she'd missed it. According to the card the governor had given her, it ended around eight, leaving her to wonder why he wanted to meet an hour after that. She didn't pretend to know anything about fundraisers and the lifestyles of the rich and pampered. Perhaps those things lingered on after the fact. Although, that didn't appear to be the case tonight.

From the corner of her eye, she noticed movement from a black SUV parked along the street. It seemed odd that with all the available parking directly in front of the library, the vehicle would be parked so far down the road. She hated being suspicious of people. It was usually unfounded, but she was raised by a man whose career relied on being naturally suspicious of others. She headed toward the brick library steps and kept watch of the man out of the corner of her eye as he followed behind. He caught up to her as she reached the steps. Her attention immediately shifted to him. If he was up to no good, she intended to see it coming. To her surprise, he was a neatly dressed man in his thirties. Neatly dressed didn't necessarily equal trustworthy, but, as their eyes met, she didn't see anything sinister lurking within them. In fact, he was quite appealing to the eyes. He immediately smiled as they continued up the steps toward the impressive doors.

"I think we missed the excitement," Harris announced pleasantly while keeping his eyes on her.

She held back her laugh. "I doubt that."

"You aren't here for the fundraiser?"

"No, I got roped into a date." She cringed at how much worse it sounded when she said it aloud.

His look was more puzzled than surprised by the comment. "Hmm, exciting date--" he remarked then teased while grinning, "--at a library."

Harris opened the thick, heavy door for her. She admired his chivalry and smiled her appreciation. He followed her inside. Jackie was immediately awestruck by the mansion still visible beyond the bookshelves. They were clearly standing in the living room or some formal sitting room. An old stone fireplace highlighted the room, standing out in breathtaking glory. To the left was the librarian's desk with a tall counter. Although newly added when the mansion had been converted, the desk was possibly antique with detailed woodwork. Jackie focused her attention back to the neatly dressed, seriously cute man standing alongside her.

"I'm pretty sure we're just meeting here," she informed him and smiled playfully in response to his teasing remarks.

Jackie was suddenly aware that she was flirting with this man and secretly shamed herself. She didn't usually flirt with the neatly dressed, businessman type. She was more into the rugged military type. She reeled in her playful side and attempted a more casual appearance.

"You're a little late yourself."

They stopped only a few feet into the main room. He turned to face her while casually placing his hands in his pockets. His charming smile almost certainly told her he'd sensed she was flirting with him.

Or was that wishful thinking on her behalf? Jackie again shamed herself and pushed any lustful thoughts from her mind.

"I'd heard the governor was here, so I thought I'd try to catch him," Harris replied.

"He should be here," she announced and almost laughed from the irony. "He's my exciting library date."

Harris' look nearly froze as he stared at her. He immediately covered with a forced smile, but it was already too late to mask what he was thinking. "The governor, huh?" he remarked then gently cleared his throat. "You're not exactly his usual type."

The comment surprised her. "What's his usual type?" Jackie suddenly asked.

"High priced call girls, strippers, teenagers--"

She stared at him a moment and attempted to keep her mouth from falling open. She felt an unsettling pang within her stomach. She was almost certain the annoyance showed in her eyes.

"Great," Jackie muttered.

Harris chuckled softly; almost seeming relieved by her reaction, and smiled in response. "I'll gladly give him your regrets if you'd like to bow out gracefully."

She felt hostility building within her. She was trapped in a cage with no way out. "Unfortunately I'm also his pilot, so I'm sort of committed," she remarked with disgust.

"Pilot, huh?" Harris asked with surprise then grinned almost boyishly. "That's, uh, wow, pretty sexy."

Jackie's mood immediately lightened by his tone and words. His directness was more of a turn-on than her usual repulsion in those situations. She entertained another indecent thought and immediately wondered what the hold was this man had on her.

"If you change your mind, you can wait in my car," he informed her while maintaining the smile she'd already grown to admire. "I'd be more than happy to take you to dinner when I'm finished."

Despite wanting to jump at his offer, she pulled her emotions back and kept them in check. "I don't even know you."

"You don't know the governor either," he countered.

Jackie hid her smile. Her father would like this man. Harris handed her his card and flashed a knowing smile. He was obviously convinced she intended to change her mind. As he walked away, Jackie wished she could, but her schedule was tight, and it would be impossible for her to back out of her dinner date now. She glanced at the card in her hand. It read 'Special Agent Harris Benton, Federal Bureau of Investigation'. Jackie's eyes suddenly lit, and she felt a shockwave of lust shoot through her entire body. Next to military men, she had a strong desire for law enforcement. Her attraction to this man was now explained. Her heart suddenly ached. She still couldn't change her plans. She was the governor's pilot for his return trip home. Jackie wouldn't allow her petty desires ruin her flying career with Titan Air.

"Hmm," came a woman's soft murmur from the desk area. "Pretty dreamy."

Jackie suddenly realized she wasn't alone and looked at the desk. A lean woman in her mid to late forties, Vicki, leaned on the checkout desk with her chin propped in her hand while staring after Harris. Her grin conveyed her lust for the man.

Jackie hid her embarrassment and found it amusing. "You overheard that?"

"Not that I was eavesdropping," Vicki announced and giggled as she straightened. "Sound has a way of traveling around here, especially when it's empty."

Jackie placed the card in her pocket and approached Vicki behind the counter. She looked around with admiration and quickly changed the subject. "This place is stunning."

"It used to be the governor's mansion before they moved into the city," Vicki proudly informed her. "The city wants to tear it down. Libraries are fading with the dinosaurs. The governor is fundraising to preserve it as a historical site. It's over one hundred years old, you know."

"I noticed the stone work," Jackie remarked. "That fireplace is gorgeous. I love old buildings."

"I know what you mean," Vicki agreed. "They give me the tinglies." She looked around with a dreamy smile. "These walls have seen it all." Vicki focused her attention back on Jackie. "Elite parties, births, deaths--" She raised her brows lustfully. "Juicy scandals."

"I'm sure you've heard some good stories," Jackie replied. "Anything shocking?"

"Oh," she announced dramatically, "plenty of that!" Vicki leaned on the desk and looked into Jackie's eyes while grinning. "You want something chilling? I could show you the old fruit cellar. It positively medieval. The place is so creepy, it'll give you nightmares."

As sick as the thought was, Jackie was completely fascinated by the suggestion. "I'd love too."

"Few people know about the fruit cellar," she announced slyly while walking out from behind the desk. "It's tucked away, almost like a secret room. You wouldn't believe the things old-timers speculate happened there."

"I can't wait to hear about it," Jackie announced and felt guilty for her giddiness over the macabre. At least she wasn't alone. Vicki seemed a little too enthusiastic to share the tales of horror and scandal.

Chapter Three

*J*ackie and Vicki walked down the carpeted, concrete steps into the massive sectioned basement filled with reference material and computers. Most of the basement had been renovated, leaving little behind of its creepy, basement appeal. There were several old doors that seemed to lead nowhere. Ironically, they were scattered about haphazard with almost no purpose.

"The old fruit cellar is this way," Vicki announced with enthusiasm. "You'll be one of the few to see it. I haven't told any of the current staff of my discovery." She glanced at Jackie several times as they walked. "I was afraid they'd gut it."

They walked in silence throughout several rooms with a maze of doorways. Jackie marveled at the many doorways. Some rooms had as many as four doors. A person could get lost in the basement archives. It was no wonder it was mostly reserved for staff. There was an opening oddly placed in the wall just ahead. Vicki slowed her approach and appeared surprised by the opening.

"That's odd," she remarked almost too softly for Jackie to hear. "Why is that open?"

They approached the strange, crude doorway and appeared in the opening to the fruit cellar. Both women immediately stopped at the sight within the stone room. Dexter punched Harris in the face, dropping him to his knees. Lyle casually sat on a crude, hand carved desk and watched as Dexter removed a gun with a silencer from his shoulder holster beneath his jacket. He aimed the gun at Harris' head. Vicki suddenly gasped in response, alerting them to their presence. Dexter immediately turned and fired at the women. Jackie shoved Vicki out the doorway, nearly tackling her to the floor just outside the room. The bullet hit the crude doorframe, splintering it. Harris knocked Dexter to the floor alongside him. Both men grabbed the gun and struggled for control of it. The gun fired almost silently. Harris suddenly gasped, being rendered momentarily motionless to the bullet penetrating his midsection. Dexter swiftly stood and aimed the gun at Harris, who was now on his knees while clutching his bleeding abdomen.

"What the--" the governor suddenly cried out.

The gun was kicked from Dexter's hand. Dexter turned with surprise to see Jackie standing before him. The look on her face was oddly unemotional. Jackie suddenly spun into a high roundhouse kick and nailed Dexter in the face. He was thrown into Lyle, who was in mid-lunge to stop her. Both men were thrown into the nearby stone wall with surprising force. Jackie pulled Harris to his feet and rushed him through the doorway. Dexter scrambled for his gun while crawling across the floor and fired at them from where he lie. The shot missed and struck the stone. Jackie kept a firm hand on Harris' arm and half dragged him through the maze of rooms, hoping she was heading in the right direction. One wrong turn and they'd find themselves at a dead end. With moderate pulling, Harris kept up with her, but his labored breathing was troubling to Jackie. She didn't have time to look back at him, and she feared looking back in case Dexter was behind them. To her relief, she saw the basement steps just beyond another doorway.

As she pulled Harris through the last doorway, she turned and slammed the thick door. She bolted it and hoped the old-fashioned lock, although built sturdy, would hold. As she turned, Harris was already sinking against the wall while clutching his bleeding abdomen beneath his jacket. Jackie didn't question or comment on his condition, she simply grabbed his arm and pulled him toward the carpeted steps. He stumbled and fell to his knees as they reached the steps. The door vibrated harshly behind them, alarming Jackie. She looked back at Harris on his knees and the blood seeping between his fingers. His black jacket prevented her from seeing just how much blood he was losing, but by the blood covering his hand, she knew it was a lot.

"Come on, you can make it," Jackie cried out.

"No, I can't," he gasped softly. "Go."

He handed her his car keys, bloodied from his hand, and the semiautomatic from his shoulder holster. She uncertainly accepted them. He removed a snub-nosed revolver from his ankle holster and clutched it in his blood-covered hand.

"I'll buy you some time," he grunted softly. "You'll have time to make it to my car."

"No, you can make it," she insisted firmly with tears in her eyes.

Harris gasped painfully while clutching his wound and shook his head. Jackie put his arm over her shoulder and hoisted him up despite the pain it caused him. Harris looked into her eyes not far from his eyes.

"You're very stubborn," he announced and smiled warmly. "I like that--"

Harris suddenly collapsed and took her to the floor with him. She pulled her arm out from beneath him and was about to pull him back to his feet when she looked at him where he lie. His eyes were open and his breathing had stopped. He was already dead. The door vibrated harshly, jolting her out of her trance. Jackie sprang to her feet with the gun clutched in her hand and ran up the stairs. No sooner had she disappeared up the steps, the door was thrown open with a thunderous crack and splintering wood.

Jackie ran across one of the back rooms, hoping she was heading in the right direction for the main door. She stopped when she noticed a trail of blood droplets across the otherwise clean wood floor. As she looked further ahead, the droplets turned to a streak of blood. She saw Vicki attempting to pull herself along the floor with blood trailing behind her. There was a bullet hole that had erupted through the hardwood floor. Misfortune would have it that it just happened to hit the fleeing librarian. Jackie ran for Vicki and helped her to her feet. Vicki appeared relieved to see her and clung to her bleeding hip. Her wound wasn't serious, but it had obviously caused her enough pain to keep her from walking on her own.

"It just came out of nowhere," Vicki gasped while clinging to Jackie for support. "I'm so glad to see you." Her tiny smile attempted to mask her pain.

"You're going to be okay," Jackie softly replied while hurrying her to the front room. "We just need to get you to the car."

"No," Vicki gasped softly. "I'll only slow you down. Get me to the desk. There's a cubbyhole where I can hide. You go for help."

Jackie considered her request then nodded as she hurried her across the room toward the front room and the desk. "I'll leave you the gun."

There was a gust of parting air, and the new familiar sound alarmed Jackie. Instinct told her to duck, but the blood erupting from Vicki's chest caused her to freeze momentarily. It took a second for her to realize Vicki had been shot through the back, exploding through her chest. Jackie watched with horror as Vicki collapsed to the floor, slipping from her grip. There was another gust of parting air, forcing Jackie to run for a nearby aisle of bookshelves. It wasn't until then that she felt a tremendous sting and burning from her arm. Once she reached the safety of the bookshelf, she leaned her back against the shelf and looked at the blood seeping from her arm. For a moment, the realization that she'd been shot was almost enough to send her into shock. It was either let the thought consume her and die or fight for life.

Jackie cringed from the pain then looked at Harris' gun in her hand. She allowed her head to rest against the bookshelf behind her and listened to the faint sound of someone approaching. It was the most frightening sound she'd ever imagined. War stories told by her father and his team flooded back to her. This was the moment she needed to become her father. She allowed panic to consume her for only a moment then shut her eyes, took a deep breath, and lowered herself into a crouching position. She exhaled softly and peeked out from behind the bookcase. Dexter was only a couple of feet away but didn't see her. She skillfully aimed the gun as her eyes fixed on the killer not far from her. She squeezed the trigger, firing twice, hitting him in the thigh and the arm. He leaped to the floor, possibly from pain or surprise, rolled out of her line of fire, and sat up, shooting back at her. Both shots hit the bookcase. He hadn't even bothered to aim. Jackie straightened and hurried along the safety of the bookcase.

"You idiot! Stop her," Lyle cried out. "Someone's going to hear the shots from her gun!"

"What do you think I'm doing?" Dexter demanded with hostility. "The bitch shot me!"

From her position behind the row of bookshelves, Jackie could see the sunroom just beyond a set of French doors. It was a calculated guess, but she had to hope there was another way outside through the sunroom. She knew she'd be safer closer to the wall, so she hurried along the aisle to the opposite end and peered around the corner to check their position. To her horror, Lyle was around the corner and knocked the gun from her hand. He punched her across

15

the face and sent her stumbling backward. That she didn't fall down was amazing. She appeared momentarily stunned from the tremendous pain to her cheek, but it wasn't enough to throw her off her game or keep instincts from kicking in. Almost certainly, to Lyle's surprise, she spun into a backwards roundhouse kick and nailed him in the face. He harshly struck the wall and was more than a little dazed. Years of her father's combat training came rushing back to her, and she suddenly wasn't afraid. Her survival instinct took over, and she was ready to inflict pain on this man.

Dexter suddenly appeared from the opposite end of the bookcase and fired at her. She didn't even hear the parting of air before feeling the sharp, stabbing pain in her leg. She clutched her bleeding leg and stared at the blood seeping between her fingers. For a split second, she was sure she was going to die. The next silent shot would be the 'kill' shot. Her eyes strayed across the floor to her discarded gun. Without hesitation, she threw herself into a roll across the floor toward her gun before he could fire the second, fatal round. She grabbed the discarded gun, rolled into a sitting position, and fired at Dexter without aiming. Dexter jumped behind the safety of the bookcase to the repetitive firing. Jackie limped at a jog for the nearby sunroom while clutching her bleeding leg. Somehow, she no longer felt the pain in her arm.

She entered the sunroom and saw there was an outer door on the opposite end. She picked up speed despite the pain in her leg, nearly struck the door, and bolted outside. Her leg was burning and pain was shooting up through her body and into her throat. She attempted to block the pain as she ran toward the front of the building. The library was brightly lit outside but there were only empty, newly built homes nearby. It seemed unlikely anyone lived in the homes or someone would have called the police after hearing her shots. Jackie ran as fast as her injured leg would carry her, even though it felt as if her leg would snap in two. Harris' SUV was just across the lawn and down the street from the library. She now knew why he parked so far from the front of the building. He had undoubtedly been staking out the library and didn't want to be seen by the governor.

The front door to the library opened, flooding excess light onto the already lit lawn. The additional light alerted Jackie that the front door had been opened. Without slowing down, she turned and fired at the doorway. Dexter narrowly avoided taking a shot to his head and dove back into the library. Jackie jumped into Harris' SUV, started it with a little too much vigor, and burned out onto the road, the tires squealing before rocketing away from the library. Jackie tossed the bloodied gun onto the passenger seat and fumbled with a switch on the panel. The red and blue lights flashed. She attempted to keep pressure on her bleeding leg while keeping the vehicle on the road. She couldn't understand why the road was getting increasingly darker. There was a strange tingling in her head and a loud humming in her ears. Everything was becoming increasingly blurry--

Chapter Four

A loud banging sound startled Jackie. She was having trouble opening her eyes, and she didn't know why. A stabbing pain sent shockwaves through her entire body. She wanted to scream, but nothing came out. She could hear voices shouting over her, and it was moderately frightening. She remembered flying her helicopter. Had she crashed? She struggled to open her eyes. She feared she fell asleep while flying and desperately needed to wake herself before the helicopter spun out of control. For a moment, she heard her father talking over her. Jackie finally opened her eyes, nearly blinded by the brilliant lights. There was another loud bang that jolted her body. The intense pain again shot through her. There was a tremendous burning sensation in her leg. Voices continued shouting all around her. For a brief moment, she saw men and women in white uniforms frantically running alongside her, but she was sure she wasn't running with them.

"You keep her alive! I need her alive," a man's voice shouted above the rest.

"You can't be in here," the doctor cried out. "Get out!"

Something covered her nose and mouth as a strange smell invaded her senses. She didn't know what was happening and fought the object suffocating her. She felt a strange, tingling sensation, and her entire body began to relax. All her pain subsided with welcomed relief.

†

*I*t seemed strange that Jackie didn't remember preparing her father's private, four-passenger single engine prop plane. In fact, she didn't even remember take-off. She loved take-off in prop planes. She loved the rhythmic thumping of the wheels rolling faster and faster down the runway, and then lift-off. That moment the plane felt weightless. The day was bright and the clouds sporadically placed in the blue sky like cotton balls. The sound of the engine was almost deafening, but that was part of the small plane experience. It had been a long time since she'd flown 'old Marge'. She looked at her father in the co-pilot's seat. Jackson Remus was an impressive man befitting the title, Navy SEAL Lieutenant Commander. He was tall, moderately muscular, and more than intimidating. His clean shaved, bald head added to his commanding presence.

She didn't know why it felt like such a long time since she'd last seen him. He'd been home for a few months, she was positive. She missed him so much, and she didn't even know why. They lived together. It wasn't as if she didn't see more of him lately. He caught her looking at him and smiled. He reserved his most sincere smiles for his daughter. Jackie suddenly heard a loud popping sound. Lights on the control panel began flashing and alarms were heard above the roar of the engine. She searched the control panel to find the source of their problem. As she looked alongside her, her father was no longer in the co-pilot's seat.

There was an unfamiliar man in a suit occupying the co-pilot's seat. She then realized she had seen him before, but she wasn't sure from where. He was clutching his bleeding abdomen in genuine agony. She saw the blood seeping between his fingers and covering his shirt beyond his jacket. Harris was dying! She struggled to control the plane, which now seemed to be sputtering and bucking in midair. She needed to help Harris, but if she released the control wheel, they'd spin out of control. There was suddenly a rush of air, startling her. As she looked to the co-pilot's seat, the door was open

19

and Harris was gone. Jackie screamed although no sound came from her mouth. No one could hear her!

✝

*J*ackie slowly woke what seemed only moments later to a rhythmic beeping sound. The sound was annoying, but she was sure it wasn't the sound of her alarm clock. She knew she should probably check the control panel and make sure the helicopter was functioning within normal parameters. It was hard to focus, and she couldn't find the control panel. The stick was a little soft in her hand, so she gripped it harder. She could finally see the control panel in front of her, but for some odd reason, she was lying flat on her back, possibly in a bed. It seemed odd, but she'd worry about that after she found the source of the annoying beeping sound. As she looked to her left, she saw a ruggedly handsome man in his mid-thirties slouched in the co-pilot's seat. He appeared to be asleep and had his feet propped on her seat. She couldn't understand why she didn't recognize him, but it was obviously her father. Who else would be in the co-pilot's seat of her helicopter?

"Dad?" Jackie asked in a voice she almost didn't recognize as her own.

The neatly dressed man with a day's worth of stubble on his face woke and looked at her. His feet immediately hit the floor. As her vision cleared, she felt tremendous pain throughout her body. She was now painfully aware that she was in a hospital bed, although how she'd gotten there remained a mystery. She attempted to focus on the man as he lunged for her bedside. Jackie realized this man wasn't her father and uncertainly looked around.

"Where's my father?" she asked and again looked at the handsome man.

"You didn't have any ID," the man informed her. He seemed polite but slightly anxious. "What's your name?"

"Jackie," she gasped softly as another shockwave of pain washed over her. She felt relief once it subsided and again looked at the man. "Jackie Remus."

"We'll notify your father, Jackie," the handsome man gently informed her.

She was having a difficult time remembering what she was doing last. She was almost certain she was in a hospital. Jackie could barely make out the outline of a stocky nurse in the doorway. All she could reason was that she'd crashed the helicopter. She wished someone would call her father. She hoped he was okay. If he'd been in the helicopter with her when it crashed--? Something suddenly clicked in her mind. She looked at the man again and thought he looked familiar, although somehow unfamiliar.

"The commander died years ago," she announced a little more firmly. "You were there, Monroe. What happened? Did I crash? Everything hurts."

"Yes, there was a crash," the man replied. "You were in a car accident. Do you remember that, Jackie?"

"Agent Falcone," the doctor scolded from the doorway. "I really must insist--"

Agent Holden Falcone held up a warning finger to the doctor with a threatening look then looked back at Jackie and smiled charmingly.

Jackie suddenly clutched the sheets and appeared frightened. "She's spinning, Dad," she gasped while watching the countryside whirling past the helicopter's windshield. "Take the stick!" She knew they were going to crash!

"Take the stick?" Holden questioned then looked at the doctor, who now hovered over her bed from the other side.

"She has a concussion and is heavily sedated," the doctor informed him. "Disorientation is normal."

Holden took her hand and clutched it firmly. She jerked and squeezed his hand with tremendous force.

"Jackie, Jackie, stay with me," he announced firmly.

Jackie clutched the stick and attempted to keep the helicopter from spinning, but it was no use, they were spinning out of control! Why was the stick warm and soft? She heard a man yelp. Jackie looked at the man standing alongside her and again realized she was in a hospital bed. Did she crash? As she stared at the unfamiliar man holding her hand, she wondered where Monroe had gone. Certainly, he wouldn't leave her at a time like this. She stared at the man and wondered if they'd met. She liked this man holding her hand. He was quite attractive.

"You're cute," she announced and grinned.

He fumbled slightly by the comment and attempted a smile. "Thanks." His look turned serious. "I need you to tell me about your injuries, Jackie. Tell me about the gunshot wounds and how you ended up in that SUV."

Jackie stared at him with a puzzled look. What was he talking about? She'd never been shot. She felt the same pain sweep through her body. A series of images flashed through her mind as she attempted to ride the wave of pain until it eventually subsided. She remembered someone shooting at her. She remembered a man flirting with her. She remembered blood! Her eyes widened in horror as she stared at him and tried to make sense of his comment and the images in her head.

"Was that real?"

"Jackie, tell me what happened?" he asked more firmly and with determination.

The image of Harris lying dead on the basement steps flashed through her mind and then another image of Vicki collapsing in front of her. Jackie suddenly began to sob. She couldn't control her emotions, and that wasn't like her.

"They're dead. He killed them!"

Holden firmly squeezed her hand, snapping her out of her emotional tirade. She once more focused on him as he leaned over her. The pain again rippled through her, causing her entire body to tense until it finally passed.

"Who's dead?" he demanded softly.

She couldn't think. She knew his name, but it wasn't coming to her. "His name, uh, there's a card in my pocket."

Holden looked at the doctor. The doctor opened a nearby bag, fished around, and removed a business card.

"It says Harris Benton, FBI," the doctor gently informed him while frowning.

The urgency in Holden's actions and voice was now evident. "Jackie, where did you last see Harris?"

"Harris?"

"You had his SUV. You had his pistol. Where is he?" Holden demanded firmly.

Jackie suddenly snapped out of her dazed state. It was all coming back to her in a tidal wave of horror and emotion. She stared at him with terror in her eyes.

"The library--the fundraiser," she gasped softly. "They killed him."

"Who? Who killed him?"

"The governor."

Holden appeared surprised and stared at her with a look of disbelief. Jackie suddenly clutched his hand, startling him. She stared into his eyes while attempting to retain her lucid thoughts.

"His goon, Dexter, pulled the trigger while the governor watched," she announced sternly. "They killed the librarian and tried to kill me."

Holden stared at her a moment longer then looked at the doctor and indicated Jackie. "Doc--" He released her hand, removed his cell phone, and ran from the room.

Jackie saw horrifying images of the library attack flashing through her mind. She trembled and sobbed uncontrollably. She wanted to stop acting so emotional but something was preventing her from controlling her actions. The doctor called the stocky nurse over to her bedside. The nurse carried a syringe with her and injected the needle into the port already sticking from the crook of her arm. Jackie felt a warm sensation flood through her entire body. Her pain was gone almost instantly. It was sweet relief. She flew the helicopter over lush fields and eventually to the East coast as the sun set. Jackie wished she had the time to fly over the coast more often. It was always so relaxing.

Chapter Five

*O*t was early the following morning. Jackie sat up in bed and stared blankly out the window. The drugs had nearly worn off and it was the first time she was able to piece together events from last night. Her encounter with the governor and his hired gun was something she could barely believe. She couldn't believe she'd escaped with her life. She couldn't believe that poor librarian lost hers. Jackie didn't know the woman, but she felt almost directly responsible for her death. If they hadn't gone downstairs--? Her thoughts again strayed to Harris Benton. He was destined to die no matter what they had done. Jackie then thought about her own father. No, she didn't want to think about him right now. Upsetting herself wasn't going to do her any good. The pain in her thigh was almost unbearable, and she rubbed it in response. The same stocky African-American nurse in her early sixties entered the room and noted her hand gingerly rubbing her leg.

"You want some pain killers, honey?" the nurse asked in the sweetest southern accent.

The nurse was Celia, and she'd spent a better part of the night at Jackie's bedside. Celia was a natural caregiver and did her best to make her comfortable while she drifted in and out during the night.

Her shift had to be ending soon, and Jackie was going to miss her over-the-top personality.

"No, they make me feel foggy," Jackie replied softly.

If the pills had helped numb her memories of last night, she'd gladly take them, but they almost made the visions more vivid and increased her nightmares when she did sleep.

"You poor thing," the nurse said sympathetically and leaned an elbow on her railing while facing her. "Is there anyone I can call for you?"

"No, my father died three years ago," she replied and attempted a smile. "There's really no other family."

"A friend perhaps?"

"None you'd be able to locate."

Celia straightened and conveyed sympathy with her eyes. Whatever she was thinking; she didn't say it aloud. "There's a policeman posted by your door, and some fed keeps asking to see you," the nurse informed her. "I don't know what happened to you last night, but you've got some serious attention from some pretty serious folks." She gave a general nod toward the closed door. "The doctor refused to let the fella into your room. He's cute, but he has a corn cob up his ass, if you know what I mean."

"FBI?" Her thoughts strayed to Harris, but she knew he was dead.

"Yeah, he was here when you came out of surgery," she informed her. "You spoke to him last night, but you probably don't remember. I'm pretty sure you called him Monroe, but I know that ain't his name."

Jackie attempted to recall with whom she had spoken last night, but she was drawing a blank. She gave the nurse a curious look. "Dark hair, dark eyes, sexy voice?"

"Don't forget 'corn cob up his ass'."

"Is he here?" Jackie asked and immediately shifted in her bed. "I'd like to see him."

"Of course he's here, honey," she announced while waving her hand. "Boy's been here all night bugging the shit out of us." Her look was concerning. "Are you sure you want to see him? I don't know that you're up to seeing no fed."

"Yes, it's important."

Celia reluctantly nodded, approached the door, and opened it. "Agent--"

Holden bolted past her before she could finish her sentence and immediately approached Jackie's bedside. Celia rolled her eyes with disapproval.

"I need to ask you some questions about last night," Holden announced boldly and without hesitation.

Jackie looked past him to Celia, who glared with her brow arched and her arms folded across her broad bosom. She shook her head before leaving the room. Jackie looked back at Holden.

"I'm fine, thanks for asking."

"I'm sorry if I seem rude, Miss Remus, but I need to know what happened to Harris Benton last night," Holden remarked firmly. "We found faint traces of blood at the library, but we didn't find any bodies."

Jackie felt her heart sink into her stomach. "No bodies?" she gasped with horror. "The librarian was just off the main room and the fed was in the basement at the bottom of the steps. They were right there."

He stared at her a moment and gave her a curious look. "Are you sure the agent was dead?"

She fought the urge to jump out of her bed. "Of course I'm sure," she nearly exploded.

Did he think she was stupid? She attempted to compose herself. She'd had a stressful night, and she didn't need to take it out on a federal agent.

"He gave me his gun and said he'd hold them off so I could get away, but I wouldn't leave him."

He looked puzzled. "Why not?"

Jackie wanted to explode. She couldn't believe he was asking such a stupid question but maintained her calm demeanor. "Because, Agent Falcone, no one should have to die alone," Jackie informed him.

Holden stared at her with surprise then attempted to remove all emotion. "Who killed him?"

"I thought I told you last night."

"You also thought I was your father," Holden replied. "You seem alert now, so if you don't mind--"

She found her temper oddly short this morning. It was almost as if she was speaking in code and no one understood her. She groaned softly and reluctantly gave in to repeating herself.

"Governor Lyle Kempton gave the order, and Dexter Smyth pulled the trigger." She studied him and suddenly realized what he was saying. "You really didn't find their bodies?"

"Makes murder harder to prove if you don't have a body," Holden replied matter-of-fact.

"But I saw him do it," she protested. "He shot me--twice, and I shot Dexter with Harris' gun."

Holden appeared surprised and became suddenly alert. "You killed Dexter?"

"No, but I gave him matching wounds," she replied. "Arm and leg; same as me."

Holden seemed anxious. "I need to make some calls and see if there were any gunshots reported last night."

He hurried across the room while removing his cell phone and passed Celia as she was entering. As he left the room, the nurse watched him and shook her head.

"He's lucky he's cute, or I'd put my foot up his ass," Celia muttered.

Jackie shut her eyes, drew a deep breath, and then looked at Celia as she approached. "I think I'll take you up on those drugs now."

"I'm way ahead of you, honey," Celia replied as she removed a bottle of pills from her pocket and gave them a vigorous shake. "After dealing with that boy half the night, I may need some of these myself."

Chapter Six

It was later that same morning. Jackie now sat in the chair alongside the bed wearing a borrowed scrub uniform. She had no clothes so Celia found something for her to wear, hoping it would help cheer her up. She possibly felt sorry for Jackie because she'd been shot and didn't have a single visitor to comfort her. Jackie's situation was complex and nearly impossible to explain why she didn't want anyone notified of her condition. Jackie stared out the window at nothing in particular. Despite the excess amount of drugs now in her system, she still couldn't get her mind off last night's horror show. The doctor had removed her IV lines earlier, since she was doing well, but she still appeared fairly bruised and battered. Some of her injuries were sustained in the car crash that followed the library attack. Despite Celia's shift having ended an hour earlier, the older nurse found every excuse to hang around and keep Jackie company. She sat on the side of Jackie's bed and stared out the window along with her.

"So who's this Monroe?" Celia asked, breaking the silence. "Is he someone I could call to come keep you company? I don't feel right leaving you here all shot up and alone."

Jackie looked at Celia and smiled. She was truly darling, but she didn't need anyone keeping her company. "Monroe was an old friend from a long time ago," she replied reluctantly knowing Celia wasn't going to let it go if she didn't give her something. "I doubt he even remembers me."

"Oh, come now," Celia announced boldly. "What man breathing could forget a pretty girl like you?"

"Honestly, Celia, I never had much time for friends or a love interest," she replied gently. "I moved around from military base to military base across the entire globe. Making friends seemed pointless. After my father died, I dedicated most of my time toward my career." She drew a deep breath and looked into Celia's sympathetic eyes. "When I fly, I feel my father is with me. In the sky is where I'm happiest."

"I understand, honey," the nurse replied with a knowing smile. "I feel the same way about church. God is the only one who gets me. Took my husband and my son from me way too soon, but I've made my peace with him."

"You're more forgiving than I am," Jackie said softly while attempting a smile.

Celia patted Jackie's lower arm. "You know what you need? You need some frozen yogurt," she announced while standing.

Jackie laughed softly at the woman's enthusiasm. "A little early for that, don't you think?"

"Honey, it ain't never too early for frozen yogurt," she announced cheerfully and extended her hand to her. "The walk will do you good."

"Really?" Jackie asked with enthusiasm. "I'd love to get out of this room."

She accepted Celia's hand and allowed her to help her up from the chair. Her leg was sore and stiff. Bearing weight was extremely painful, but she didn't mind. Her short, supervised trips to the bathroom had quickly become boring. The opportunity for a real walk sounded too good to be true. She clung to Celia's arm and allowed the nurse to escort her to the door. As they stepped into the doorway, the officer at the door stopped them.

"I'm sorry," he announced firmly. "I can't allow you to leave the room."

Celia appeared nearly as stunned as Jackie was. "On whose authority," Celia suddenly bellowed.

"Agent Falcone gave specific orders," the officer replied. "You'll have to take it up with him."

"I'll take my foot up his ass," Celia groused. "Now move yourself before you get the same."

"That's threatening a police officer, ma'am," he calmly replied. "Would you care to reconsider that last statement?"

Before Celia could speak, Jackie tugged on her arm. "It's okay, Celia," she said gently. "Don't get into any trouble on my account. I'm sure Agent Falcone has his reasons. I'll be fine. You should probably go home anyway."

"Not until I get you some frozen yogurt," she announced and guided Jackie back to her chair. She helped her sit and straightened. "You just relax, and I'll be back in a jiff." Celia hurried for the door, gave the officer a stern sneer, and then left.

Jackie returned to staring out the window, once again at nothing. Only a few minutes had passed when she heard a familiar male voice at the door. She looked up as Holden entered the room. Jackie angrily bolted up from her chair despite the shooting pain through her leg.

"What's with the officer outside my door?" she suddenly exploded with rage and hostility she'd cleverly kept hidden from Celia. If she had let the nurse know it bothered her, she'd undoubtedly lose her job. She'd already ruined enough lives for one week. "He says I can't leave my room! He won't tell me why, but he says it's on your orders!"

Holden abruptly stopped his approach, appeared surprised by her burst of hostility, and held his hands up defensively. "The officer is for your protection, Jackie. I'm investigating the possible murder of a federal agent, and you're either my star witness or my prime suspect."

His words nearly floored her. "What the fuck is wrong with you?" she cried out. "They were going to execute him! I did everything I could to save him!"

"I guess they took you off the happy pills," Holden muttered under his breath.

"I'm the one who had to watch Harris Benton die, Agent Falcone," she lashed out hotly. "My father taught me to never leave our men behind. Where were you when your man was dying? Where was his backup?"

Holden seemed stunned by the scathing remark. He again held his hands up defensively and attempted to remain calm and soothing to her explosive temper.

"I'm sorry, I didn't mean to accuse you of killing Agent Benton," he replied gently and lowered his hands. "I'd just like to ask you a few more questions. Please--"

Jackie slowly returned to her chair and cringed with discomfort. She was in agonizing pain now, but she didn't want to let him know, since it had been her own doing jumping up as she did. Jackie gently rubbed her thigh then glared at him.

"Did you see Dexter's injuries?" she asked. "That should be enough to corroborate my story."

He appeared slightly uncomfortable and fidgeted. "The governor and Dexter are out of the country on business. They left last night after the fundraiser."

Jackie was stunned by the comment. "How? I was supposed to fly them back."

"Your boss said they called him to report you weren't at the departure location, so he sent out another pilot to bring them back," Holden replied.

She didn't know why she was surprised, but she was. "Take me to the library," Jackie said gruffly. "I'll walk you through the entire evening. There has to be bullet holes to corroborate my story. You'll believe me then."

"I don't think your doctor--" Holden began.

"I don't give a shit what the doctor says," she launched back. "You have authority, don't you? Use it!"

She'd caught him off guard and rendered him speechless. He turned to leave and nearly collided with Celia, who stood in the room with two cups of frozen yogurt. Her mouth hung open with surprise as she watched him leave the room. She looked at Jackie with a stunned look on her face.

"Damn, girl!"

Chapter Seven

*A*s Jackie limped through the doors of the library with use of a borrowed cane, pain shot through her leg and straight into her throat. Her arm was just mostly sore and gave her little trouble, which seemed odd. She wore a black FBI jacket over her borrowed scrub uniform. Thankfully, she was able to wear her own black boots. They were casual with a low heel. Even with the low heel, they were causing discomfort to her injured leg. The fact that they were black hid the traces of blood staining them. Sadly, the blood on them had been more than just her blood. Despite Holden's tough fed persona, he remained close by her side and lent a hand when she became unsteady. She would have found it endearing or possibly comical if she hadn't been feeling anxiety about returning to the library.

Jackie and Holden were accompanied by two women from the forensics unit, a local police officer, and Agent Fields, Holden's partner at the bureau. Agent Fields was at least ten years older than Holden. He was relatively fit for a middle-aged man, but Jackie figured most federal agents were required to remain in shape. Despite Fields being older than Holden, it appeared as if Holden was the senior agent of the pair. It was her opinion that Fields was better at taking orders than giving them. He didn't have the same commanding presence as Holden. She likened Holden to the men in her father's platoon. No matter what their rank, every one of them owned a room when they walked into it. Even in the general population, Jackie could spot a former Navy SEAL from twenty feet away. The six made their way slowly through the main room and entered the adjoining room where Vicki had died instantly from the bullet penetrating her back and undoubtedly directly through her heart.

"This is where Dexter shot Vicki in the back as we tried to escape," Jackie informed Holden as the forensic team followed them to the location she indicated.

Jackie had little difficulty pointing out the exact spot where the librarian collapsed on the floor. All that remained was an excessively clean spot on the hardwood floor. She had to admit, the governor went to great lengths to clean the place in a short period of time, but he had to know forensics would be able to extract traces of blood deep within the wood. The forensics team was already picking up traces with their black lights. She then retraced hers and Vicki's steps just a few feet to where the bullet had come through the floor, initially tearing into the woman's hip. The floor had been patched and wood putty filled the hole. The putty hadn't completely dried, and one of the forensic scientists was easily able to dig out the soft putty to expose the hole.

"After the librarian was killed, I ran into that room," she announced and indicated the adjoining room just off the sunroom. "That's when I got into a physical altercation with Dexter and the governor."

"I've never met Dexter Smyth," Agent Fields remarked while studying her, "but I hear he's pretty intimidating. You actually held your own against him in a fistfight?"

"Not really a fistfight," Jackie replied. "I don't hit so much as kick. Considering the company I kept while growing up, I wouldn't consider Dexter intimidating. More like a bully with a gun. He's not really a skilled fighter."

Jackie guided them to the next room over. Fields and Holden exchanged looks and raised eyebrows.

"She's one tough girl," Fields muttered.

"To survive what happened here last night, she'd have to be," Holden replied then followed Jackie.

As they continued through the back room attached to the sunroom, the pain in Jackie's leg was nearly excruciating. She had wished she'd taken Celia up on the offer of an additional dose of oxycodone, but she didn't want to show weakness in front of Agent

Falcone. She wanted him to realize she was strong and could tolerate the pain even if she secretly couldn't. She didn't know why she had to be so stubborn. Definitely a trait passed down from her father that she abhorred. Finding the bullet holes in the bookshelves was an easy task. They'd used the same putty to fill in the holes, which was nearly a shade off. Finding one bullet they'd missed would give further credit to her story, but they weren't having that sort of luck. Jackie had a difficult time pinpointing where Dexter may have lost blood. She knew she shot him twice, but they couldn't seem to find any residue, even with their special lights.

Tackling the basement steps was near agonizing for Jackie. She felt as if her leg would break under her own weight and each step caused her indescribable pain. She finally stopped halfway, feeling exhausted and nauseous. Despite her protests, Holden placed her arm over his shoulder and supported most of her weight down the last few steps. When they reached the bottom, she found it difficult to release him. She fought the urge to vomit, though she desperately wanted to. Her head was now pounding in rhythm with the stabbing pain in her thigh, and she felt oddly weak. It was hard to believe she'd managed to escape with her injuries last night, but those same injuries were unbearable not twenty-four hours later.

"That's where Harris died," she said weakly, indicating the floor while making an effort to release Holden.

He allowed her to pull away just near the railing, which she immediately clung to for support. Forensics was able to find traces of blood beneath the carpet in the porous concrete. Although only speckled, it covered a large area. Holden turned away, seemingly showing no emotion, and stared across the room at nothing. Jackie had seen that look before. It was silent rage. Holden was a ticking time bomb. For the first time, he was probably admitting to himself that one of his own had actually been killed. Agent Fields gave him space, possibly not wanting to be too close in case he did explode. As forensics scoured the room for any traces of bullet holes, Jackie led Agent Fields and the local policeman in the general direction of the fruit cellar toward the back of the basement. Holden was mysteriously absent. Jackie paused by the solid wall where she was certain there had been an opening. Confusion swept over her. She knew she hadn't been wrong. There was a stone room. She had been in it. It was where Dexter shot Harris. Fields and the officer stared at her with the same puzzled look.

"This place is a maze of rooms and doors," Agent Fields announced and casually looked around. "Are you sure it wasn't one of the other doorways?"

"No, it was here," Jackie protested firmly. "The fruit cellar entrance was right here. I'd swear--"

Holden finally joined them and stared at the solid wall with no visible doorway. He looked back at her and raised his brow in question.

"So where is it?" Holden demanded with increasing hostility, almost as if he stopped believing everything she'd told him due to this one setback.

As she stared at the wall, images of last night continued to fill her head. Vicki's words returned to her. She looked at Holden.

"Vicki said it was a secret passageway, hidden away," Jackie informed him. "She'd stumbled upon it."

Holden didn't seem convinced. "Looks like a pretty solid wall to me."

"I'm telling you," she nearly exploded. "The fruit cellar is beyond this wall. He probably stashed their bodies inside. Open this wall, and you'll find both of them."

"That should be a fun court order to get," Holden scoffed. "Judges are funny about giving permission to knock holes in walls of historic buildings."

"I know I'm not asking," Fields muttered.

"There has to be a way to open it," Jackie protested. "If Vicki found it--"

She looked around the wall itself while deep in thought. The officer smirked and looked at her as if she were crazy. Holden ran his fingers through his hair and avoided looking at her. He obviously wasn't happy with her or was just miserable in general after seeing where Harris died.

"It would have to be a trigger as old as the building itself," she muttered more to herself while scanning the surrounding area for any visible release.

Jackie started pushing on individual stones, but all seemed secure and solid. Holden glanced around with limited patience then stared at a slightly smaller, lighter colored stone near the ceiling. He reluctantly pushed on the stone. A section of stone grinded away from the wall. Agent Fields and the police officer jumped with surprise, not expecting the wall to move. No one was more surprised than Holden. He moved Jackie away from the small opening, removed his gun, and gently pulled the jagged looking doorway open to reveal total darkness. Agent Fields and the officer removed their weapons as well and stepped in front of Jackie, keeping her behind them. Holden removed a flashlight from his pocket, shined it around the room, and then felt the wall.

A light flickered and brightened the room. As Holden, Fields, and the officer entered, Jackie stepped in behind them. The room was exactly how Jackie remembered it from last night. To her surprise, there weren't any bodies. Harris' blood remained on the floor where he'd been shot, and she easily noticed the bullet hole in the wall just inside the entrance. They hadn't bothered cleaning up evidence within the fruit cellar, possibly thinking they'd never find it, but Jackie just couldn't believe the bodies weren't there. Holden frowned and replaced his gun to his shoulder holster.

"Well," he said with a deep sigh, "so much for hiding the bodies in the fruit cellar. He must have loaded them into a car and disposed of them elsewhere."

"A little risky, don't you think?" she asked and leaned against the wall for support. Her leg was causing her serious pain now. "He couldn't have known I'd wreck the car. He didn't know he had that kind of time."

"Then he called others to assist," Holden informed her. "The bodies obviously aren't here. We have Harris' blood, bullet casings, and a bullet in the wall over there." He looked back at Jackie. "We have more than enough evidence to back your version of what happened last night."

"I suspect we won't catch up with the governor or Dexter until his injures have healed," Fields announced.

"I'm sure Dexter is smart enough to have ditched the gun someplace where we'll never find it to match the bullets we'd recovered," Holden added.

Jackie studied Holden and drifted off into her own world. Holden stared at her a long moment in silence. She snapped out of her trance when he finally spoke.

"Without the bodies, what little physical evidence we have won't put either away--especially implicating the governor in murder," Holden informed her then drew a deep breath. "We might get lucky with Dexter, if his scars match where you say you'd shot him." There was an uncomfortable silence. "Your testimony is all we have, Jackie. The only thing getting them a murder conviction is your account of what went down. I don't think I have to tell you what position you're already in."

Jackie allowed her eyes to stray to the stained blood on the floor. The entire scene played out in her mind like a horror movie on an endless loop. Jackie was still stunned at what she had gone through and witnessed just last night. She knew she tried to save Harris, but she'd been a second too late.

"I knew him maybe five minutes--" she said softly while staring at the bloodstain on the floor.

Holden appeared puzzled. "Excuse me?"

"Agent Benton," she announced and met Holden's gaze. "I only knew him for five minutes, but I liked him."

"He was a good man," Agent Fields interjected softly.

"I really don't see what choice I have," she announced proudly. "I need to testify. The governor and Dexter need to pay for what they did."

Holden fidgeted slightly and drew a deep breath while staring into her eyes. "Thank you."

Chapter Eight

*O*ne week later. Jackie sat in the large conference room within the federal building. She alternated rocking in the leather chair and resting her chin on her arms across the table. She was bored and the officer standing just inside the room by the closed door wasn't much for conversation. He was young and appeared to be operating according to the official police rulebook. Perhaps if he hadn't been so serious, she wouldn't mind her incarceration nearly as much. Jackie heard arguing voices just outside the conference room and immediately sat up straight, becoming alert. She easily recognized Holden's voice, as it was dominant. She was actually surprised she'd remembered his voice. She hadn't seen him since their visit to the library the day after the killings.

Of course, that may have had something to do with her recovery being spent at the state hospital in lockdown. She had to admit, Holden placing her in a high security mental institution was ingenious, but she couldn't say she enjoyed her accommodations. She had spent the week on an empty floor with special, government trained doctors, nurses, and guards. The company wasn't bad, but she found it difficult to sleep knowing there were criminally insane killers on the floors beneath her. The possibility that she'd be forgotten and left there to rot had also occurred to her on more than one occasion. Paranoia and boredom often went hand in hand. As the arguing voices outside the door trailed off, her enthusiasm faded. She again rocked in her comfortable chair and glanced at the young officer standing guard.

"I've been here two hours," Jackie groaned lowly. "I think rigor mortis is setting in."

The officer offered her a sympathetic smile for the first time. He then seemed aware of his own aching body, having stood the entire two hours. He shifted uncomfortably. The arguing was again heard and the door finally opened. Jackie was ready to jump out of her chair. She needed to stretch her legs and perhaps breathe some fresh air. The entire week of confinement was killing her! Holden and two U.S. Marshals, Phil and Carter, entered the room. She'd briefly met the two, middle-aged Marshals that morning. They were a little too straight for her liking. Phil had thinning, light brown hair and more of a youthful face. He was lean, but almost certainly built athletic. Carter had a little more girth to his stature. To her, he was possibly former military, but he almost seemed too much of a pretty boy. Of course, she'd met a few 'pretty boys' who were Navy SEALs as well. Looking like James Bond only toughened them more. No SEAL wanted to be told he was a pretty boy, even if it were true. The customary beating usually followed after that sort of comment.

Holden approached Jackie at the table. She wasn't sure why, but she was oddly enthusiastic to see him. He actually looked good to her. Not that she didn't think he was attractive when she'd first met him, but he did have that dry, federal agent personality. Smiling wasn't high on their list of priorities. Still, she was happy to see him. The situation now was different from when they were last thrust together after the murders. It gave her a chance to admire him for the handsome man he was and even entertain a wayward sexual thought or two. Holden paused before her chair and met her gaze with his own, serious look.

"U.S. Marshals will be in charge of protecting you until the trial," he informed her.

That was it? Not even an insincere 'hey'? As she stared at him, she began to wonder why she had been so glad to see him and if he could be a bigger prick.

"Good morning to you too, Agent Falcone," she retorted while folding her arms across her chest.

Celia had been right about the corncob up his classified posterior. Holden needed to work on his delightful personality. On the bright side, she was no longer entertaining any sexual fantasies involving him. He'd successfully turned her off in one failed swoop. Her snarling comment took him by surprise. He managed a tiny smile and reluctantly played along.

"Good morning, Jackie."

"That's better," she replied and folded her hands across her lap. "Please tell me you come with good news."

His charming disposition was short-lived and it was back to business as usual. "Well, on the bright side, you're being sprung from your padded cell, but it's all downhill from there." He sat on the edge of the desk near her and retained his serious look. "I'm not going to lie to you, Jackie, you're on the governor's hit list at this point whether you testify or not. Protective custody is your only option."

He didn't have to tell her, she was already aware of her situation. If she hadn't been, her weeklong vacation at the insane asylum was enough to tell her she was in trouble.

"Right before Harris died, he looked at me and smiled," she informed Holden. "If I let them get away with killing him, that smile will haunt me forever." Her look was serious. "Nothing will stop me from testifying."

"You don't know how much that means to me," Holden replied with a more sincere smile.

Jackie drew a deep breath and asked the question she feared. "How long until the trial?"

"We haven't officially charged either yet," Carter announced as he casually sat across the table from her. "We're still trying to locate the governor and his assistant, but it's going to be at least two to twelve months."

She suddenly shot a glare at Carter as her mouth fell open. "It's been a week," Jackie scoffed and attempted to control her rising temper. "How can you not locate a prominent figure like the governor?"

"All we know is he's still overseas somewhere," Phil announced in a tone meant to soothe her increasing hostility. He failed. "The CIA has been trying to track him down in France, where his passport indicated he had visited last." Phil then glared at Holden. "But certain federal agents--"

Holden immediately stood, turned toward Phil, and glared at him. "I've been more than cooperative with the CIA," he snapped lowly and indicated Jackie with a firmly pointing finger. "You know damned well I should be in charge of protecting this witness. Agent Benton was one of ours--not yours."

40

"Protecting witnesses falls under U.S. Marshals' jurisdiction, Agent Falcone," Carter suddenly interjected from across the table. "You're free to leave this meeting anytime." He pointed toward the guard behind him. "The door is right behind you."

Jackie could no longer control her temper, and the 'boys acting like boys' mentality was wearing thin. "Maybe if you boys stopped comparing gun calibers, you'd be able to do your jobs!"

Her outburst was enough to silence all three. Phil and Carter exchanged looks, as if wondering what they'd gotten themselves into with the seemingly innocent young woman.

"She's a little tenacious," Holden casually informed them while holding back his laugh. He placed his card on the table before Jackie. "If you need anything--call." He then looked at Phil and Carter and hid his smile. "She's all yours. Enjoy, Gentlemen."

As Holden turned to leave, Carter reached across the table for the card. Jackie slammed her hand on the card and glared at Carter. Holden glanced back. Jackie took the card and stuck it down her shirt. Holden chuckled and left the room.

Chapter Nine

It was three weeks later, which translated into three weeks of Jackie's two to twelve month prison sentence. The charming, two-story log cabin style lake house had multilevel decks overlooking the massive, picturesque lake surrounded by woodlands. For a prison, it wasn't without its charm. The impressive dock had a small speedboat attached alongside it. It was mostly used for trips to the general store on the opposing side of the lake. There was also a local's bar somewhere near the store, not that Jackie was allowed to go to the bar; or the store; or in the boat; or on the lake. The sun was setting, giving the lake a romantic glow; not that Jackie was allowed outside on the deck. With the thick woods all around, most of the homes along the lake maintained privacy, so it didn't appear as if there was another living soul around for miles. Seclusion was why the U.S. Marshals chose that particular house. Although it didn't look it, there were multiple security sensors surrounding the house. Unfortunately, the silent alarm was set off several times a day by woodland wildlife.

The first floor of the lake house contained an open floor plan with a large living room and modern kitchen, accented by a massive stone fireplace. An open staircase spiraled alongside the fireplace leading to the second floor's interior balcony. There were several rooms on the open, second floor and a second, spiral iron staircase that led to the kitchen. The second floor was specifically designed with multiple escape routes. Jackie, Carter, and Phil sat at the sturdy, rustic kitchen table playing a relatively friendly game of poker. Each had a card stuck to their forehead with the face value exposed. Jackie placed her cards down and grinned. She'd won yet another hand. Both men groaned, tossed their cards down with disgust, and removed the extra card from their foreheads. Jackie scooped her winnings toward her.

"You're going to owe me your pensions at this rate," she announced and hid her mocking smile. "At least make it a little sporting."

"Maybe if you'd stop cheating," Carter mumbled under his breath.

Jackie eyed him sharply. She didn't cheat! Although, she could if she wanted too. The two marshals weren't the best poker players and probably wouldn't even notice if she had stacked the deck. But being they were bad players, there really wasn't a need to cheat. The third U.S. Marshal, Pam, sat by the kitchen door while flipping through a magazine. She was obviously bored and possibly read the same magazine several times. Pam wasn't unattractive, but she had that certain prudish appeal about her, which made her seem older than a woman in her early forties. Jackie suspected the woman felt superior to her fellow colleagues. She acted more like their overly strict mother and didn't seem to appreciate either man making the best of their situation.

"You've been playing poker for three weeks straight," Pam scoffed in response to Jackie's comment without looking up from her magazine.

"What else is there to do?" Jackie asked, growing tired of the woman's constant nagging.

Jackie suspected the female marshal was secretly jealous of her bonding with the men. Truth be known, Jackie had always been more comfortable around men. She rarely spent time with women growing up. Despite the number of female soldiers on the various bases where she lived, there never seemed to be that many in her immediate circle. She barely remembered her own mother and her father never brought any women around, so women were almost foreign to her.

"You won't let me on the lake," Jackie informed her while attempting not to sound as if she were whining but it was difficult to achieve. She felt like whining. "Beating the boys at poker is all I have."

Pam finally glanced up from her magazine and gave her a scolding look. "I wish you wouldn't encourage them, Jackie," she remarked firmly.

Jackie didn't think she was a bad influence, and she felt almost offended that the prudish woman tried to make her feel she was. Despite knowing it was wrong purposely to push the woman's buttons, Jackie looked around the table and smiled enthusiastically at both men.

"Who's up for strip poker?"

Phil and Carter chuckled in response and hid their matching grins. Pam scolded them with a look. They immediately fidgeted and attempted to behave. Mother wasn't amused.

"Where did you learn to play poker?" Phil asked as he passed the cards to Jackie, being her turn to shuffle.

"My father's Navy buddies were always over playing poker between missions," she casually announced while skillfully shuffling the cards. "Men who specialize in killing people with their bare hands don't like losing at poker to little girls."

Both men laughed. Pam frowned and continued to flip through her magazine with added irritation. Jackie dealt the cards and allowed her boredom to surface.

"Can we do something tomorrow?" Jackie asked in a slightly whiny voice. She was already bored out of her mind. "I can't look at these walls for another two to twelve months." She mentally rolled her eyes and snorted a soft laugh. "Ironic, I'm the one who got the prison sentence."

"You know the rules, Jackie," Carter informed her with some sympathy. "Early morning run around the lake then you're inside the rest of the day."

It wasn't as if they weren't equally bored, but at least their tour of duty would be ending soon, and they would get to go home to their loved ones. Jackie would continue to rot in her lakeside paradise.

"I already have cabin fever," she announced firmly and picked up her cards with disgust. "If you don't want me going crazy and taking you guys with me, we'll need to find something more physical to do inside."

Phil and Carter eyed her from above their cards and grinned. Their snickers drew her attention to the devious looks they wore. Jackie groaned and rolled her eyes.

"Not sex, you perverts," she scoffed.

Jackie was getting tired of sitting around all day with nothing better to do than listen to Pam degrade the male marshals; Phil complaining about his teenage son; and Carter sharing intimate details of his marital problems with his sexually lethargic wife.

Pam was almost heard cringing with annoyance. "I hope our relief shows up before sexual harassment charges are filed," she muttered.

Jackie didn't bother looking at her. She couldn't bear to see her prudish, pinched lips again. "If I'm here long enough, the guys might file them against me," Jackie remarked then tossed her cards down and groaned. "Come on; one swim," she begged. "I'll even agree to skinny-dipping. Just let me go in the lake."

Carter looked up and was about to speak when Pam tossed down her magazine and glared at them.

"No lake! No nudity!"

Jackie turned to Phil with a serious look on her face. "Your girlfriend is a real buzz kill."

Carter chuckled in his throat. Pam's cell phone suddenly chirped like a chipmunk sending out Morse code. It was an awful sound, but at least it was moderately faint. Pam looked at the caller ID and immediately rolled her eyes. She reluctantly answered the phone with no warmth.

"Yeah--?" There was a slight pause as the caller spoke. "We're fine. She's an absolute angel," Pam scoffed under her breath. There was another pause. Pam's eyes shifted to Jackie as the caller spoke. She didn't appear pleased. "No, I don't think so."

Jackie looked at Pam and immediately became excited at the prospect that someone actually wanted to talk to her. "Is it for me? Who is it?" she asked while jumping from her seat. "I'll talk to anyone."

"It's Agent Falcone," Pam muttered.

"The other kill joy," Jackie announced to 'her boys' and lunged for the phone. She took the phone and grinned while speaking into it. "Hi, babe, how's it hanging?"

"Hey, Jackie, it's Agent Falcone. I'm coming up with the replacement marshals," Holden replied from the other end. "Do you need anything?"

"Good poker players," she casually replied. "The competition is getting a little stale."

"I'll see what I can do," he responded and didn't even seem fazed by the request.

"Will you be hanging with us?" she asked and cast a look at Phil and Carter while grinning.

"I'm not exactly welcome," Holden replied with little emotion. "Something about not playing well with others. They'll probably let me stay a day or two."

"Hmm, forty-eight hours," she cooed into the phone. "We can get into some serious trouble in that time. Don't forget your handcuffs."

There was an awkward pause. Jackie knew she blindsided him with that comment. She could almost hear him blushing through the phone.

He was heard gently clearing his throat and spoke with a slightly crackling voice. "Anything else?"

"No, I suppose not," she replied with a depressed sigh. "I need to go. They're about to start the orgy without me. Love you, babe."

Jackie made a kissing sound into the phone and disconnected the call. She handed the cell phone back to Pam, who glared her disapproval. Jackie smiled and winked at her. She returned to the table and collapsed into her chair while frowning. Carter and Phil watched her and appeared equally humored.

"I love the way you handle him," Carter said with a throaty laugh. "Those feds can be real pricks."

"Especially Agent Falcone," Phil interjected. "There's a man who needs to get laid."

"Well, I'll do what I can," Jackie informed them with a bored sigh, "but I doubt he'll give it up willingly. He's a bit of a Boy Scout, you know."

Pam's chair scraped the floor as she abruptly stood. No one had to look at her to know she was annoyed.

"I've had enough," Pam scoffed. "I'm making rounds early. I'll keep my transmitter turned on."

Pam touched her left ear containing a small, barely seen ear transmitter so she could maintain radio contact with the other marshals. She left through the nearby kitchen door, shutting it securely behind her with added aggression. Jackie was always glad when Pam made rounds. She didn't like her hanging around and ruining their bad behavior.

Jackie gave both men serious looks. "Next time we have a sleep over, don't invite her."

Both men laughed softly.

"I hear you," Carter muttered.

Both men glanced over their cards, appeared disgusted, and folded simultaneously. Jackie tossed her cards down as well, groaned softly, and stood.

"I hate to take your money and run, but it's nearly seven and way past my bedtime," she informed them. "Night, boys. Give Pam a kiss for me."

"Good night, Jackie."

Jackie headed across the massive living room for the elegant stairs to the second floor and listlessly climbed them. She entered the second room, shut the door behind her, and approached the window on the opposite end. She opened the curtains to reveal the stained glass window with bars built directly into the glass. There was a small clear glass opening, which was approximately two inches, for her to gaze out onto the lake.

"Nothing like a cage with a view," she muttered and closed the curtains with disgust.

She approached the queen-sized bed and tossed herself onto the multi-colored bedspread with a loud sigh. She stared at the ceiling and watched the ceiling fan gently spin above her. For nearly twenty-one evenings, she watched a cobweb dangle from the spinning fan blade. One day, she intended to climb up there and remove it. Evenings were mind numbing, well, more so than during the day. She'd spent hours each night thinking about the new life she'd accepted. It wasn't easy convincing herself it would all be worth it after the trial, but she continued to repeat it silently in her head every night before bed. One hundred times, if necessary. 'It'll be worth it putting the governor behind bars.' Truth be told, if she had a gun and the governor before her, she'd probably shoot him just to end her suffering.

"Oh, Dad," she whispered softly. "I wish you were here to tell me what to do."

As she stared at the ceiling, all she could think about was her father. If he were alive, she'd be safe. He'd whisk her away to a place where the governor and his goon would never find her. He always felt he had to be her protector, even when she didn't need or want him to be. Her subconscious mind overtook her, and she drifted back into a happier time. At least it seemed that way on the surface.

†

*T*hree years earlier. Jackson had just finished his inspection of the four-passenger, prop plane. The elegant name painted on the side read, 'Old Marge'. Jackie silently crept up behind her father.

He tossed the clipboard onto the co-pilot's seat, seemingly unaware of her stealthy approach. She jumped on his back while clinging to his neck from behind. Jackson grunted from the sudden impact and additional weight but made no effort to defend himself against his would-be attacker.

"You're getting slow in your old age," Jackie teased with her head on his shoulder while hanging off his back.

Jackson laughed, patted her arm around his neck, and cast a slight look at her face near his.

"Lucky for you, you're not nearly as stealth as you'd like to believe you are," he remarked.

She kissed his cheek with added drama and jumped off his back. Jackie maintained her humored look as he turned to face her. "Don't even pretend you saw me coming."

"Princess, I saw you sneaking around the field the last five minutes," he informed her.

Princess wasn't the term of endearment most would believe it to be. When the commander called his daughter 'princess', it was a rub the same as calling his hard-core Navy SEAL comrades 'ladies'. It was meant to offend her, and it usually did. Jackie was far from a princess.

"Sure you did," she scoffed then smirked.

"If I hadn't, you'd be scraping your hide off the tarmac," he announced while grinning.

There was probably some truth to that, and Jackie was very aware of the consequences that came with sneaking up on the commander. Fortunately, while in a non-combat role, he rarely drew his weapon. Although none was seen on him, he undoubtedly had one tucked away somewhere. Jackie looked over the old prop plane with approval then back at her father.

"What's with 'old Marge'?" she asked of the plane on the tarmac before them. "I thought you retired her after you trusted me enough not to crash."

"If you'd bothered to read my note at home on the frig, you'd know I'm giving a flying lesson this afternoon," he replied matter-of-fact.

"I read your note," she announced then casually shrugged. "Just not all of it. Your penmanship sucks. I stopped at, "I'll be at the airfield--" She gave him a quizzical look. "Since when do you give flying lessons?"

"Just a favor to one of my former military buddies," he informed her.

Jackie's eyes lit up. "Oh?" she quickly asked with enthusiasm. "Which one?"

She always enjoyed spending time with her father's military buddies. Obviously, some more than others, but she enjoyed their visits between missions. In six months, her father would finally retire from the military, and they'd have plenty of time to spend together. On the down side, she wasn't sure how often she'd see the rest of the team after that. Some had joked that they too would retire after he did. The team had survived a long time together. To her, they were all family.

"Abbott," he replied.

"Abbott?" she questioned, considered the name, and then realized she'd met him several times briefly, but he hadn't been with the commander's team very long. He was discharged almost a year ago, so she hadn't seen him in a while. "Oh, yeah, I remember him. The party guy. Bad poker player; bluffs a lot. Can't handle Tequila."

Jackson chuckled. "That's Abbott. I'm flying him out to that old, abandoned airfield for his first lesson. I probably won't be back until dinnertime."

"Can I come along?"

Her father considered it a moment and appeared uncertain. "Well, that depends if he minds. I don't want him to feel nervous his first time flying."

"I don't make people nervous," she pouted.

"No, but you're distracting," Jackson replied firmly. "He may not want to be distracted."

A ruggedly built man in his late thirties approached them, saw Jackie, and grinned cheerfully. "Two Remus' for the price of one! How did I get so lucky?" Abbott pulled Jackie into his arms and hugged her long and lovingly. He pulled back just far enough to take her in. "You've grown!"

"It hasn't been that long," Jackie teased then admired his unusual ring. "Is this new?" she asked and indicated the ring he wore on his right ring finger.

"Well, sort of," he replied with a chuckle. "That's my Purple Heart. You could say it's my good luck charm. I had it melted down and made into a ring after my discharge."

Her father seemed to disapprove but didn't comment. Abbott grinned cheerfully and placed his arm around her shoulder.

"Did I ever tell you how I received that Purple Heart?" Abbott asked.

She shook her head while studying him with great interest as her father rolled his eyes. Abbott chuckled at Jackson's reaction to the comment and released Jackie.

"It was on one of those classified covert missions we're not allowed to talk about. Your father saved my life after I'd been severely wounded by enemy fire."

"Must we rehash war stories in front of my daughter?" Jackson remarked.

"Who better?" Abbott announced cheerfully.

Jackie hugged her father and smiled proudly. "I never get tired of hearing about your heroic acts, Dad."

Her father returned the embrace while seemingly embarrassed and kissed her on the forehead.

Chapter Ten

*J*ackie woke from her light sleep with a startled gasp and stared at the ceiling fan rotating lazily above her. It took her a long moment to realize she was still lying on top of the quilted bedspread in the safe house bedroom. Faint sounds from the lake could be heard through the sealed windows. She uncertainly looked around the room with some disorientation and realized she must have inadvertently fallen asleep. She hadn't been sleeping well since the murders at the library, and when she did, they were usually nightmares involving Dexter and the governor. Some nights, she didn't survive the experience. On rare occasions, she managed to save either Vicki or Harris, although, usually never both. The dream she just had about her father disturbed her more than she'd ever admit. Although she loved being able to see her father in her dreams, the reminder that he was dead when she woke was almost too much to bear. It was as if she'd lost him all over again each time she woke. She placed her hand to her forehead and held back her sobs.

†

51

*O*t was nearly half an hour since Jackie went to her room for the night, and Pam had gone outside to make rounds. Carter picked up the scattered cards and chips, stacking them neatly, while Phil peered outside through the kitchen door window. He couldn't hide the concerned look on his face. He touched his earpiece transmitter and spoke aloud.

"Pam?"

There was no response through his transmitter. Phil frowned and looked at Carter with possible concern for their fellow U.S. Marshal.

"I hate when she doesn't answer me," Phil scoffed as he became further agitated and worried.

"She's probably just cooling off," Carter remarked while stacking the chips in the plastic tray. "You were a little hard on her this evening."

Phil was surprised by the comment and stared at his partner. "Me? I'm pretty sure you were the ringleader."

He snorted a soft laugh. "She'll probably report us for having a good time with Jackie."

"I don't like this," Phil announced, again staring out the window. He shook his head while looking at Carter and appeared serious. "I'm making the call."

As Phil removed his cell phone and pressed a button, Carter removed his gun and hurried across the living room for the second floor stairs. Phil became alert when someone picked up the phone on the other end.

"It's Phil," he announced into his cell phone. "Pam went outside almost thirty minutes ago and isn't responding on her transmitter. I'm going to check on her." There was a moment's pause. Phil nodded. "Yeah, Carter's heading upstairs to watch her. I'll call you back in five."

Phil shut his phone, removed his gun, and headed outside. There were few outside lights on by design, leaving the exterior dimly lit, mostly from the moon shining off the lake. Sounds of wildlife from the area surrounding the lake were almost deafening. There were no other sounds. Phil cautiously walked along the deck while keeping his back partially to the wall and his gun lowered near his hip. The last thing they needed was a lookie loo taking a stroll and reporting a man with a gun sneaking around one of the cabins. There was still no sound other than that coming from the lake and woods. If Pam was patrolling, her footfalls should be heard along the wooden deck. At the very least, there should have been sounds coming from her transmitter. Turning it on while patrolling was by the book, as was Pam. If something had happened, she would have given them some sort of signal. Had she been unable to respond, they would have heard something through her transmitter. As he approached the rear deck, he could see Pam sitting on one of the deck chairs with her back to him, facing the lake. Phil groaned softly and relaxed while lowering his gun as he approached.

"Damn it, Pam," he said gruffly and paused alongside her chair by the railing. "You gave us a scare. Why the hell didn't you respond to my calls?"

†

*J*ackie lie reclined on top of the multi-colored bedspread in her tank top and sleep shorts while reading a book. It was a steamy romance novel, which she borrowed from Pam. With some of the love scenes, she was surprised it was something Pam would even consider reading. Having never read a romance, Jackie was convinced they were sappy love stories for desperate women with no prospects of ever finding a man. Instead, she found the story was actually captivating, judging by the tingling sensation it sent throughout her body. As she read the next paragraph, her mouth fell open with surprise.

"Oh, wow," she moaned softly and quickly turned the page. As she read, her hand covered her mouth and a slight gasp escaped. "She's one naughty girl."

Her bedroom door abruptly opened without warning, causing her to jump. She instinctively shoved the book under the bedspread as she sat up. She wasn't permitted to lock the doors, but none of the men had ever busted into her room unannounced before. Mild panic pulsated through her body. She watched as Carter hurried across the room with his gun in hand, approached the window, and looked through the small, clear pane.

"What is it?" she asked with concern.

"Pam's not answering," he replied without looking at her and continued to scan outside through the small opening. "Nothing to worry about just yet. Just a precaution."

His words didn't comfort her. Jackie hurriedly slipped into her jeans, sweatshirt, and shoes then quietly sat on the bed. She watched Carter and attempted to listen for any unusual sounds. When Carter

53

didn't notice anything outside, he returned to the bedroom door and touched his earpiece.

"Phil? Anything?" He awaited a response, but there wasn't one. "Phil? Do you copy?"

Again, there was no response. The look on Carter's face was enough to send shivers down Jackie's spine. Carter hesitated only a moment then looked at Jackie. She didn't like what she saw in his eyes.

"We're going--now."

Jackie sprang from the bed and quickly joined him by the bedroom door. She'd played enough paintball battles with her father to know the drill. She needed to remain glued to Carter and be the eyes in the back of his head. Carter peered outside the bedroom door, making certain the area was secure, and then motioned for her to follow him. Jackie shadowed him and kept watch behind them. She understood the concept to the open floor plan of the lake house and the open railing to the studio below. From their vantage point, they could view the entire first floor. There was no sign of either marshal. Carter and Jackie hurried down the open stairs to the main room. He made certain nothing moved before hurrying her to the front door.

Carter looked through the peek hole and studied the area carefully before quietly unbolting the door. He again looked around outside then hurried Jackie to the SUV. They moved against the vehicle while keeping low. He wasn't taking any chances, and Jackie felt confident in his abilities. Carter wasn't the most serious man during their poker games, but he was certainly field ready when called upon. There was a gust of air that immediately sent chills through Jackie. She'd heard that sound before at the library. Carter gasped, clutched his side, and struck the SUV. He immediately fired in the direction of the silenced shot. Jackie instinctively ducked and got a closer view of his wound. It wasn't caused by your average handgun. This was a much larger weapon. He'd been lucky it'd only grazed his side. A direct hit would have torn him apart. Another shot hit the car, leaving a large hole in the metal. Carter threw open the passenger side door and aggressively motioned to her.

"In!"

Jackie jumped into the SUV and leaped into the driver's seat, allowing room for the marshal. Carter jumped in after her, handed her the keys, and slammed the door. Jackie started the SUV, threw it into gear, and burned out on the gravel driveway. She didn't know where she was going, but she intended to make record time. The front tire suddenly blew and the vehicle swerved wildly, turning the SUV toward the lake and away from the back road. Jackie attempted to control the vehicle while Carter clutched his bleeding side.

"Don't stop for anything!"

"You don't have to worry about that," Jackie announced with panic in her voice.

The windshield suddenly chipped, startling her. Jackie let out a scream and attempted to keep the SUV going straight after jerking the wheel. She looked at Carter alongside her for further instructions. He was slumped in the seat with blood streaking his face. As his head jolted, she saw the right side of his skull had been blown from his head and out the passenger side window. Panic flooded her only a moment before she returned to attempting to steer the SUV away from the lake house and the lake itself. What sounded like an explosion was actually the rear tire blowing from another shot meant to cripple the vehicle. The SUV suddenly pulled right. She fought the jerking steering wheel to retain control, but it was too late. The lake was suddenly in front of her. Jackie screamed.

The SUV with two flat tires on the passenger side veered into the lake alongside the dock. The front of the vehicle sank into the water halfway up the driver's side door. The gunman, dressed entirely in black, quickly approached the partially submerged door and yanked it open. Jackie sat facing the door with Carter's gun in her hand and aimed at him. She fired twice shooting him with both rounds in the chest. The shooter fell into the water with a splash. Jackie jumped into the water, hurried around the car with Carter's gun clutched in her hand, and ran from the lake for the nearby dock. Gusts of air flew past her as dirt exploded near her feet. She bolted toward the dark area beneath the cabin's deck and the safety of darkness. Jackie fired blindly behind her without even looking and tripped over something in the darkness just before the deck. She fell roughly to the ground and flipped onto her back.

She saw Pam's lifeless body lying broken, having fallen or been thrown from the upper deck. Closer inspection revealed a small hole through her left ear. She'd been shot with precision through the transmitter in her ear. Jackie held back her horrified gasp and scrambled over Pam's body just within the darkness beneath the deck. There were no shots fired, so she knew she was no longer visible to the shooter, but that didn't mean he wouldn't be closing in fast. She looked at Pam's body just in the edge of the deck's shadow. Jackie needed her cell phone. As she leaned forward to check her pockets, she realized the bullet that had gone through her left ear had exited out the right side of her head, taking most of her skull with it.

Jackie fought the nauseous feeling in her stomach and avoided looking at Pam's remaining hollowed out skull. She quickly searched her jacket pockets and removed the cell phone. Jackie pressed a single button then looked around while shivering from the cool night air chilling her soaked body.

"Yeah, Pam," came Holden's voice void of enthusiasm from the other end.

Jackie whispered into the cell phone, "They're dead. He's here!"

"Jackie?" Holden was heard gasping. "I'm on my way. Find a place to hide."

"There is no place to hide," she whispered with panic in her voice.

There was a gust of air followed by splintered wood from the support beam near her head. Jackie randomly fired back in the direction of the shot.

"Who's firing?" Holden suddenly yelled from the other end.

"Who the hell to do you think?" Jackie cried into the phone, no longer attempting to keep her voice down. She'd already been made, so it no longer mattered.

Jackie shoved the phone into her pocket, removed Pam's gun from her shoulder holster, and fired wildly while running for the boat attached to the dock. The wood on the dock splintered behind her running feet. Jackie dove into the boat and fired randomly while untying it from the dock. Silent shots were fired back, striking the water disturbingly close to the boat. Jackie crouched alongside the driver's seat, threw the boat into gear, and fired back at the shooter while speeding away. She maintained speed for several minutes until she was safely out of view of the cabin and nearly to the other side of the lake. Jackie stopped the boat a safe distance from any homes and conducted a quick search of the boat. She found a tackle box, searched through it, and removed a fishing knife. She stared at the knife a moment then recovered Pam's cell phone and pressed the same button. It barely rang before Holden answered.

"Jackie? Are you okay? Where are you?" Holden gasped from the other end.

"Carter and Pam are dead," she informed him while looking around the secluded lake. There was a house in the near distance with one light on inside. It appeared to be the only house around. "I don't know what happened to Phil. I shot one of them, but it wasn't Dexter."

"Listen carefully, Jackie," Holden said from the other end while attempting to sound calm. "The local sheriff will be there any minute. I'm about thirty minutes away." She could hear the sound of his vehicle's siren. "Where are you?"

"I'm in a boat on the lake," she replied and again looked to the nearby house. "There's a house not far from here with an old boathouse next to the dock."

"I know exactly where you are," he announced from the other end. "I'm coming for you, Jackie. I just need you to hold on, okay?"

Jackie drew a deep breath and looked at the knife in her hand. She nodded even though he couldn't see it. "Okay," she replied softly.

Jackie disconnected the call, placed the phone in her pocket, and then drove the boat closer to the boathouse with as little sound as possible. She cut the engine alongside the dock, using the boathouse to keep anyone within the house from seeing her. She looked at the knife in her hand, took a deep breath, and dragged the blade across her forearm. Jackie gasped with agony from the stinging sensation as she self-induced an inch long cut, which bled freely. Jackie dropped the knife while clutching her arm and took several deep breaths. She recovered the bloodied knife, placed it in her pocket, and ran her hand across the blood on her arm. She carefully dragged a bloody handprint along the outside of the boat. Jackie jumped onto the dock, tossed one of the guns into the boat, and put it in gear. She sent the boat across the lake then removed the second gun and fired twice into the air. Jackie turned and ran into the woods as the house lights came on.

Chapter Eleven

*J*ackie shivered from her still damp clothing as she walked through the woods parallel with the dark, back road. She carefully wiped her blood and fingerprints from the knife, using her damp sweatshirt. Luckily, her sweatshirt was dark, so the blood wouldn't be visible once she reached a populated area. Once she was convinced the knife contained no traces of her DNA, she tossed it into the woods. Even if someone eventually found it, without seeing any visible blood, she doubted they'd think anything of the find. She had no idea where she was, but she knew the road had to lead somewhere. She knew for a fact she was heading away from the lake house almost certainly crawling with police by now. She'd been walking nearly thirty minutes before she saw lights through the wooded area. As she approached, she discovered it was the local tavern, tucked away within the woods, and packed with mostly pick-up trucks. There were two things she was counting on being so far from civilization. Country boys leaving their pick-up trucks unlocked and, more importantly, the boys forgetting their cell phones inside their unlocked pick-up trucks.

Jackie hurried across the parking lot and looked into several trucks. Going inside the tavern wasn't an option. Her damp clothing would cause unwanted attention. After the third truck, she discovered what she needed most at that moment. She opened the passenger side door and removed a cell phone from the cup holder. She hurried to the side of the tavern, hiding within the shadows, and pressed several numbers. Despite having Pam's cell phone, she couldn't use it to make any 'private' calls. She didn't need the FBI learning she was still alive, but more importantly, she didn't need them knowing whom she had called. She shivered, feeling colder than she had before, now that she had stopped walking. She attempted to control her chattering teeth as the phone rang relentlessly. Soon the voicemail would pick up, and leaving a message wasn't an option. She saw Holden's SUV fly past with its lights flashing. He'd been right on time. Now that she was standing in a clearing, she could hear the sirens on the other side of the lake.

Someone picked up the other line. "Hello?" came the puzzled, male voice.

Jackie had never been so happy to hear a familiar voice in her life. She nearly jumped while clinging to the phone. "Monroe, it's Jackie," she announced a little too quickly and with more urgency than she was attempting to convey.

"Jackie!" The male voice belonging to Monroe was overly enthusiastic. "You better be calling to say you've finally decide to run away with me."

She wanted to melt into his voice, but her fear took hold. "I'm in trouble, Monroe. Real trouble," Jackie said in a tone she knew he'd pick up on. She kept her back to the tavern wall and looked around as if expecting someone to jump out at her at any moment. "I need someone I can trust--someone smart."

There was a strange silence. "Are you okay?" Monroe suddenly demanded with a sense of urgency. "What do you need? Where are you?"

She nervously looked around. "I'm in a town called Harmony Lake outside a bar, Harmony Lake Tavern. Do you know anyone near here?"

"I know someone everywhere," he informed her. "Give me a second to look." She could hear the clicking of his fingers tapping feverishly on a laptop keyboard. The typing continued as he spoke. "I have a guy about twenty minutes from Harmony Lake. What do you need?"

"I need an exit and a change of clothes," she said and felt relief for the first time in over an hour.

"Give me a minute. Don't hang up."

"I won't."

There were several clicks as he put her on hold then silence. Jackie looked around and shivered. The cold, damp clothes against her skin was becoming unbearable. More clicks were heard as he came back on the line.

"His name is Bogart," Monroe informed her over the phone. "He'll be there in fifteen minutes and flash the headlights so you know it's him."

"Bogart?" She knew she wasn't in any condition to question Monroe's judgment in acquaintances at the moment, but it slipped out.

"He's not someone you'd take home to mother, but I trust him," he replied, answering her silent question. "He'll take you wherever you want to go. I'd come and get you myself, but I'm, well, indisposed."

With Monroe, that could mean just about anything. The last thing she wanted was for him to attempt to reach her. She had to move and couldn't wait that long, especially if he was where she thought he was.

"Monroe, I need to vanish," she informed him firmly and with seriousness.

There was another strange silence.

"I can't get back into the country for at least two days," he announced with the disgust evident in his voice. "Most of my best contacts are going to be hard to reach. I'll have to find less ethical contacts for you. I know people who can help, but you're going to need money."

"I can get money."

"Call me when you're safe," he informed her. "I'll have your next contact by then. With any luck, we can meet up at Casa d'Monroe in a few days."

She knew that was code for his house on an island just off the coast of Florida. "Thanks, Monroe." She hesitated then said softy, "You know I love you."

"I know," came the gentle reply. "Stay safe."

Jackie disconnected the call, wiped her prints from the phone, and tossed it alongside the building. She took a moment to wipe the tears from her eyes then hurried back to the safety of the dark woods.

t

*H*olden stood on the dock by the boathouse alongside the portly, country sheriff. Both watched as the small speedboat was towed toward the dock. The bloody handprint on the boat's side was clearly visible. Holden held his breath, shut his eyes, and shook his head with obvious disgust.

"A couple in the house heard gunshots," the sheriff announced then nodded toward the boat on the lake as it approached them. "They saw the boat slowing across the lake with no one inside." He eyed the bloody handprint and frowned as well. "Looks like someone went overboard."

"I need fingerprints," Holden announced firmly while scanning the approaching boat and the blood in particular. "I want to know whose blood that is on the side, and I'll need divers in this section of the lake."

"Divers? Do you know where you are?" the sheriff suddenly demanded. "You're in the middle of backwoods nowhere. Fingerprints we can do. Divers ain't exactly common around these parts. Nothing to see much under there but lawn chairs and beer bottles."

"I'll make some phone calls," Holden announced with limited patience. "Just get some boats with lights out there for now. If she's floating around alive out there, I want her found. If she's dead, I want her brought back to life."

The sheriff gave him a dumbfounded look. He wasn't winning any points with the country cop. Holden removed his cell phone and pressed 'Pam' on the call screen. The phone immediately went to voicemail. He frowned and disconnected the call. As some local fishermen tied the boat to the dock, Holden scanned the interior. He leaped into the boat and picked up Pam's gun by the barrel with his fingertips. He smelled the gun and appeared curious. He looked around while in thought, catching the attention of the sheriff as he ordered his men to search the area with boats. He finally looked at Holden.

"Something curious?"

He didn't look at the sheriff but instead stared at the boat. He shook his head while remaining distant. "This is one of the U.S. Marshal's guns. She must have had this on her, but it wasn't fired," he announced more to himself. He studied the gun a moment longer. "In fact, the safety is still on."

"Maybe she didn't know how to switch off the safety," the sheriff remarked.

Holden looked at the sheriff and snorted a laugh. "Trust me; she knows how to operate a firearm." He shook his head while remaining deep in thought. "She'd managed to elude several trained killers and even took one out with a marshal's gun, yet this gun wasn't fired. That means she had a second gun at some point. How would a resourceful young woman like that *with* a loaded gun be ambushed in a boat in the middle of a lake? Something doesn't seem right."

Holden looked toward the woods. The sheriff stared at his profile with a look void of intelligence. Holden turned back toward the sheriff and appeared curious.

"How far of a walk is it to that country tavern?"

"Twenty maybe thirty minutes," the sheriff replied. "Depending on how thirsty you are, I suppose. What? You honestly think she survived an attack like that and decided to go grab herself a beer at the tavern?"

Holden inhaled deeply and scratched his brow. It was obvious the country cops in the small, tourist town weren't hired according to their IQ.

Chapter Twelve

*J*ackie remained hidden within the woods and closely watched the tavern while huddled by the base of a large tree. A newer truck pulled up to the tavern. It no sooner stopped when the headlights flashed. Jackie felt a rush of relief that Monroe's contact had arrived. A ruggedly handsome country boy in his late twenties, Bogart, got out of the truck and leaned casually against the hood while looking around with the appearance of disinterest. She straightened alongside her tree, realizing her legs had stiffened considerably, when Holden's vehicle pulled up to the tavern. Jackie tensed with alarm and watched the federal agent. Her heart immediately pounded. She didn't dare move in fear he might see her hiding in the shadows. Holden walked past Bogart and headed inside the noisy tavern. Bogart casually watched him until he disappeared inside then opened the passenger door of his truck without even looking at her. Had Bogart seen her? It didn't matter; that was her cue. Jackie darted from the woods and jumped into the truck. Bogart casually shut the door behind her, rounded the truck, and didn't even acknowledge her as he got inside. He started the truck and drove away from the tavern and Agent Falcone.

Jackie shivered while clinging to her chilled arms. She was relieved they were safely on their way, putting distance between both the feds and the governor's men. Bogart barely eyed her, turned the heat on, and then nodded to the backseat.

"Clothes are in the duffle bag."

Bogart wasn't much for conversation, and he certainly didn't seem the curious type.

"Thanks."

Jackie climbed into the back and opened the bag. The thought of dry clothes was more important than the notion of changing in the backseat with possible prying eyes. She'd save modesty for another day.

"Ironic that our mutual friend failed to mention you were attractive," Bogart remarked simply.

She didn't bother looking at him. "Probably because talk like that got his ass kicked."

Bogart grinned in response. Jackie removed her wet clothes as quickly as possible and slipped into the dry ones. Bogart casually tilted the rearview mirror for a better view of the PG-13 show in the backseat.

"Where are we going?" he asked and finally minded the road. "Monroe was vague as usual."

"I need to get home to Vernon Heights."

"Vernon Heights?" he suddenly asked and glanced at her through the mirror. "That's six hours away."

"Take me as far as you can," she announced. "I'll manage the rest of the way."

"That's not the deal, sweetheart," he said firmly. "Monroe said to take you where you needed to go." Bogart groaned softly, smirked, and tilted his head. "So we're going to Vernon Heights." He was silent a moment then appeared curious. "Was the fed looking for you?"

She looked at him through the rearview mirror from her position in the back. "You knew he was a fed?"

"The stench of arrogance and the signature suits are a dead giveaway."

Jackie climbed back into the front, passenger seat and belted herself in. At least changing into dry clothing made her a little more comfortable, but the horror of what happened at the lake house still haunted her.

Bogart indicated the cut on her arm with a nod. "There's a first aid kit under the seat."

Jackie removed the first aid kit from under the seat and cleaned the cut on her forearm. It stung more than she thought it would. Considering she'd been shot just last month, she didn't think a little cut would hurt as much in comparison.

"Fed do that?"

She snorted a soft laugh. "No, that was self-inflicted. I needed a diversion."

"Hmm, classic," he said with a charming grin. "If you were looking to fake your own death, I hope you remembered to wipe your prints off the weapon."

"Yeah, I did."

"Sexy and smart." He glanced at her and appeared curious. "Did you ice someone?"

"The other way around," she replied. "If that fed catches me, he's going to put me back into protective custody. I may as well be sitting in a kill box."

"You need to disappear."

She groaned softly and rested her head against the seat. "It's on my 'to do' list."

"Well, if anyone can make you disappear, it's Monroe."

"That's what I'm counting on."

✝

It was a little after one in the morning. The duo had been on the road nearly four hours with another two hours remaining on their journey. Jackie feared falling asleep. Despite the fact that the governor's men couldn't possibly track her at the moment, she just couldn't shake the nagging feeling that someone was following them. She finally curled into the corner of the passenger seat and shut her eyes only for a moment. She barely heard Bogart say something about needing coffee. When her eyes opened, she saw the out-of-the-way diner with a few pick-up trucks parked outside. She was alone in Bogart's truck. Jackie suddenly straightened and felt alarm rush through her. What if Bogart wasn't trustworthy? Could he be selling her out? No, Monroe trusted him, and that was good enough for her. She shifted in her seat and double-checked the gun neatly tucked down the back of her pants. She felt safer knowing it was still there. When the truck door opened, Jackie jumped with surprise and felt her hand go for the hidden gun. Bogart climbed in and handed her a cup of coffee and a muffin. She didn't think she was hungry, but her stomach disagreed the moment she saw the fresh muffin.

"Saw you on the news," Bogart teased while grinning. "*Tourist disappears on Lake Harmony.*"

She cocked her head and stared at him with some surprise. "They didn't mention me by name?"

"Sweetheart, I don't even know your name, and I'd like to keep it that way," he informed her. "I don't need the feds crawling up my ass with a microscope. They don't need added reason to come after my ass."

"Why would he withhold my name?" she questioned aloud although more to herself. "If the governor thinks I'm dead, he'll stop hunting me."

"Who's to say," Bogart replied and started the truck. "Those feds are a crafty bunch of bastards. They do everything for a reason. Even when they take a piss it's by the book." He suddenly grinned and appeared pleased with himself. "Probably why they've never caught me. I don't play by no book."

Despite their limited conversation on their four-hour journey, Jackie was getting a pretty good read on Bogart. He played a dumb hick, but he was smart--borderline genius smart. She'd met plenty of men like him in her father's platoon and around the base. He was excessively charming when he needed to be, but she was almost positive he'd turn into a rattlesnake if provoked. She found it odd she liked him. As they pulled onto the main road, he became somewhat chatty. The added caffeine may have helped.

"Another two hours and we'll be entering Vernon Heights," he announced. "I'll be needing directions to your place."

"It's easy to find," she replied.

"You know, if either fellas following you suspect you're alive, they'll be watching your house," Bogart informed her and raised his brows. "Could be dangerous showing up at your own place like that."

"I'm a little smarter than I look," she replied. "I'll case the place before I go inside."

He chuckled softly. "Someone sure raised you right," Bogart said then eyed her several times while driving. "I may have to stick around just to see how this all plays out."

"I've already taken up enough of your time," she replied and sipped her coffee. "I couldn't ask you to do that."

"It's not like I have any place else to be," he retorted. "I'm sort of freelance at the moment."

She eyed him and held back her smile. "Freelance *what?*"

Bogart glanced at her and chuckled at the comment. "That's classified, sweetheart."

"Can I assume you've cased a place before?" she asked with a teasing look.

"I'm offended you'd even ask." He alternated looking at her and the road. "I've been breaking the rules since I was in kindergarten," he announced proudly.

"It could be dangerous just being caught in my company," she reluctantly informed him then frowned at the thought.

Bogart eyed her lustfully. "If you're trying to turn me on, it's working."

Jackie couldn't help but smile at his lust for danger but avoided looking at him. She wasn't playing that game. Although she didn't doubt he was amazing in bed, casual sex wasn't really her thing, and this wasn't the time or place. As silence overtook them, she allowed the events of the night play out in her mind. She fought the tears welling in her eyes. She kept thinking about Pam, Phil, and Carter. Their families were going to be devastated. It was troubling that three highly trained U.S. Marshals were taken out so easily. How the governor's men even found them was a mystery to her. It didn't seem possible. How far was the governor's reach? The thought frightened her.

✝

Jackie's split-level home was nestled in a quiet development with other charming homes in what would be considered an upper middle class neighborhood. Despite her absence, the yard was well manicured. The home appeared to be in excellent condition, and it was obvious someone had been tending to the yard and garden on her behalf. It was after three in the morning and streetlights dimly lit the small development. The homes remained fairly dark as most of the residents were asleep, which worked to their advantage. Bogart's truck was parked two homes away along the curb. There were few vehicles parked on the street, since most of the homes had large driveways. Remaining inconspicuous was a challenge, even for Bogart. Jackie and Bogart watched the house from within his truck for nearly forty minutes in silence. No one appeared to be casing the house, apart from Bogart. He inhaled deeply and finally looked at her.

"I'm going to check it out," he announced. "I'll let you know if it's clear."

"Are you sure?" she asked with apprehension. "Maybe we should wait a few more minutes."

Bogart opened his door and gave her a serious look. "I've had four cups of coffee," he informed her with added urgency. "Waiting isn't an option."

Jackie reluctantly nodded and watched him leave the safety of the truck and head toward her house. Home never looked so good, but it somehow seemed foreign to her after her lengthy absence. Her father had bought the house, knowing she needed some sense of normalcy. They had spent most of her childhood base hopping. When he'd finally gotten to a point in his career where he didn't have to move from country to country, and she was old enough to spend time at home alone, he opted to buy the house for a stable environment. She was possibly the only sixteen-year-old living alone months at a time, but she was trustworthy and excessively mature. Besides, she was never really alone. There was no shortage of her father's military buddies who seemed to show up and invite themselves to stay for extended periods of time. She knew most of them and didn't mind the company.

Bogart finally reached the house, walked the entire perimeter, and then peered through several windows. Jackie was grateful for the darkness and hoped none of the neighbors were peeking out their windows at the late hour. He made a convincing burglar. He walked onto the porch and knocked on the door. Not surprising, no one answered. He looked back to the truck and nodded. Jackie quickly jumped from the truck and hurried to join him on the porch. She removed the hidden key from beneath the porch swing and unlocked the door. Bogart entered behind her.

Chapter Thirteen

Jackie immediately headed for her father's study as Bogart darted into the nearby bathroom. She crossed the room, which was dimly lit by streetlights shining through the part in the curtains. Jackie closed the curtains then turned on the smaller light on top of the desk. She wasted little time approaching the cabinet beneath a small bar and opened the door to reveal a hidden safe. She quickly unlocked the safe and removed a large amount of cash and a little black book. She placed the marshal's gun in the safe and shut it. Jackie stuffed the cash and book into a duffle bag from the nearby closet. As she approached the desk, she eyed a photo of her and her father along with seven men from his team. She picked up the photo and stared at it.

It was taken seven years ago on New Year's Eve. She was eighteen and was graduating high school that spring. Her father clung to her on her right side, and a baby-faced, fashionably dressed man clung to her on the left. Monroe looked so young back then. Abbott was leaning on Monroe's shoulder, holding two fingers up behind his head. Classic Abbott. Behind her was a face she hadn't seen in a long time. Zach had his head on her shoulder between her and Monroe, almost as if attempting to keep them apart. His twisted smile was a reminder of how devious he could be--and usually was. She traveled back to that day and the sound of laughter echoing from their living room. The men from her father's team had secretly gotten her drunk beneath her father's nose. Naturally, he knew what they were doing, but he pretended he didn't. It was the best New Year's Eve she'd known. Her father and his team made it home alive and spent the entire week at their house. It was the best gift she'd ever received.

Jackie snapped out of her daze, somehow not wanting to be reminded of such fond memories right now. She stuffed the photo into the bag then opened one of the desk drawers. She removed a semiautomatic and several clips then tossed them into the bag as well. Bogart entered the study with a bottle of beer in his hand. She briefly glanced at him. He didn't seem to care about drinking so early in the morning. Then again, since he'd been up all night, technically, it was late at night for him. She continued to search the desk drawers.

"Place is clear," Bogart announced while drinking his beer. He flashed a piece of paper in his hand. "Someone left a note for you on the frig."

She cast a sharp look at him and the paper he held. She tensed and gently cleared her throat. "Would you mind putting that back where you found it?"

He appeared slightly surprised by her comment. "Sure," Bogart replied. "You going to be here awhile?"

"Just long enough to get some clothing and then I'm out of here," she informed him as she rubbed her chilled arms while looking around. "I could really use a shower, but I don't feel safe here. I feel like I'm being watched."

"You go on and take that shower," Bogart informed her firmly then offered a jovial smile. "I'm here. Ain't no one gonna get in here without my knowing."

She was hesitant to believe him let alone trust him, but she felt grimy from her impromptu swim in the lake. She gave it some thought then reluctantly nodded.

"I'll make it a quick shower," she announced then gave him a firm, serious stare. "You need to remain alert, Bogart. If the governor's men show up, they won't hesitate going through you to get to me."

He grinned and appeared humored. "Let them try," he announced. "You grab that shower and let me worry about the governor's henchmen. Plenty of people want me dead. Ain't none got me yet."

"As long as you're sure," she replied while grabbing her bag. She still wasn't convinced about letting her guard down, but something told her Bogart could handle himself.

"Need a ride somewhere else?" he asked with a curious look. "Ain't like I have much else to do."

"Thanks, but I have a car," she informed him.

"License plates are traceable," he remarked firmly. "You're in luck though. I have a few spare ones in my truck." Bogart smiled and winked at her. "You know, in case of an emergency. Where's the car?"

She wasn't about to ask, and she didn't want to know. "In the garage." She indicated the note in his hand. "Don't forget to put that note back."

He eyed the note and then her. Her obsession with the paper seemed to peak his curiosity. Bogart saluted her, grinned, and left the study.

✝

*J*ackie entered the second floor bathroom just off her bedroom. It was a semi-private bathroom with a door on each end, so the bathroom could be shared by the two bedrooms. She locked both doors and started the shower. She removed the semiautomatic from her duffle bag, flipped on the safety, and hung the gun by the trigger guard from a hook on the back shower wall. She intended to take the quickest shower in the history of showers. Jackie hastily threw her clothes to the floor and jumped into the shower beyond frosted glass doors. As she rushed through washing her hair, she attempted to hear past the sounds of the rushing water and kept her eyes fixed on the semiautomatic hanging on the back wall of the shower. Anyone attempting to sneak up on her while in the shower would be in for a rude surprise. She finished rinsing her hair and quickly lathered her body. As the last of the soapy water washed down the drain, she heard what sounded like a dull thud from just outside the bathroom.

Her heart nearly stopped as she froze and attempted to listen more closely. She was almost positive she heard the bathroom door opening. As she stared at the frosted shower doors, she swore she'd seen a shadow. Jackie grabbed the gun from the hook, held it in her wet hand, and reached for the glass door. When the shadow moved, she felt panic sweep through her entire body. She threw open the glass door with the gun aimed at the open doorway. Bogart stood in the doorway with a bag of cookies in his hand. When he saw the naked woman holding a gun aimed at him, he dropped the bag and held up his hands.

"Don't shoot, it's just me!" he cried out then swept his eyes over her naked body. His eyes were wide as he stared helplessly. "Holy shit!"

Jackie cried out with frustration, grabbed a towel from the bar with her free hand, and held it to her naked body. The gun remained trained on Bogart. She waved the gun at him with anger and embarrassment.

"Get the hell out of here!"

That she had to tell him to get out was unbelievable! Bogart darted out of the bathroom. Jackie's shoulders sagged as she groaned and lowered the gun. Bogart's hand appeared along the floor and snatched the bag of cookies before disappearing out the open door. Jackie got out of the shower, took two quick steps to the open door, and slammed it shut with disgust. She again locked the door and hastily dried herself as the gun lie on the bathroom sink only inches from her. She quickly slipped into her clean clothing, grabbed the gun and her duffle bag, and left the bathroom through the same door Bogart had exited. Bogart leaned in her bedroom doorway and ate cookies from the bag without a care. She looked at him then the gun in her hand and wondered what was preventing her from shooting him. It was too late. The time to shoot him would have been when he first walked in on her. Now, shooting him would just seem rude.

"What the hell is your problem?" she exploded without releasing the gun, although she refrained from aiming it at him.

"Me?" he cried out. "You're the one showering with a loaded weapon. You're scary!"

"And you're lucky I didn't shoot you," she lashed back at him. "What were you thinking? Why the hell would you walk in on a woman in the shower?" She hesitated, considered her question, and came to an alarming conclusion. She immediately turned hostile. "I may just shoot you yet."

He didn't appear unusually concerned, but he was extremely defensive. "I heard a clunk," Bogart announced. "I thought you might be in trouble, so I thought I'd check on you." He raised his brow and glared at her defensively. "I'd think you'd be smart enough to lock the door--all things considered."

"I did lock the door," she scoffed with annoyance.

"Um, no, I don't think so," he replied. "If you had, I wouldn't have just been able to walk in."

Jackie hesitated and stared at him. "That clunk," she announced with concern for the first time, "it wasn't you?"

"If it had been me, why would I need to check on you?" he demanded.

She suddenly felt alarm and looked around the room. She looked to the bathroom door then at Bogart in silent question. Jackie nodded to a baseball bat near her bed then to the hallway. Bogart only needed a second the catch on. He tossed his bag of cookies aside, grabbed the bat, and entered the hallway. Jackie returned to the bathroom and approached the locked door to the adjoining bedroom. She only stood there a moment before hearing a crash from the adjoining bedroom. Jackie unlocked and threw open the door. A cat spat at her and ran through the bathroom and into her bedroom, its fur standing on end. Bogart approached the bathroom door from the adjoining bedroom and shook his head.

"You could have told me you had a cat," he remarked. "I nearly brained the poor thing."

"I don't own a cat," she firmly replied. "That's the neighbor's cat. I wonder how it got inside."

"I'm guessing it slipped inside with one of your many admirers," Bogart replied and twirled the bat to his shoulder then made a slow motion swing.

She groaned softly, shut her eyes, and placed her hand with the gun to her forehead. "I really have to get out of here," she muttered softly.

As she looked at Bogart, he continued with imaginary batting practice. His lack of concern for the entire situation stunned her, considering she nearly shot him. If she were honest with herself, she still wanted to shoot him.

†

*J*ackie entered the attached garage from the kitchen doorway and looked at the shiny black mustang with a slight layer of dust covering it. It was ten years old yet appeared brand new. Bogart leaned against a work counter while eating cereal from a box and admired the car.

"Nice. Where'd you get it?"

"It was my father's," she informed him. "Being out of the country on missions a lot, he rarely drove it. I only drive it on special occasions."

"Eluding the FBI?" he teased. "Sounds like a special occasion to me."

"Unfortunately, I'll have to abandon it," she replied with a defeated sigh.

He straightened, lowered his cereal box, and looked at her with surprise. "That's a sin."

"I spoke with Monroe," she informed him. "He gave me another contact, so I'd better go."

"Well, good luck," he announced cheerfully. "I'd say see you around, but I doubt it." He grinned teasingly. "If it's all the same to you, I think I'll hang out a bit, maybe watch a little television and catch a nap."

"Make yourself at home."

"By the way, your cereal is stale."

"Yeah, it's four weeks old."

He chuckled in response then ate another handful despite how bad it must have tasted.

Despite his faults, he was starting to grow on her. "Thank you, Bogart."

"Anytime, sweetheart."

Bogart smiled charmingly and opened the car door for her. She returned the smile and got inside. She pressed the garage door opener within the car. The garage door automatically opened, and she carefully backed out. Bogart took his box of cereal and headed inside.

Chapter Fourteen

After driving nearly two hours, the black mustang pulled up to a country house on a back road around six in the morning. Jackie stopped the car in the driveway before the three-car garage and contemplated shutting off the car. It was too early to knock on the door, and Monroe didn't provide a phone number for her new contact. As she debated her next move, the garage door suddenly opened. She couldn't see anyone in or around the massive garage. She uncertainly put the car into gear and pulled in alongside another sports car. As she turned off the car, the door automatically closed. Jackie got out of the car and looked around. Despite only showing three bays from the outside, it was actually a six-car garage, being two cars deep. There were four cars, three furthest away from the bay doors and the sports car alongside hers. Two were rare, classic sports cars and the other two were newer models.

She shut the car door and looked around for any sign of the homeowner. It seemed odd that she'd been invited inside but wasn't greeted. She couldn't deny the pang of distrust in the pit of her stomach. Normally, she wasn't so distrusting, but the last four weeks had taken their toll on her. It also didn't help that she had some idea the sorts of people Monroe considered 'acquaintances'. He didn't offer any warnings about Othello as he had Bogart, so she assumed he didn't warrant any distrust on her behalf. Still, it was difficult feeling secure around strangers these days. The door attached to the house opened, but there was no one there. Now she was feeling apprehensive. Something didn't seem right. She turned back to her car and removed her bag from the passenger seat. The gun was readily available at a moment's notice, and she felt better knowing she had access to it.

As she shut the car door and turned toward the house entrance, a large Rottweiler dog sat in the opening and stared at her with its head tilted. She loved animals, but she didn't love her current situation or the way the dog stared at her. Did the dog know she was invited? Or did it think she was an intruder? She attempted a smile even though she knew the dog would sense her emotions and not her facial expressions.

"Nice puppy," she announced nervously.

The dog suddenly tilted its head while staring at her. She was almost certain the dog thought she was its new chew toy. Upon closer inspection, she saw the dog was wearing a wireless transmitter affixed to its collar. A computer monitor suddenly flickered on near the door and the face of an unfamiliar man appeared.

"You must be Jackie," the man announced enthusiastically. "Meet Darth. Darth will show you to my dungeon."

She stared at the face on the monitor and forced a smile. "Othello?"

"The one and only," he replied pleasantly while grinning. "Come on down!"

Jackie gently cleared her throat and approached the serious looking dog in the doorway. The dog barked gruffly, stopping her in her tracks. Darth stood and turned back into the house. Jackie released her nervous breath and followed the dog.

†

*O*thello's basement, more fondly known as 'the dungeon', was filled with computers, monitors, and security of every kind. Jackie followed Darth down the stairs and immediately stopped at the bottom to look around the organized chaos. In addition to modern technology on every countertop and wall, there was an equal amount of trash and clutter. Her host seemed to enjoy a wide variety of take-out, judging by all the empty pizza boxes and Chinese food cartons. A heavyset man with wild, black curly hair, Othello, turned on his elegant desk chair, looked at her, and grinned.

"Nice to meet you, Jackie," Othello announced. "I don't usually get up at such an ungodly hour, but for Monroe, I'll always make an exception." He cleaned off the chair alongside him and appeared embarrassed by all the take-out boxes lying around. "You'll have to forgive the mess. I don't entertain much." He hesitated and considered the comment then laughed heartily. "Actually, I haven't had a face to face conversation in months. Come, sit."

Jackie approached him at his desk filled with monitors closely watching every inch of his house and property. As she set her bag down and sat in the chair, Darth immediately greeted her. His face was nearly even with hers and looked as if he intended to stare her down. She was sure the dog wanted to eat her.

"I think he likes you," Othello announced cheerfully then immediately turned serious. "You should probably pet him before he takes offense."

Jackie uncertainly pet the dog. He placed his large head on her lap and seemed to enjoy the attention. She indicted the wireless transmitter attached to his collar.

"What's with the transmitter?"

"Oh, I like to maintain radio contact with Darth at all times," he replied. "He's very smart. He's like my personal assistant. Monroe says you need to disappear." Othello leaned back in his chair and grinned. "I can give you a license, passport, birth certificate, the works--but it's not cheap."

"What about a pilot's license?"

He stared at her a moment then chuckled. "Oh, a challenge," he announced with a sly smile. "*Are* you a pilot?"

"Yes, I was working on my commercial airline license until my world fell apart."

He raised a daringly clever brow. "And you'd like to make the great escape in a private plane?"

"Yes, my father has one at a small field about an hour from here."

Othello made a buzzing sound, startling her. "Wrong! You're a pilot with your own plane. The feds will be on your ass before you know they're there." He suddenly grinned. "I have a better idea. It's brilliant, but it's going to cost you extra."

"How much?"

He took little time to consider the question. "Give me the car, and we'll call it even."

Jackie tossed him the keys without hesitation. Othello turned toward his computer and speed typed.

"I'm going to give you the works and tell you exactly what to do," he announced while grinning like an evil genius. "What's your destination?"

"Florida."

He glanced at her and appeared pleased. "Oh, so you're off to see the wonderful Monroe of Oz, huh?" Othello slid a basket of temporary hair color toward her with his foot. "Pick a color and get started. The bathroom is in the back."

†

*B*ogart slept reclined in the corner of Jackie's sofa with one arm clutching the puffy pillow against his side, a bag of chips scattered across his chest, and the sleeping cat on his lap. Despite it being after six in the morning, the glow of the television was the only source of light within the room. The curtains remained closed, keeping the room relatively dark. A shadow loomed over the sleeping man. The cat woke and suddenly hissed, alerting Bogart to company. Bogart opened his eyes and stared at a neatly dressed man standing over him. A second man stood across the room in the doorway. Both resembled hitmen for the mob. The cat dove off Bogart's lap while hissing and hid behind the nearby recliner. Bogart straightened slightly without making any sudden movements and studied both men.

"Can I help you?" Bogart asked while looking at the man directly in front of him.

"We're with the U.S. Marshals," the man announced with little emotion. "We're looking for a fugitive."

"Good for you," Bogart replied and looked at each man then returned his attention to the first. "Doesn't explain why you've disturbed my nap."

"This is her house," the man informed him. "Since you're sleeping in her house, I'm going to assume you're acquainted with her."

"Nope," Bogart informed him. "I'm just trespassing. House was vacant."

"Nice try," the man replied. "Where is she?"

Bogart alternated looking between the two men then flicked a chip from his chest. "I don't suppose either of you boys has any identification on you.　You seem a little well-dressed for U.S. Marshals."

The man standing in front of Bogart suddenly lunged forward, grabbed him by the shirt, and aimed the barrel of a gun between his eyes.

"Here's my identification," the man snarled.　"Either you tell me where she is or there will be some pain involved."

Bogart stared at the gun aimed at his forehead then met the man's gaze only a foot from his face.　He tensed slightly but managed a grin.　"Well, since you were nice enough to give me some options, I'll go with option number two."

The man stared at him and appeared bewildered by the comment.　Bogart revealed a stun gun, hidden in his hand behind the pillow, and shoved it into the man's crotch.　The man jerked and jolted from the impulse sent through his sensitive area.　The second man reached inside his jacket for his gun.　Bogart grabbed the first man's gun as he sank to the floor and shot the second man in the leg. As he fell to the floor, Bogart casually stood and shook his head with disgust.

"I hate guns," he scoffed while approaching the second man writhing on the floor while clutching his bleeding leg.

Bogart kicked the gun from his reach.　He squatted before the writhing man, took a deep breath, and scratched his temple with the barrel of the gun.

"So," he announced with a dreary sigh, "what am I supposed to do with the two of you?"

✝

*J*ackie approached Othello sitting before the monitor while drying her hair with a towel that had seen better days.　She looked over his shoulder and lowered the towel.　He handed her a small stack of items, which included a license, passport, and other credentials, including a pilot's license.　He admired her now auburn hair.

"Hmm, nice choice," he remarked.　"I'm a sucker for redheads."

She eyed the credit card then looked at him with concern.　"Not to complain, but I don't want to add credit card fraud to my newly found crime wave."

"Relax, it's your money," he announced. "I opened a debit account in your new name. If you get a hotel, you're going to need a credit card. Cash equals suspicion. Spend wisely. You only have a thousand dollars on that card." He handed her printed instructions and a cell phone. "Memorize your travel instructions then shred them over there." He indicated his state-of-the-art shredding machine. "The cell phone is untraceable. I also went through your bag. The gun won't float, so I removed it."

She gave him a sharp look about the gun comment but quickly dismissed it. She looked over the instructions on the paper. She was stunned by what was on the itinerary. She looked back at him with her mouth hanging open.

"You're kidding, right?"

Othello grinned. "I'm a certified genius."

"You're a certified something," she muttered while marveling at her itinerary. She had no idea how Othello thought she'd pull off this little stunt.

✝

*H*olden appeared exhausted early that morning as he entered his extremely tidy office with a cup of coffee in one hand and a file in another. There were several accommodations on the wall as well as framed photos of him with various influential people. The only homey presence in the otherwise all-business office was a twelve-inch zombie action figure on his desk. Agent Fields rushed in behind him and appeared moderately enthusiastic.

"You're going to love this," Fields announced while grinning, proud of himself.

Fields set his laptop down on Holden's desk, carelessly knocking the zombie figure over while hastily doing so, and pressed a button on the laptop. Holden sat on the edge of his desk, casually returned the zombie to its correct position, and then watched the grainy security footage from Jackie's house. Jackie, hiding beneath her hat, was seen entering her house with a strange man just behind her. Holden suddenly jumped up from the edge of his desk, spilling half his coffee, and stared at the computer screen with a stunned look that quickly turned enthusiastic.

"I knew she was alive!" Holden shook spilled coffee from his hand and appeared interested at the monitor. "Look at the time that was taken. How did she get there so fast?"

"Probably this guy," Fields said and indicated Bogart on the screen while hitting pause. "Face recognition comes up Steve Turner, AKA Bogart, a grifter. One of the best."

Holden stared at the grainy image of the man and shook his head with amazement. "How would she even know someone like that? All of her known acquaintances are squeaky clean."

"You have to admit," Fields announced and glanced at him, "it's odd that she only has acquaintances and co-workers. A nice looking girl like that should have boyfriends lined around the corner and a ton of childhood friends." Fields eyed Holden and tilted his head. "You said she had no visitors and asked no one be called. Just strange for someone her age."

"Her family moved around a lot when she was growing up," Holden replied. "She probably didn't have time to make many lasting friendships. I suspect she's been a bit of a recluse since her father's accident. According to her boss at Titan Air, she's been putting all her free time into her commercial pilot's license." He looked back at the screen and studied Bogart's image. "I know I didn't have time for friends and relationships when I was establishing my position with the Bureau."

"Yeah, well, we're not all robots like you," Fields remarked with a soft laugh.

Holden glared at him with disapproval. Fields maintained his devious smile then concentrated on the grainy footage displayed on his laptop.

"She left in a black mustang with unregistered New York plates," Fields remarked. "I put out a call on the car and plates, but she had a good few hours head start already."

"I've got to give her credit," Holden announced. "She's making one hell of an effort to disappear."

"Should I put the call out to pick her up?"

"No, let the governor think she's dead awhile longer. If the state police locate the car, tell them to call it in. I don't want them attempting to confront her. She's clever. I don't want to give her the opportunity to disappear again."

"Ironically, only two hours after this footage was taken, two men were seen entering her house but not leaving. I believe they disabled the cameras upon their arrival. Shortly after, two men fitting their description were picked up only fifty miles from her house," Fields informed him. "They were walking naked along the interstate with their wrists bound behind their backs. One man was shot in the leg."

"So you think this Bogart guy stayed behind and ran into these guys at her house sometime after she'd left?"

"I believe so," Fields replied. "If we could locate Bogart, we may be able to find out where she went."

"Good luck finding him. Guys like that know how to vanish without a trace." Holden suddenly appeared curious and looked at his partner. "Is there an airport near her house?"

"There's a small field about an hour away," he replied. "Major airport is about two hours."

"Let's watch both just to be safe," Holden announced and again played the grainy footage. He suddenly straightened and considered something he obviously hadn't before. "Any private planes registered to her or her father?"

"I'm pretty sure there's one at the small airfield," Fields announced and appeared to read Holden's mind. "You said she's a pilot, didn't you?"

Holden suddenly appeared alarmed. "Get someone over there to watch that plane and look for that car. If she gets away in a private plane, we may never locate her."

"I'm on it."

Chapter Fifteen

$\mathcal{R}$ichmond International Airport was packed and bustling during the late afternoon rush hour flights. Taxis, cars, and transfer vans packed the curbs at the massive passenger drop off and pick up area in front of the airport. Police assisted in keeping traffic flowing, although added police presence was noticed. The sheer number of people in and out of the airport at their busiest time was staggering. Jackie walked through the airport terminal in her freshly pressed co-pilot's pantsuit uniform, hat, and airline security badge. Her official airline bag rolled behind her as she walked with a determined gait toward her plane. She saw several officers ahead of her, apparently looking for her, but she managed to act disinterested and didn't even flinch as she passed.

Jackie then caught a glimpse of Holden talking to one of the security guards while flashing her picture. Her heart pounded so hard, she thought the veins in her temples would explode. She felt herself panic slightly but kept her head high, focusing on her destination, and continued toward her gate without slowing. The attendant at the exterior door checked her paperwork and allowed her to pass through the secured, passenger entry door to the gangway leading to the awaiting plane. It wouldn't be long before passengers were called to board the plane, and with a little luck, within the hour, she'd be far from the airport and all those interested in finding her. She couldn't believe how nervous she was while walking the gangway to the plane. She felt at any minute Holden would come running after her, stopping her flight. As she boarded the turboprop regional airliner, she was immediately greeted by the pilot, a cheerful looking man in his late forties, and a fairly attractive flight attendant in her early thirties.

"You must be new," the captain announced cheerfully and hid the fact that he'd given her a quick once over. "I'm Captain Vincent Wells."

He extended his hand to her, which she immediately accepted while returning the smile.

"Brianna Lesher," she announced and released his hand. "I've only been with the company a few weeks."

"My first female co-pilot," he announced a little too eagerly. "I'm honored." Vincent suddenly grinned. "This flight just got more interesting."

"Down boy," the flight attendant muttered while taking Jackie's bag.

The pilot laughed at the flight attendant's joke, or was it jealousy she was displaying? The way she looked at Vincent told a different story. Jackie had heard stories of flight crew fraternizing while on extended layovers. She had to wonder if those stories were accurate. If so, it sounded like anything goes. Vincent suavely guided her into the flight deck. She was grateful it was a smaller, turboprop plane rather than a larger jet, but she couldn't deny she felt a slight tinge of panic. She was suddenly uncertain for the first time about the flying aspect of her charade. She knew what she was doing, since she'd been training a long time for her commercial license. Still, she suddenly felt very anxious not having a senior pilot hovering over her shoulder giving endless instruction and criticism.

As passengers started the boarding process, she felt even more anxious about flying the plane. For a fleeting moment, she actually considered bailing and turning herself in to Agent Falcone. Once they closed the flight deck door, the captain skillfully tended to his duties and turned surprisingly professional. Something clicked inside Jackie. All her fears slipped away, and she sank into her new role of co-pilot. She had to admit as they were taxiing down the runway, she never felt so alive. When she looked at the sky as the plane lifted off, she knew this was where she belonged. Flying was all she ever wanted to do.

†

*A*s the passengers departed the small aircraft, Jackie, alongside Captain Vincent, thanked their passengers for flying their airline. It was an amazing feeling, and she now knew she was ready for commercial piloting. Once everyone had departed the plane, Jackie and the captain shook hands.

"That was probably the most fun I've had on one of these flights," Vincent announced cheerfully and seemed reluctant to release her hand. "Are you sure you don't want to grab a bite to eat?" His smile conveyed possibly more than just dinner.

The flight attendant overheard his invitation and gave him a scathing look that he didn't see. Jackie saw it but it didn't have any influence on her response.

"Thanks but I'm meeting some friends."

"Well, I hope we get to work together again soon," Captain Vincent announced cheerfully.

"Yes, me too."

Jackie accepted her rolling bag from the flight attendant and headed onto the gangway. She was almost certain Captain Vincent was about to have his head handed to him by the jealous flight attendant.

†

*T*he small, no-frills beach house sat on a remote section of Florida beachfront, which appeared rarely traveled. It wasn't the best-kept beach, far from most of the tourist destinations, but it was private. It was a little after seven o'clock that evening when a taxi pulled up to the house. Jackie got out with her rolling bag containing her duffle bag, approached the house, and rang the bell. Only a moment passed before the door opened to reveal a woman in her mid-twenties, Shannon. Shannon smiled enthusiastically and hugged Jackie with giddy delight.

"Jackie, it's great to see you!" She took a step back and stared at her. "I can't believe you're really here!"

"Trust me," Jackie announced with a knowing smile, "it was a long journey."

As they entered the quaint house, a man in his late twenties, Wayne, appeared behind Shannon.

"You must be Jackie," he announced with a pleasant smile. "Shannon's done nothing but talk about you since you called an hour ago to say you were in town."

They politely shook hands, and he immediately took her bag from her.

"I'll put this in the guestroom for you," Wayne announced. "I'm sure you could use a drink."

"Yes," Shannon announced gleefully. "I've made us a pitcher of Cosmos. They're in the frig. We'll sit on the deck and catch up on old times."

Jackie, Shannon, and Wayne were soon sitting on the deck with their drinks while enjoying the ocean in the evening setting. Jackie had to admit it was beautiful. She also felt relaxed for the first time in over a month. It seemed impossible that either interested party would know where to find her. She was nearly home free. Just one more day--and another Cosmo or two.

"Shannon was so excited that you called," Wayne announced while keeping close watch of her. "It's not often I get to meet her college friends."

Shannon playfully frowned. "Probably because I dropped out after my first semester."

"I'm sorry to have called you on such short notice. There was a mix-up with my schedule, so now I have a long layover between flights. I remembered you lived near the airport and thought I'd take a chance catching you at home," Jackie announced then gave them a concerned look. "I hope I'm not putting you out."

"No, of course not," Shannon quickly interjected. "We're happy to have you over, Jackie. I just wish you didn't have to leave tomorrow afternoon."

"I'll visit longer another time, I promise." Jackie looked around the serenity of the secluded beach. "This is what you've always wanted," she announced and looked back at her friend. "A handsome man and a house on the beach."

"The house is only a rental," Shannon playfully pouted. "We can't afford to buy a place like this, but the handsome man is 100% mine."

Jackie was happy Shannon was finally in a committed relationship. Her first and only semester at college was filled with countless men and endless parties. It was no wonder she dropped out. At the rate she was going, she was failing all her classes, and her grades reflected her party girl lifestyle. Jackie wasn't sure what she thought about Wayne. Shannon and Wayne hadn't been dating that long, if she recalled their last email only a few months ago. Wayne stared at her with a look that set her on edge. Most of Shannon's boyfriends in college were womanizers. She was guessing Wayne was probably not the exception, but that wasn't the vibe she was getting from him. There was something else behind his eyes. His constant staring made her uncomfortable and distrusting. Despite his attempt at dressing the part of a gentleman, she got the distinct impression he was a bit of a bad boy and would eventually break Shannon's heart.

Shannon raised her brows lustfully. "What about you? Any men in your life?"

Jackie considered the irony of the question, held back her chuckle, and smiled. "Oh, there are one or two actively pursuing me at the moment."

"Gonna let one catch you this time?" Shannon teased.

"Not if I can help it," Jackie replied and hid her smile. "You know me, I like my freedom."

"You act like it's going to kill you."

Jackie sharply eyed her and raised a brow. "You never know; it might."

Chapter Sixteen

*T*he beach was beautiful and peaceful for seven in the morning. Despite the early hour, it was possibly the latest Jackie had slept since her deadly encounter with the governor. She finally felt relaxed and free for the first time. It was a feeling she had taken for granted not so long ago. She would soon be at Casa d'Monroe, and the governor would be a quickly fading memory. Jackie walked along the beach, enjoying the sunshine and peacefulness of the secluded area. She removed Othello's untraceable cell phone from her pocket and pressed several numbers. She placed the phone to her ear and barely heard the phone on the other end ring.

"Jackie?" came the familiar voice.

"How did you know?" she asked with surprise. "Othello said this phone was untraceable."

"Yeah, but he gave me the number, so I'd know when you called," he replied from the other end. "Are you okay? Are you safe?"

"Yes, I'm fine," she replied and paused by some rocks. She looked out to the ocean and sighed. "Othello was great. His hide in plain sight theory worked perfectly."

"I'm glad to hear," Monroe replied. "Othello's a good man, but sometimes, he's a little out there. Where are you?"

"Florida."

There was a long pause. "You're still in Florida? Why didn't you go to my place on the island?"

"My flight got in late, and I missed the last ferry out. I didn't realize the last ferry left at six," she informed him. "I thought it was seven."

"Only during the summer," he replied. "After Labor Day, it's six. The first morning ferry doesn't leave until ten."

"Yes, I found that out last night while I stood on the dock looking like an idiot," she replied. "It's okay; I'm at a friend's house."

There was an odd silence. "What? No, no, Jackie! They know your friends," he suddenly cried out through the phone. "You shouldn't be there. Get out; get out now!"

She didn't understand his concern, although, Monroe did tend to be overly dramatic at times. It wasn't as if she hadn't thought it through with extreme care. He could be such a worrier.

"It's okay, they don't know about Shannon," she explained and hid her amusement. "No one does. I only knew her for one semester at college before she dropped out. We weren't even roommates."

"I don't like it, Jackie," he said firmly. "My flight is preparing to land. I have to go. I don't want to miss my connecting flight, or I'll be stuck in this shithole overnight. After I land, I'll secure you a helicopter, and you can fly to the island."

"Don't be ridiculous," she chirped. "The ferry will be leaving in three hours. I'll be at your place before you'd even secure a chopper. We'll meet up at your place later this evening, I promise." Jackie looked toward the house and saw an unfamiliar car pull up. She suddenly felt alarm sweep through her. She attempted a calm voice into the phone. "Listen, I'll call you back once I'm on the ferry."

Jackie disconnected the call and hurried for the house, being careful to remain out of view of the deck and any windows. It wasn't possible that they'd found her. No one knew about Shannon. Sure, there had been the occasional email, but she corresponded with a lot of acquaintances. Even Shannon didn't know she was visiting until an hour prior to her arrival. Jackie reached the side of the house and peered around the corner at the newer car by the curb. She could see someone enter the house but couldn't see his or her face. She couldn't risk it. Jackie climbed through the bedroom window and into the guestroom. She hurried across the bedroom to the open door and peered into the hallway. She heard voices coming from the living room. Jackie silently shut the door, pulled her duffle bag out from under the bed, and dropped the bag out the open window. She was about to follow her bag through the window when she heard a tap on the door as it opened. Jackie turned, leaned against the windowsill, and appeared casual. Shannon stood in the doorway while grinning.

"Oh, great, you're up," she announced cheerfully. "I know this is awkward, Jackie, but I want you to meet one of Wayne's friends from work. He's cute and has no plans for breakfast this morning. I hope you don't mind."

Jackie felt her entire body suddenly sag with relief. "Oh--" she announced softly and laughed. "Uh, yeah, that would be great."

Jackie followed Shannon from the bedroom and down the hall. They crossed the living room into the kitchen and approached the deck doors. Wayne could be seen sitting on the deck, his back to them, with a glass of scotch in his hand. Jackie was puzzled. It seemed a little early for him to be drinking, especially the hard stuff. What sort of man had Shannon gotten involved with this time? Shannon stepped onto the deck through the glass doors and unexpectedly shut them behind her, surprising Jackie.

"Hello, Jackie," came Holden's familiar voice from behind her.

Jackie quickly turned to see Holden standing only a few feet from her. Her entire body twitched. How did he know where to find her? How had he managed to sneak up on her like that? A thousand thoughts rushed through her mind; the first being the closest exit.

"I'm impressed," he announced and offered a moderately charming smile. "You almost had me convinced you fell overboard at the lake."

Holden approached her. Jackie quickly shot looks around the kitchen for an exit. Holden suddenly stopped as if attempting not to frighten a wild animal.

"Don't even think it, Jackie," he said firmly. "I'm placing you back into protective custody."

She was stunned by his words and had to keep from laughing. "Protective custody? Your protective custody cost three marshals their lives," she suddenly lashed out then turned hostile. "I didn't even last three weeks in your so-called safe house. How many people need to die before this goes to trial?"

He appeared to tense then turned sympathetic. "I'm not going to let anything happen to you. You have to trust me."

Shannon and Wayne watched through the glass deck doors. Jackie glared at them with a venomous look. She wouldn't mind punching her *former* friend in the mouth. They quickly minded their own business. She looked back at Holden.

"Do you honestly think you stand a chance against the governor's men?"

"Yes, and I should have been the one protecting you from the start," he announced firmly. "I'm not going to let him get to you, you have my word."

"Your word when you're dead doesn't mean a whole lot," she muttered under her breath. Jackie finally groaned with defeat while subconsciously running her fingers through her hair. "But seeing I have little choice, my things are in the guest bedroom." She gave him a cold look and nodded toward the couple sitting on the deck casting curious looks into the house. "How much did they get for selling me out?"

"They're not being compensated," Holden informed her. "I'm sure they know that."

Jackie suddenly snorted a laugh. "Wanna bet? I'm sure that'll come as a shock to them." She folded her arms across her chest. "I guess that explains why Wayne kept staring at me last night. I should have seen the dollar signs in his eyes."

She turned toward the glass doors and again caught the two peering inside. Jackie mocked them with her smile, rubbed her fingers together symbolizing money, and shook her head. Their expressions immediately dropped as they exchanged looks. A heated debate quickly ensued. Jackie chuckled then looked back at Holden.

"We can go now," she announced and nodded toward the hall. "The guestroom is that way."

Holden stepped aside and allowed her to walk past him. She wasn't exactly surprised that he didn't trust her. Even she didn't trust herself not to do something stupid. She walked past him without comment. He followed her down the hall and into the guest bedroom. As he stepped through the bedroom doorway after her, Jackie kicked out behind her, striking Holden in the chest, and sent him backwards into the door. The door slammed shut as his body struck it. As he straightened from the surprise attack, she spun into a roundhouse kick. He caught her ankle, surprising her, and threw her backwards onto the bed. She hadn't been expecting his quick reflexes to her attack, nor the pain it had caused her previously injured leg. As she lie on the bed, she clutched her injured thigh with agony and appeared unable to move. Holden casually approached her and removed his handcuffs.

"I didn't mean to hurt you, Jackie," he announced in a calm tone. "I'm sorry I have to do this, but you give me no choice. We have to do this the hard way. I'm placing you under arrest for striking a federal agent."

Jackie remained lying on the bed while gingerly rubbing her sore thigh. Holden reached for her wrist. Jackie suddenly grabbed his arm, kicked him in the side, and pulled him to the bed alongside her. She jumped on top of him and swiftly cuffed his wrist to the brass bed rung. He appeared stunned by her amazing reflexes. She pinned his free wrist to the bed, straddled his waist, and hovered over him. It wasn't as if her leg didn't hurt, but it didn't hurt as much as she made it seem. She stared into his stunned eyes with an unusual calmness.

"It's nothing personal, Agent Falcone, but the only way I'm going to survive until the trial is by looking after myself," she informed him.

He remained stunned by his predicament then stared back at her and assumed a more authoritative tone. "I can't let you do that, Jackie. Now unlock the cuffs."

Her expression didn't change, and she didn't look away. "I wasn't asking permission; I was making a statement," she casually informed him. A sly grin crossed her face. "Now don't take this personally--"

While keeping his left wrist pinned to the bed, Jackie felt around his waist behind him. He bucked beneath her in an unsuccessful attempt to throw her off him. She'd only momentarily lost her balance but remained on top of him. Jackie revealed the second pair of handcuffs and smiled while dangling them. Holden wasn't humored and again attempted to toss her off him. He managed to free his left wrist from her grip and attempted to reverse their roles by trying to pin her to the bed with his body. He made an effort to subdue her wrist holding the second pair of handcuffs. She had to admit that his body pressed against hers while he attempted to get her beneath him was almost as pleasant as it was distracting. She kept her leg securely wrapped around his hip while attempting to keep him from pinning her to the bed beneath his body. Her free leg was her only leverage against his weight and gravity. Anyone walking in on them would almost certainly get the wrong impression of their activities.

Holden's sheer weight alone was working against her, and if he managed to get on top of her, she'd never be able to toss him off without physically harming him. They continued to wrestle in their compromising position for only a minute or two when Jackie felt she was losing ground. Soon he would be on top of her, and he'd have her at a disadvantage. She was left with only one option. Jackie kissed him passionately and aggressively on the mouth, momentarily freezing him. In the split second he'd been taken by surprise, she snapped the handcuff to his left wrist, broke off the kiss, and threw her body into his. She propelled him onto his back, with her again on top, and snapped the cuff to the brass headboard. Holden immediately pulled against his cuffed wrist. Jackie half collapsed on top of him while panting with some exhaustion. She'd never cuffed a man to a bed before, and considering the effort it took, it was almost sexually satisfying. Holden appeared equally worn from the wrestling match and panted heavily as well.

She took a deep breath and slowly sat up while straddling his hips, allowing her hands to touch his chest as she straightened. She grinned while looking down at him, enjoying a lustful thought or two. She interrupted her sexual fantasy, realizing she needed to focus on her task at hand. Jackie playfully reached within his blazer and removed his gun from its shoulder holster.

"Don't do it," Holden firmly gasped as he helplessly watched her take his weapon from him.

Jackie gave him a reassuring smile that conveyed her intentions and then tossed the gun to foot end of the bed. She grinned playfully.

"Sorry, but I have to frisk you."

"Jackie, I mean it!"

Jackie searched his jacket pockets then caressed his side as she leaned over him and reached behind him to feel his back pockets. The heat of his body felt good against hers, and she wasn't ashamed to admit it. Her hand behind him found something of interest. She straightened and revealed a revolver from a concealed belt holster in the small of his back.

"My God, it's like disarming Germany."

Holden was furious or embarrassed. It was difficult to tell.

"This isn't funny, Jackie."

Of course, that was just his opinion. She was actually enjoying herself. Jackie tossed the revolver to the bed with the first gun, grinned her response, and seductively slid her body down his hips to search his pants pockets. She hesitated, looked down with surprise at the firmness contained within his pants, and then met his gaze with a lustful smile.

"Well, I see you're enjoying being frisked."

His face conveyed hostility despite his body's reaction. "Get off me and unlock the cuffs," he said firmly.

She was now enjoying her 'search and seizure' a little too much and grinned in response. "Who knew the big, tough fed would be turned on by a little rough play?"

Jackie searched his front pants pockets while maintaining her cheap grin. She couldn't help but take in several eyefuls of the enthusiasm his pants were sporting. Perhaps it was just their wrestling match, but she was almost surprised at her own rising desire. Her search of his pockets produced its intended result, sadly, too fast. She removed his rental car keys and casually dangled them in front of him.

"Do you mind if I borrow your car?"

"If you unlock the handcuffs, I'll forget everything else," Holden growled in a failed attempt to sound convincing.

Jackie moved up his body, again straddling his hips, leaned over him, and placed her hands on either side of his head. She hovered just inches from his face and smiled her lustful intentions. He immediately tensed beneath her. Despite his attempt to remain in control, the bulge in his pants beneath her throbbed its own intentions. Jackie couldn't pretend she didn't feel his reaction and fought to resist her own impulses to act upon it.

"Might be more fun if you just admit what you really want," she cooed softly while brushing her lips past his.

Holden tensed while breathing heavily and allowed a soft groan to escape involuntary in response. Jackie kissed him quickly but passionately on the mouth. In that split second, Holden jerked against the handcuffs keeping him from her and thrust upward against her. Before he could return the kiss, she quickly broke it off, realizing her actions could be considered sexually assault against a federal agent. She slowly sat back up while fighting her own sexual desires and seductively ran her hands along his chest. Holden tensed beneath her and watched her with possible anticipation to her next move. She couldn't deny how badly she wanted to feel his naked body against hers, but she was sure that feeling would pass quickly. Besides, she had more important things to do. She quickly and secretly collected her emotions, so she could maintain control of the situation. She smiled sweetly and pushed all sexual feelings aside.

"I'd love to stay and corrupt that little Boy Scout in you, but I have a prior engagement."

"Don't do this, Jackie," he suddenly warned with less conviction in his voice.

She wasn't sure, but she felt he was more disappointed than irritated. She managed a playful grin and enjoyed one last twitch from his body beneath her.

"Don't worry," Jackie cooed. "Next time you can handcuff me to the bed."

Jackie flashed a lustful smile, winked, and swiftly jumped off him, landing gracefully alongside the bed. She dangled the handcuff keys before him then dropped them on his chest.

"Later, love." Jackie headed for the open window, paused with reflection, and looked back at him with all seriousness. "Oh, and tell Shannon she won't be getting a Christmas card from me."

Jackie blew him a kiss, took in one last eyeful of his aroused state, and left through the open, bedroom window. Holden groaned softly and allowed his head to fall back on the pillow. He then looked at the handcuff keys on his chest and frowned.

"Great."

Chapter Seventeen

*H*olden's stolen rental car sat near the ramp in the crowded airport parking lot late that afternoon. Seemingly, out of nowhere, several police cars with flashing lights surrounded it. Four armed police officers jumped out of their cars with guns drawn and cautiously approached the vehicle. They peered inside then lowered their weapons. The car was empty. All four officers appeared disgusted and shook their heads. One radioed their findings. Within the airport terminal, Holden and a security guard walked at a fast pace through the crowded terminal. He briefly looked at every woman they passed and appeared disgusted each time it wasn't Jackie. Holden's cell phone chirped. He pulled it out of his inner pocket with some hostility and placed it to his ear.

"Falcone--"

"We found your rental car. It's in the parking garage on level four," a police officer said from the other end. "She couldn't have gotten far."

Holden suddenly snorted a soft laugh while looking around the terminal. "With a fake passport, she could be anywhere in the world," he snapped hotly. "Check with security. See if they found anything on the tapes. Maybe we'll get lucky."

As Holden disconnected the call, his phone rang again. He pressed the button with disgust and answered slightly gruffer than unusual.

"Falcone--"

"Hey, babe. Miss me?" Jackie chirped cheerfully from the other end.

Holden suddenly stopped and looked around, although, it was unlikely she was calling from nearby. "Where are you?" he demanded.

"Somewhere where you'll never find me," she replied casually. "I'd like to live long enough to testify."

He ran his fingers through his hair and seemed to hold his breath. "Look, I'm willing to forget about this morning," Holden announced while attempting a gentler tone. "Just tell me where you are, and I'll come and get you."

"Hmm--? I don't think so."

His frustration quickly surfaced. "I'm starting to lose my sense of humor, Jackie."

"I'm doing you a favor," she announced firmly. "If you can't find me that means the governor's henchmen won't have a reason to kill you."

"You might enjoy it if they did," he remarked lowly.

There was an awkward silence. "How could you even think something like that?" Jackie snapped with irritation in her voice. "You may be a prick, but I wouldn't wish that on you. After what happened to Harris, how could you even suggest something so depraved?"

Holden immediately fidgeted and started pacing a small area near the guard. "You're right. I was out of line, and I'm sorry," he said gently. "Forgive me?"

There was a moment of hesitation from her end. Her tone immediately softened as well. "Yeah, I forgive you."

Holden followed the security guard to a restricted area while keeping his cell phone to his ear. A massive wall of security monitors revealed the entire terminal at a single glance. A police officer watched security footage leading up to the time Holden's rental car was discovered. Holden sat on the nearby console with his cell phone still to his ear.

"Harris was my friend, you know," he attempted to reason with her. "I want to put those bastards away, but I need you alive in order to do that." He carefully considered his words. "I know you wouldn't deny Harris retribution."

"We want the same thing, and I'll be there for the trial," she informed him. "You can reach me on this phone. It's untraceable, by the way, so you can stop trying to trace it. I know what I'm doing, but you need to back off."

The phone suddenly disconnected, leaving him disgusted. Holden replaced his phone to his jacket pocket, closed his eyes, and groaned softly as his head fell into his hand.

"Tough day at the office, dear?" the officer sitting before the monitors teased.

He lifted his head and groaned softly. "She's like a tiger. Very beautiful, very playful, and fun to watch in action," he replied. "But if you get too close, she'll tear you apart."

The officer snickered, looked back at the monitor, and hid his grin. "I heard she handcuffed you to a bed," he remarked without looking at him. "What was that like?"

Holden closely watched the monitor over the officer's shoulder and showed little reaction to the question. "Very erotic."

The police officer suddenly became interested and looked back at him with surprise. "Erotic?"

"Close enough to foreplay for me to count it," Holden muttered without looking away from the monitor.

The officer and guard stared at him with their mouths hanging open. Holden continued to watch the screen then snapped his fingers, spotting something.

"There!"

The vehicle was seen on the security footage pulling into the parking lot. A well-disguised man got out. He turned in such a manner that his face remained cleverly hidden.

"She's not very attractive," the security guard remarked while grinning.

"That's not her," Holden snarled and shook his head with disgust. He appeared to sink into thought only a moment. "She's not here. He's a decoy." He shook his head and remained deep in thought. "Where is she finding all these street-smart people who keep helping her?" He gave the police officer a firm nod. "See if you can identify the man."

"He gets into a cab three minutes after he parks," the security guard replied. "You never see his face. He knew where the cameras were and completely avoided them."

"Call the cab company about that fare," Holden announced. "Maybe we'll get lucky."

Holden removed his cell phone, pressed a single button, and awaited a response from the other end.

"Agent Fields," came the reply.

"Fields, she slipped away again."

"What do you need?" Fields asked.

"I need a list of people Jackie Remus knows in the Florida area. Someone's helping her--someone smart." He suddenly hesitated then reconsidered his comment. "Scratch that," he announced with added enthusiasm. "Get me a list of men from her father's old platoon. Find any connections between them and Florida."

"We investigated them already," Fields insisted. "There was nothing to indicate she'd been in contact with any of them since her father's funeral."

"So it would appear," Holden remarked. "But nothing about this girl is what is seems. She's likeable, you said so yourself. So why doesn't she seem to have any friends? It's too convenient." Holden paced the security office with his cell phone firmly to his ear. "Tell me everything we know about Lieutenant Commander Jackson Remus. I want to know everyone he knew."

Chapter Eighteen

 *T*he small motel near the ocean was well-maintained and very busy for the week after Labor Day. The two-story motel had fewer than fifty rooms with guestrooms opening directly to the outside walkway. It was a little after seven that evening and several guests were returning from their lengthy day on the beach. Jackie, in her cap and sunglasses, entered the office with her duffle bag. Agent Falcone's surprise visit at Shannon's beach house had disrupted her entire schedule. She was forced to spend most of the day traipsing around Florida while Monroe worked his magic finding another contact to dispose of the rental car. She again missed the last ferry to her island destination, but she was lucky to have avoided police as it was. Holden was better prepared with local police, and they were actively scouring the airport and nearby marina.

Monroe had missed his connecting flight as well and remained inconveniently out of the country for another night. Monroe missing his connecting flight was actually a mixed blessing. If he had made it back to the states, he'd insist on coming for her himself. She couldn't risk him coming to her. Holden undoubtedly had half of Florida's state troopers casing all major airports and rinky-dink airfields as well. They'd easily trace any chopper or plane rental Monroe could secure on short notice and red flags would fly in every direction. Monroe didn't need any additional suspicions swirling around him. He got into enough trouble on his own. Attempting to catch the ferry tomorrow remained her best option to reach Monroe on the island. She'd have to be very cautious, and they'd both have to be patient.

Jackie approached the old desk in the outdated lobby that had seen better days. The tacky nautical décor reminded her of some cheap seafood restaurant. As she approached the desk, she was greeted by the clerk in his early twenties. Truman looked like a cross between a surfer dude and an escaped mental patient. He was excessively tan with nearly white, shoulder length hair. His green, beady looking eyes were set close together. He immediately smiled while greeting her with a polite nod.

"I have a reservation," she announced pleasantly. "Lana Watson."

Truman checked the computer for her reservations then looked at her and grinned in response. "Yes, Miss Lana Watson. I have you down for two nights in our ocean view standard room," he announced cheerfully, as if they had anything other than standard rooms at the motel. "Compliments of *Maxim Magazine*. Writer or model?"

She immediately fidgeted to the desk clerk's cheap grin. Monroe was responsible for making her motel arrangements while stranded in parts *unknown*. She had to admit, her friend had a warped sense of humor.

"Photographer's assistant, actually," she replied and gently cleared her throat, secretly cursing Monroe. "I'm checking out possible locations for our next issue. I'm told you have some very private beaches here."

"Plenty of seclusion for your magazine's content."

"I'd appreciate it if you didn't mention I was here," she remarked and tilted her head. "You understand."

"Oh, definitely," Truman announced a little too eagerly. "Your company sent a package by special courier."

He handed her the card key and a box marked 'fragile'. She accepted the package. Special courier was probably code for one of Monroe's *acquaintances*.

"Thanks."

"Call if you need anything."

Jackie offered a polite smile, replaced her sunglasses, and left with her package. She headed up the closest stairs for her room on the second floor facing the ocean. She entered the room and was pleasantly surprised by its modern updates and cleanliness. She locked the door behind her and immediately closed the curtains. Jackie removed her cell phone while flopping on the slightly creaky bed and pressed a button. Monroe answered before it had a chance to finish ringing the first time.

"Jackie? You checked in?"

"Yeah, thanks for the reservations, though I'm not sure about the flashy cover story," she remarked then grimaced although he couldn't see it. "*Maxim Magazine?*"

"Hey, hide in plain sight, remember," he announced with humor in his voice. "I heard they found the fed's car at the airport."

"Did your friend get caught?"

"Flash? Get caught? Are you kidding?" Monroe said from the other end and chuckled. "He knows every security camera in the city. All they'll ever see is his cap and shoes." There was a long pause. "They're watching the ferry, so that's out."

She groaned softly. "I sort of suspected as much."

"I needed to get a little creative, so I'm sending a friend for you at eight tomorrow morning. He'll be at the marina. Slip twenty." There was an awkward silence. "I don't want to alarm you unnecessarily, Jackie, but don't turn your back on this guy. He's slightly unbalanced."

"I can handle unbalanced," she replied. "Thanks for the heads up though."

"Did you get the package?"

"Yeah, what is it?"

"Just a token of my affection," he teased. His tone turned serious. "I'm no longer comfortable with you going straight to my house from the marina. You have more admirers than I'd anticipated. Some of my contacts are already aware of your situation from some of their less ethical acquaintances. Your friend, the governor, has the underground buzzing. The FBI isn't the only interested party who knows you're in Florida."

Jackie's expression dropped as she sank on the bed. "The governor knows I'm in Florida?"

"I'm afraid so," Monroe replied gently from the other end. "It's okay. As long as you meet that prick boat captain at the marina tomorrow morning, he'll get you safely to the island. I'll meet with you tomorrow evening at the island's annual fair. It'll be extremely crowded. Crowds work in our favor. Eight o'clock by the Ferris wheel."

Her fears were overwhelming, and his concern wasn't helping ease her tensions. "Why so late?"

"Security is a little tight here," he replied. "You know how these third world shitholes operate."

"Is everything okay?" she asked with concern for her friend. Now she had a pretty good idea where he was, and it didn't make her feel any better for his safety.

"Oh, yeah, fine," he replied. "A few cows breached security on the runway. Happens all the time."

Jackie was unusually quiet a moment. "Should I ask?" she questioned while grimacing.

"Eh, probably not," he replied. "Let's just stick with the cow story."

Compared with Monroe's problems, Jackie's problems were just a minor nuisance. He enjoyed getting into trouble and actually thrived on it.

She held back her nervous laugh then smiled gently. "Thanks, Monroe. I owe you one--"

"You owe me too damned many. One day, I may even decide to collect," he informed her and added a soft chuckle. "Now that's a lovely image." He turned serious. "In forty-eight hours, no one will find you until you want to be found."

"That's what I'm counting on."

"And I've taken out a few additional insurance policies for good measures," he informed her.

Jackie hesitated and stared blankly at the tacky framed print on the wall. "You mean--?"

"Whiskey Tango Foxtrot has gone dark."

She immediately sat up straight on the bed. "All of them?" Jackie gasped with astonishment.

"Oh, yeah," he gloated.

Jackie could barely contain the tears of joy welling in her eyes. She wiped her tears and smiled even though he couldn't see it. "Thank you, Monroe."

"For you, anything, darling," he replied gently. "Good night, Jackie."

"Night, Monroe."

Jackie disconnected the call, set her phone aside, and opened the box. In contained a semiautomatic in a leather shoulder holster with two extra clips and a revolver in a belt clip. She removed them from the box and placed them in her duffle bag. She didn't know how Monroe managed the things he did especially being off in some

Godforsaken country with little more than his laptop and a cell phone, but she was glad he was resourceful.

It was nearly an hour later. Jackie flipped through the television channels and felt excessively bored. She was starving, but she didn't want to risk leaving the safety of her room. She'd live with the hunger until she was on her way to the island. Fair food sounded appealing. With extra time on her hands, she considered Monroe's comment about the boat captain she was to meet at the dock. If Monroe felt the need to warn her, there had to be something not right with the guy and it was concerning. Unbalanced could mean just about anything. There was a knock on the door, startling her. Jackie jumped from the bed and collected herself before approaching the door. They couldn't possibly know where she was, but she wasn't taking any chance. Resisting the urge to grab one of the guns from her bag, she nervously looked through the peek hole first. It was the front desk clerk, Truman! She groaned while rolling her eyes, decided it was best to see what he wanted, and opened the door. His expression revealed very little.

"Yes?" she questioned the young man, attempting to sound patient but missed the mark.

"The FBI was here looking for you," he informed her with a serious look on his face. "We need to talk."

Jackie stared at him a moment and, despite her panic, she showed little reaction. She stood aside and allowed him to enter. She shut the door behind him, leaned against it, and appeared casual.

"Is he waiting for me?"

"I told him I didn't see you," Truman remarked. "I think he bought it."

She fidgeted slightly as a thousand thoughts exploded in her mind. She straightened while attempting to remain casual. "Thanks, I appreciate that, but it's not how it looks."

"Oh? And how is it?"

"We lived together," she announced without hesitation. "He's extremely possessive and didn't take my moving out very well. Now he's using his position with the Bureau to get me back." She added a soft groan for added effect and rubbed her temple. "He won't leave me alone."

"Well, he checked in," he informed her and gave a nod. "He's just a few doors down."

"And I'll be checking out." Jackie took a step toward her bag on the bed.

Truman stepped into her path and offered a cheap smile. "He has a warrant for your arrest."

"Yeah, for striking a federal officer--namely him," she snapped then glared at him and wondered what the young man was up to, although, she already had a pretty good idea. "I thought you were defending me?"

"Only if you make it worth my while."

She showed no reaction, but she was disgusted with his fumbling attempt at blackmail. It was best just to pay the little bastard and avoid confrontation.

"How much?"

Truman smiled lustfully and gave her a quick once over. "I'll take it in trade."

She almost felt sorry for the poor, clueless bastard. His raging hormones were about to get his ass kicked, and he didn't even know it yet. She glared at him with impatience in her eyes and folded her arms across her chest.

"I'd rather take him back and tell him you hit on me," she remarked then raised a cocky brow. "I'm sure that'll go over real well."

Jackie attempted to push past him. Truman suddenly backhanded her across the face, tossing her into the table. She was startled by his aggressive outburst. He took two quick steps to the door and locked it. Truman turned to face her as she held her cheek and glared at him with a wildly unpredictable look. At least she no longer felt sorry for him.

"If you could afford to scream, you would have," he remarked while smirking deviously. "You can't report me, so that makes you fair game."

Jackie casually leaned against the table, rubbed her red cheek, and smirked. His barbaric philosophy was just adding to her desire to knock him senseless.

"It's not nice to hit a lady," she hissed.

"I doubt you're much of a lady."

She slowly straightened and grinned at the comment. "Yeah, you've got that right," she retorted without taking her eyes off him. "I hope you like it rough."

Truman smiled and reached for her. Jackie caught him by the wrist, twisted his arm, and dropped him to his knees. He cried out in agony. She could easily snap his arm, but she was proving a point not aiming to maim. She glared down at him and tilted her head as he remained paralyzed with pain.

"How's that working for you?"

Truman punched her in her injured thigh with his free fist. Jackie released him and clutched her injured leg. He had successfully nailed her in the one spot that could possibly disable her. Truman stood, flexed his sore arm, and then lunged for her. Despite the pain in her leg, Jackie jumped across the bed. Truman hit the nightstand, knocking the lamp to the floor with a crash. Jackie sprang to her feet on the other side of the bed, facing him. Truman leaped across the bed for her. Jackie swept his legs out from under him with her arm. He fell to the bed with a bounce, rolled off it, and hit the floor with a thump. He'd hit the floor hard and was momentarily dazed. Jackie snatched her bag and casually limped across the room toward the door.

As much as she wanted to dispense some punishment on the little bastard, the crashing lamp had caused enough noise. It was time to make her escape before someone came checking. She was nearly to the door when Truman tackled her into the dresser. She was momentarily stunned by the collision with the flimsy dresser. Truman grabbed her by the throat, attempting to suffocate her into submission, while reaching for her pants. She was already contemplating her next move when the door suddenly burst open to reveal Holden with his gun aimed.

"FBI!"

Jackie rammed her knee into Truman's ribs then spun into a roundhouse kick and struck him in the face. She was through playing games with this punk and held little back. Truman was thrown across the room and forcibly into the bedside stand, vibrating the wall. Jackie spun into a return kick for Holden and knocked the gun from his hand. Holden jumped with surprise and held his hands up defensively.

"Jackie, just calm--"

Jackie kicked him in the side and knocked him into the television. While she was preoccupied with Holden, Truman attempted to bolt past her. Jackie grabbed his arm, jolting him to a halt, and forced him to meet her gaze. She looked into his eyes and sneered her hostility.

"I think you forgot something--"

She kicked him in the groin, nearly lifting him off his feet. Truman barely had time to clutch himself as he dropped to the floor. Holden approached her with his hands up.

"Enough," Holden boldly announced.

Jackie spun and was about to kick him in the groin as well. Holden instinctively blocked with a loud gasp. Jackie stopped short of his crotch. Both relaxed. Holden exhaled, visibly shaken, and leaned against the dresser.

"I saw my entire life flash before my eyes," Holden gasped softly.

Jackie leaned against the dresser next to him while breathing heavily and gingerly rubbed her sore thigh. "Yeah, well, you're lucky I'm a lover and not a fighter."

Holden cast a look of surprise at her. She held back her laugh to his look. He then indicated Truman writhing in agony on the floor.

"Kind of young and clumsy for one of the governor's men," he announced.

"That's because he's not one of the governor's men."

"I realize that," Holden remarked. "How did you manage to piss off the front desk clerk?"

"Why do you always assume it's my fault?" she demanded then casually indicated Truman on the floor. "He was soliciting sexual favors in exchange for his silence." She cleverly raised her brows along with a sly grin. "He was annoyingly insistent."

Truman slowly pulled himself to his knees in a half-hearted attempt to make it to his feet. Holden casually retrieved his gun, replaced it to his holster, and then eyed Jackie's bruised cheek with a frown.

"He do that?"

"Yeah, he said he liked it rough," she replied. "I'd say I obliged. The prick wouldn't believe you were my extremely jealous ex-boyfriend with a history of violence."

"Dating you? I'd almost have to have a history of violence," Holden snorted. "Possibly some mental issues as well."

Truman still appeared to be in some pain as he stumbled to his feet. Holden grabbed Truman by his shirt and slammed him against the nearby wall.

"Is this how you treat women?" Holden demanded while indicating Jackie.

"I'm sorry, man," Truman exclaimed nearly down to tears. "I'm really sorry. It won't happen again!"

"If it does, I'll personally shoot you in your favorite body parts," Holden growled.

Truman stared into Holden's eyes and nodded while trembling. Holden tossed him across the room toward Jackie, who didn't move from her reclined position against the dresser, and the open door. Truman jumped away from Jackie with a frightened look and hurried from the room. She casually shut the door behind him and snickered softly.

"He'll be scarred for life, if we're lucky," Jackie announced, pleased with herself.

"So have I earned a little trust?" Holden asked as he approached her.

She briefly looked at him and felt that odd pang of sexual desire once again. Their altercation that morning was suddenly the only thing on her mind. She avoided looking at him and attempted to cover her emotions.

"I'm too tired and sore to argue anymore tonight," Jackie replied and again rubbed her aching thigh. "All I want is a hot bath and some sleep."

Holden indicated her discarded duffle bag on the floor near the door. "Is this everything?"

Jackie reluctantly nodded. Holden picked up her bag and opened the door for her.

"My room's a lot cleaner."

Chapter Nineteen

*N*early an hour later, Jackie appeared from the bathroom in Holden's motel room wearing a pair of shorts and a tank top as she dried her hair with a towel. She carried her duffle bag with her and set it on the floor alongside her bed furthest from Holden's bed. Holden sat casually reclined on the bed closest to the door while juggling a carton of take-out Chinese food and the television remote control. As she took in an eyeful of him, she couldn't deny how sexy he looked with his legs stretched out and crossed at the ankles. She allowed her eyes to stray to his crotch and immediately shamed herself. Holden flipped through the television channels while frowning then tossed the remote control onto her bed with disgust. Jackie poked through the take-out bag on the dresser and found something that smelled appealing. She was so hungry, anything sounded appealing, even eating in a two-star motel room with Agent Falcone. She collapsed onto her own bed and picked up the remote control.

"Nothing X-rated," he warned.

She glared her disapproval at him. "Please, I'm all talk. If you knew my father, you'd understand," Jackie announced. "Six-foot-two Navy SEAL, built like a tank, and able to kill a man with his bare hands without breaking a sweat."

Holden nearly choked on his food then gently cleared his throat without looking at her. "Judging by your fighting skills, I'm guessing he taught you. Was he an expert in martial arts?"

"He was a master of everything," she replied. "Knives, guns, swords, batons--" She sighed deeply. "Numb chucks, throwing stars, crossbow--" She then considered her comment and continued. "Harpoon guns, stun gun--" She eyed Holden with a curious look. "Did I miss anything?"

"Explosives?"

"No, they had a slightly crazy, unstable guy for that," she casually remarked then made a face. "Now there's a man you *wouldn't* want to meet. My father said when Zach died several small countries threw ticker tape parades celebrating his death."

"Big funeral, huh?"

"A small one, actually," she announced then hesitated and muttered, "considering they only found his big toe." Jackie eyed him and smiled slyly. "But he went out just as he promised he would-- with a bang."

"Sounds like someone else I know," Holden announced while casting a look at her. He partially turned on his bed to face her and appeared serious. "And while we're on the subject, I'd appreciate it if you aren't the one who kills me."

"I wouldn't do that," she said matter-of-fact as she casually ate from her Chinese carton. "I have tremendous respect for law enforcement."

"Is that what you were conveying this morning?"

She glanced at him and grinned. "You didn't seem to mind being frisked," she teased. "Or is being aroused while on duty frowned upon?"

Holden gave her a disapproving glare. "It was completely disrespectful toward a federal agent."

Her smile suddenly faded. "Oh, I'm sorry. I didn't know," she gasped softly with embarrassment then grimaced. "I'm usually perceptive to a person's sexual orientation."

He stared at her with his mouth hanging open and appeared offended. "I'm not gay."

"Okay. No need to whip it out and prove it," she quickly announced, although she enjoyed the colorful image. She then casually shrugged. "Growing up military allowed for a lot of roughhousing with the men in my father's platoon." She continued to eat from her carton. "What you consider sexual harassment, I call shore leave."

There was an awkward silence. He looked into his food carton and poked around, appearing almost disinterested in the conversation. "Do you keep in touch with them?"

She cast a strange look at him. She knew his disinterest wasn't genuine. He was fishing. She hated that he had to turn all federal agent on her--and when they were just starting to get along.

"No, I haven't spoken to them since my father died," she casually replied.

He cast a glance at her and raised his brows sharply. "Then explain the dozens of lengthy, untraceable calls we found on your phone records over the past few years."

His comment surprised her although it shouldn't have. She should have known he'd be poking around into every detail of her life.

"What are you insinuating?" she suddenly demanded to know and set her food carton on the nightstand between them.

"Come on; give me some credit, Jackie. Four men from your father's old SEAL team suddenly vanish without a trace when their former commander's daughter is in trouble," he remarked boldly. "What do you think I'm insinuating?"

She felt annoyed by the entire conversation and wasn't about to let him suggest they were up to something. "If they're organizing to help me, I certainly didn't ask them to."

"Then I don't suppose that phone you've been using would have calls to any of those untraceable numbers we'd found, huh?" he casually asked.

Holden set his carton on the nightstand, stood, and approached her duffle bag on the floor beyond her bed. Jackie pounced on the bag to prevent him from opening it. Holden joined her on the floor and attempted to take it. Within a split second, Jackie removed the gun and aimed it at him. He stared at the gun she held then eyed her without flinching.

"We both know you aren't going to shoot me," he bluntly informed her.

Jackie stared at him without emotion, but she wasn't sure how long she could maintain her bluff. She quickly removed the cell phone from the bag, smashed it against the nightstand, and then tossed the gun back into the bag with disgust. She hated that he had been right. She'd never willingly shoot him.

He hesitated and stared at the smashed phone on the floor. "I guess I should be grateful that wasn't me." Holden removed the gun from her bag and examined it. "Cute. Illegal possession of an unregistered firearm. Obstructing justice, pulling a weapon on a federal agent, assaulting a federal agent--" He shook his head. "And that's just the last two hours."

She folded her arms across her chest and muttered, "Everyone has off days."

He groaned softly and attempted to plead with her from where he sat on the floor leaning against the bed. "I can protect you, Jackie, but I need you to trust me."

She cast a look at him and wondered how badly he wanted her trust. It wasn't fair that he was so cute yet so underhanded. "You want to protect me?" she demanded while studying him. "Fine, but just us. No one else can know our location." She sat back on her feet and stared at him without emotion. "We can chill out on a remote beach, sip tropical drinks, and work on our tans until the trial."

"I can't do that. I have superiors to answer to."

Her look was serious as she searched his eyes. She wanted to trust him so badly, but she wasn't sure she'd ever be able to. She couldn't even rationalize with him, since he clearly had his own agenda. Then again, so did she.

"No one else has to die, Agent Falcone."

"I could lose my job."

"You could lose your life!"

They stared into each other's eyes for a long, awkward moment in silence. She briefly allowed her thoughts to stray. The two of them alone together for the next two to twelve months almost sounded appealing. She wondered if she'd be able to corrupt the Boy Scout in him. She subconsciously had to keep her eyes from straying to his crotch. It had been a long time since she wanted a man so badly that he was able to cloud her judgment.

Holden tensed, almost as if he had heard her thoughts. "Supposing I agreed. Where's safe?"

Her heart suddenly pounded at the mere suggestion. She was almost surprised he was even considering it. Her sexual desire seemed to take over and left her brain and good senses behind. She already had them rolling around naked on some tropical beach. Another fine image.

"If you're opposed to a phony passport, there's a ranch in Colorado," she informed him and quickly sat forward with renewed enthusiasm. "My friend can rent a puddle jumper, and I'll fly us there. We could leave right away."

"Not that I'm agreeing to anything, but I should remind you that you destroyed your cell phone and mine can be traced," Holden informed her. "Using my cell phone to call your contact would lead the Bureau right to us."

Jackie removed Othello's cell phone and grinned deviously. "That was Pam's phone."

"You're good," he remarked then stared at her a moment in silence.

She attempted to read his expression. The way he looked at her sent a shockwave of pleasure through her body, reminding her just how long it had been since she'd been with a man. All she could think about was how badly she had wanted him that morning. Jackie cursed herself for thinking such things and reeled in her sexual desire. She could think about scratching her itch later.

"I suppose if I want your cooperation, I have little choice," Holden finally announced. He shifted uncomfortably while staring into her eyes. "Make the call."

Jackie studied him a moment, grinned deviously, and pressed a button on the cell phone. There was a moment's pause as she waited for the person on the other end to answer. She suddenly snapped to attention at the responding voice.

"Hey, it's me," she said cheerfully into the phone. "I hope I didn't catch you in mixed company." She grinned slyly, winked at Holden, and awaited a response. "We have a change of plans. I need a puddle jumper. Agent Falcone has agreed to accompany me." She hesitated then chuckled lowly. "Oh, please, he's too much of a Boy Scout." There was a moment of hesitation as she eyed Holden with a raised brow. Her eyes swept quickly over his body. "He says he's not."

Holden rolled his eyes and groaned.

"Yeah, I love you too." She disconnected the call and smiled at Holden, pleased with herself. "He'll have it set up for eight tomorrow morning."

He stared at her a moment longer, fidgeted uncomfortably, and looked away with some embarrassment. "We should probably get some sleep," he announced gently. "We have a long day ahead of us."

She nodded in agreement. As Jackie stood, Holden extended his hand to her to help him up. She took his hand and helped pull him to his feet. Holden suddenly twisted her arm behind her back and tackled her to the bed face first. Jackie fought against him, but her attempts were futile. He swiftly handcuffed her right wrist to the wooden bedpost, released her, and avoided the kick for his groin that instantly followed. Jackie flipped onto her back and pulled against the handcuff.

"You bastard! You tricked me!"

Holden removed his cell phone, pressed a number, and waited for an answer. He was oddly out of breath despite his limited physical exertion.

"Yeah, Fields, I've got the clone phone. Our boys should be able to pull the number of her contact from it," Holden announced then hesitated and eyed Jackie while listening to Fields on the other end. "She's restrained but most certainly pissed. I think her head's about to spin around. What time will my backup arrive?" He fell silent and listened to the response. "Okay. Eight tomorrow morning. We'll be here."

Holden disconnected the call, replaced his cell phone to his pocket, and glanced at her before heading back to his own bed. She followed him with hostile eyes.

"All bets are off, Agent Falcone," she snarled.

"You're just pissed because I did it to you before you could do it to me," he scoffed and flopped onto his bed. "I'm not exactly thrilled about taking on a handful of rogue ex-Navy SEALs." He gave her a serious look. "I want your father's team at a safe distance until after the trial."

"Now I'm wishing I had kicked you in your lady parts," Jackie snapped.

Holden ignored her, reclaimed his carton of take-out, and leaned against the headboard. He ate his dinner and watched an old movie playing on the television. Jackie sneered at him and tugged on her cuffed wrist. It wasn't going to end well for Agent Falcone, she was positive of that. Unfortunately, he was too dense to see it.

Chapter Twenty

$\mathcal{D}$t was early the next morning, and the rising sun was peeking into the motel room through the part in the blackout curtains. Holden slept on top of the duvet while remaining fully dressed, possibly in anticipation of problems, whether from the governor's men or his restless witness. The distinctive sound of a handcuff snapping shut broke the silence. Holden jerked awake and snapped his head to the right. His right wrist was already cuffed to the bedpost. He didn't even have time to react before Jackie pounced on top of him. She pinned his left wrist to the bed, and firmly held her knee between his legs snug against his crotch. Holden gasped to the pressure between his legs and stared at Jackie as she hovered over him. She glared at him with an evil, twisted smile.

"Play time is over, Agent Falcone," she growled. "Welcome to this girl's Navy, bitch."

"Jackie, don't make--"

"Don't Jackie me," she hissed with hostility. "I trusted you, and you fucked me over."

"Those men--"

Jackie pressed her knee more firmly against his crotch. He gasped with surprise and moderate discomfort. She no longer wanted to listen to anything he had to say.

"You made it personal by going after my friend. That was a mistake," she growled lowly. "I'm going to protect him even if it means hurting you."

He stared at her a moment in silence, apparently considering his current situation and his next move. "I think I'd rather have you flirtatious."

"Consider yourself lucky I'm not squeezing and twisting," Jackie snarled.

"Jackie, I'm sorry," he quickly remarked with a hint of panic in his voice. "It was necessary."

"You're only sorry because my knee is just short of crushing your boys."

"Please, a little mercy here!"

Jackie frowned and eased the pressure against his crotch. Holden exhaled with relief. Whether she intended to hurt him or not didn't matter, it only mattered what he thought she'd do. Judging by his reaction, he believed she intended him bodily harm. He underestimated her loyalty to her friend.

"Be reasonable," Holden announced while breathing more naturally now. "Several officers are going to be swarming the area in less than two hours and there'll be even more waiting at the airport surrounding that plane. You have nowhere to go."

She rolled her eyes with disbelief to how gullible he had been then studied him from where she remained hovering over him. This time, she wasn't even thinking about how handsome he was as her face remained close to his.

"Do you really think he'd arranged that?" She snorted a soft laugh. "Go back to spy school. You should realize that what I told him was merely code for 'that prick has me, and I didn't know if I can trust him'." Jackie raised a cocky brow. "And, incidentally, he thinks you're probably gay too."

Holden frowned to her crude joke not being humored. Despite his efforts to stop her, this time she easily removed his second pair of handcuffs and cuffed his left wrist to the headboard. She was getting a little too good at subduing him and cuffing him to objects. She grinned somewhat playfully but with something more sinister lurking behind her eyes. She was no longer that playful tigress, and he knew it.

"I'll put something on T.V., so you won't be bored for the next two hours while waiting for your friends."

Jackie swiftly jumped off him and turned on the television loud enough that no one would hear him if he yelled. As the porn movie started, the familiar background music pulsated in time with the woman's cries of ecstasy. Jackie carelessly tossed the remote control across the room along with his cell phone, which had been setting on the nightstand.

Holden frowned at her sadistic selection of entertainment. "Thanks for not humiliating me."

"Anytime," she announced cheerfully.

Jackie grabbed her duffle bag, blew him a kiss, and slipped from the room. Holden jerked on his right, cuffed wrist then glanced at Jackie's bed beyond his bed. A pillow was propped against the wooden bedpost that was now broken in half. She had used the pillow to muffle the sounds of the splintering wood.

✝

*J*ackie walked along the marina dock only fifteen minutes after her *conversation* with Agent Falcone. She made excellent time on her short walk from the nearby motel. She wore her baseball cap and sunglasses to help conceal her face while carrying her duffle bag securely over her shoulder. It was another beautiful morning and the sounds of the ocean and seagulls added to its ambience, but Jackie was in no mood to enjoy it. Her encounter with Holden had her bothered, and she wasn't even sure why it bothered her as much as it did. She certainly didn't expect him to see things her way. It was his job as a federal agent to believe he had all the answers and believe he was right beyond all doubt. What he didn't realize; she was in a better position than most to take care of herself. The few resourceful people she knew were highly connected to other *more* resourceful people. It was an enormous network of people owing other people favors. In the dead center of that enormous network was Monroe. The man she trusted with her life.

Once she met up with Monroe, she was convinced that the governor would never be able to touch her. In her coded conversation with her resourceful friend, he had offered to send the cavalry to her rescue last night, but she quickly shut it down. Jackie knew she was capable of escaping Agent Falcone if he had turned on her. She had been secretly hoping he'd see things her way, but it was a childish fantasy to think he would. Having Monroe making some wild move from some foreign country just to fly in and attempt to save her, when she really didn't need saving, would only result in putting him on the 'watch' list or worse. Her life wasn't in danger, so she wasn't going to allow Monroe to expose himself. Jackie noticed one or two police officers lurking around the marina, but she was easily able to slip past them. Both had obviously been on duty all night and were tired now. She walked past several docked boats before reaching slip number twenty. Jackie suddenly stopped, noted the expensive yacht, and eyed it with an approving grin. She was already impressed with Monroe's most recent contact. As she walked up the gangway, a neatly dressed man in his early fifties, wearing a hat and sunglasses, appeared on deck not far from her. He stared at her with a look that quickly turned hostile while placing his hands firmly on his hips.

"That son-of-a-bitch!" the yacht's captain suddenly cried out, startling her.

Jackie took a step back and stared at the man with distrust. Perhaps she'd complimented Monroe a bit too hastily. He did warn her about the captain.

The captain suddenly smiled cheerfully. "Monroe didn't tell me I was picking up the commander's daughter!"

He extended his hand to her while grinning. Jackie felt relief flood her body, accepted his extended hand, and allowed him to help her onboard. Once she was safely on deck, she attempted to get a better gage of the man's concealed face.

"You knew my father?"

"Of course I knew him," he boldly announced then grinned. "Don't you remember me?"

The captain removed his cap and sunglasses to reveal a face Jackie hadn't seen in years. Jackie stared at him with near horror and held back her gasp.

"Zach?" she suddenly cried out. "But I thought--I thought you were dead!"

He suddenly chuckled with amusement. "Hey, there are many levels of dead, Jackie. If I wasn't dead--I'd be dead, you know what I mean?"

Jackie laughed overjoyed and happily hugged him. He returned the warm embrace and then pulled back just far enough to kiss her quickly on the lips. He grinned slyly and released her. She felt her cheeks immediately redden from the quick kiss. She'd forgotten how exuberant Zach could be. Monroe was a prick! He knew he was sending a familiar face, but he chose to surprise both by not telling either about the other. He wasn't totally wrong though. Zach was unbalanced. And after being listed as dead for the last five years, there was no telling if that instability had increased. Actually, with Zach, there was no telling anything. Despite his innocent, docile appearance, Zach was a frightening creature.

"We'll catch up after we cast off," he announced cheerfully. "I assume you're in a hurry.

"I've got about an hour before the cavalry arrives and frees one very unhappy federal agent."

"Well it's nice to know you're following in your father's footsteps--" he announced with a grin, "--pissing off all the right people."

Chapter Twenty-one

It was a little after seven o'clock that morning, and the motel seemed peaceful for the early hour. Truman remained at the front desk within the lobby, having worked a double shift. Business had slowed considerably after the holidays and several employees had been laid off. He looked bored while playing games on the computer to pass the time. He gingerly tugged on the crotch of his pants while making a face of discomfort. He still hadn't fully recovered from Jackie's assault on his testicles.

"Excuse me," a male voice announced from across the desk, startling the young man.

Truman quickly straightened and immediately appeared to regret the sudden action. He looked at the intimidating man standing on the other side of the desk from him. Dexter flashed a badge and maintained his serious look.

"I'm with the U.S. Marshals' office," Dexter announced then indicated the equally intimidating man, Oscar, standing just inside the lobby doorway. "This is my associate."

Truman looked from the badge then to both men with some surprise. Dexter placed a photo of Jackie on the lobby desk before Truman.

"Have you seen this woman?" Dexter asked. "We have reason to believe she registered at this motel last night under an assumed name."

Truman glanced at Jackie's photo on the desk then looked back at Dexter. He smirked with arrogance. "Maybe I have. What's it worth to you?"

"Stop jerking us around, kid," Dexter snapped. "We know she's here. What room is she staying in?"

"I never said she was staying here," Truman remarked in a clumsy attempt to solicit a bribe.

Oscar locked the door and closed the vertical blinds. Truman glanced past Dexter to see what the other man was doing by the door. He was about to speak when Dexter grabbed him by the back of the neck and slammed his face against the desk. His face struck the desk with a tremendous thump. As Truman pulled his head back, his nose bled freely and was possibly broken. Truman screamed and clutched his bleeding nose. Dexter didn't release the back of his neck.

"Let's try again," Dexter growled and pounded his index finger on the photo on the desk, which now contained droplets of Truman's blood. "Where is the girl?"

"A man claiming to be a federal agent came for her," Truman cried out in agony and fright. "I think they went to his room. Room 210. Please, don't hurt me!"

Dexter released the back of the young man's neck and casually straightened Truman's shirt while he cried and clutched his bleeding, broken nose.

"See," Dexter announced with a cheap grin on his face, "that wasn't so difficult, now was it?"

Dexter turned and approached Oscar by the door. Oscar removed his gun with silencer from his shoulder holster and, without hesitation, shot Truman in the head from across the lobby. Truman's head snapped back, and he collapsed to the floor behind the desk. Both men left the lobby, making certain the door was locked behind them. Dexter and Oscar walked around the building and headed up the outside stairs to the second floor facing the ocean. Dexter looked at the blood droplet on his white shirt, frowned, and dabbed it with his handkerchief.

"Is it just me, or do kids bleed easier these days?" Dexter asked his associate.

"You were standing in the splash zone," Oscar remarked casually. "You need to take a step to the side. You weren't always so careless."

Dexter returned his handkerchief to his pocket and frowned his disapproval to Oscar's comment. They checked each room number as they casually walked along the balcony. Holden's room was just up ahead. Dexter stopped Oscar two rooms away.

"No excuses," Dexter informed Oscar in a soft tone while glaring at him. "Once I break open the door, we shoot anything that breathes. No one comes out alive. We've wasted enough manpower on this girl."

Oscar nodded. "Won't be a problem."

Both men reached inside their jackets for their hidden weapons when Holden's motel room door suddenly opened, startling them. Dexter and Oscar holstered their weapons and took a step closer to the wall to avoid being seen. Holden stormed from the room with a police officer on his heels. They headed for the stairs in the opposite direction.

"I want the airport and the marina scoured for her," Holden announced with hostility. "I want her found before she escapes again!"

"How did she manage to handcuff you to the bed?" the officer asked as he hurried after Holden. "And why were you watching porn movies?"

"Shut up," Holden growled as they vanished down the second set of steps.

Dexter and Oscar exchanged looks then hurried for the opposite set of stairs to avoid being spotted.

"How the hell does she keep getting away?" Dexter demanded.

"Any idea where she's going?" Oscar asked as he followed Dexter to the ground floor walkway.

"No, but hopefully our friend has some theory," Dexter replied while removing his cell phone then looked at Oscar. "I'll send some men to the airport to watch for her. We'll head for the marina and look around there."

†

*J*ackie stood at the helm of the yacht, skippering the expensive ship as they sailed along the slightly choppy, secluded waters. She felt relaxed and enjoyed being in control of the amazing craft. It wasn't nearly as exciting as flying was, but she was enjoying the experience all the same. Zach leaned casually against the railing and watched her while grinning at her pleasure. After a few minutes, his look turned more serious.

"I wonder why Monroe didn't tell me you were the one in trouble."

She cast a glance at him and grinned. "Well, you know Monroe."

He suddenly chuckled and hid his smile. "You mean Monroe knows me."

"That might have something to do with it."

"That's so typical," he scoffed, shook his head defiantly, and threw his hands in the air. "Shoot people with a barrage of bullets and it's peachy keen. Blow up shit and you're labeled the angel of death."

She cast a sharp glare at him. "I heard you blew up a freighter."

"Just a small one."

"I won't nitpick," she announced with little interest in any details of Zach's mission and returned to watching the ocean rush past. "I'm just happy to see a friendly face."

He suddenly snorted a laugh and straightened by the railing without taking his eyes off her. "You'd be the only one to think I have a friendly face."

That was far from the truth. Zach looked friendly and even acted friendly. Most people would think he was a gentle, kind man by just looking at him. As he studied her, Zach shook his head in disbelief and near disgust.

"I can't believe it's been nearly five years since I last saw you," he announced. "I'm starting to think you've been avoiding me on purpose."

She glanced at him and tried not to laugh. "Your being dead probably had something to do with it," she replied while containing her grin.

"I suppose that could make get-togethers more difficult," Zach replied.

"I went to the funeral."

"I didn't bother attending," he announced with disinterest. "I'm not much for funerals." Zach appeared curious and tilted his head. "Was it nice?"

"Yes, very."

"Was the commander drunk?"

"Of course," she replied while grinning.

"Well, that's what's important," he announced.

She glanced at him several times with an odd look now on her face. There was something that she suddenly found troubling. He immediately noticed her concerned expression and grinned almost humored.

"You have that look," he remarked. "Something on your mind, dear?"

She became uncomfortable, shifted at the helm, and then sheepishly glanced at him. "We buried a toe," she replied gently and immediately grimaced at the thought. "If you didn't die, whose toe did we bury?"

Zach grinned and chuckled in his throat. His smile mocked her. "Why do you ask questions which you don't want to know the answers?"

She rolled her eyes and attempted to hide her smile. It was true. She forgot. Never ask Zach about the things he does. Zach finally approached her at the helm, stood behind her, and peered over her shoulder as she steered the expensive yacht through the slightly choppy waters.

"You don't need Monroe," he informed her while placing his hands on her shoulders. He gently massaged her shoulders from behind. "I can take you to some of the most beautiful, remote islands anywhere. I mean, let's face it. You wouldn't need more protection than me."

She enjoyed the shoulder massage, knowing how tense she'd been the last few weeks. Zach was absolutely correct; she wouldn't need more protection than him, but the thought of traveling alone with him for any length of time was at best frightening. He was wildly unpredictable, and, honestly, she didn't trust him not to blow up that remote island.

"I appreciate the offer, but Monroe already has my disappearance planned."

"Ah, the hell with Monroe," he scoffed then placed his arms around her waist. He rested his head affectionately on her shoulder like an innocent child. "That prick was hitting on you when you were barely sixteen. He'd love to get you alone somewhere isolated and exotic for a few months. I, on the other hand, am a perfect gentleman."

She slowly turned her head to look at his face only inches from hers and noted his grin. She raised her brows and gave him a curious look.

"Didn't you back me into a corner once?"

Zach removed his head from her shoulder and took a step back from her. "That doesn't count. I was drunk," he replied firmly. "Besides, you were nineteen and legal."

Jackie eyed him behind her and laughed. He gave a general nod across the ocean.

"There's a secluded beach on the other side of the island," he announced matter-of-fact. "I thought you might enjoy a little beach time."

"That sounds wonderful," she said with a soft groan at the thought. "I could use a little relaxation in the sun. I've been wound pretty tight lately."

"A little skinny dippin' will cure that."

Jackie eyed Zach's devious grin with a skeptical look. She'd forgotten how charming and *horny* Zach was. Even so, she wouldn't trade him for the world. It was great having him resurrected from the dead. The only question remaining on her mind was whether or not he'd actually hacked off his own toe while faking his death. Or did he just happen to *find* a spare one lying around? She didn't know which thought was more disturbing.

Chapter Twenty-two

The skies appeared to be darkening later that afternoon as the winds picked up slightly. Zach's expensive yacht was seen anchored just off shore of a remote, secluded beach on the small island not far from Florida. An inflatable launch was pulled onto the beach where the pair had been soaking in the sun after a lunch of freshly caught lobster. Jackie relaxed on the beach in her shorts and tank top while holding a glass of wine. It was actually her third glass, and she was feeling pretty good. Her relaxed mood probably had something to do with allowing Zach to massage her feet. He was grinning boyishly and appeared to be in his glory. Jackie enjoyed the thorough foot massage as she stared at the dark skies rolling in, interrupting their sunny afternoon on the beach.

"Is there a storm approaching?"

"A nasty little bitch of a hurricane is skimming the coast," he informed her without looking up from her feet. "It's not expected to hit here. Expect some high winds later tonight."

Jackie marveled at how much he sounded like a weatherman. Living on a boat probably sharpened his nautical knowledge, not that he was ever a slouch in that area. Most SEALs were well-adjusted to water. She found herself distracted by the dark skies and drifted into her own, private thoughts. Zach studied her a moment and appeared curious.

"You seem terribly distracted," he informed her. "Would you feel better if I waited with you for Monroe?"

She snapped out of her daze and looked at Zach. "No, I wouldn't want to impose more than I already have."

"Seriously?" he demanded and appeared offended. "Does it look like I have anything else to do today? Besides, you're family. We take care of our own."

"You know, with everything that's been going on and all the violence I've seen recently, I can't understand why I'm so bothered by one federal agent," she said aloud and instantly regretted it. Zach was going to jump all over that comment.

"The guy you handcuffed to the motel bed?" He grinned lustfully. "Was there more to that bondage scene than you're telling me?"

She glared at him with a disapproving look then groaned softly. "I just thought--I thought I could reason with him. I really thought I got through to him, and he turned around and tried to flush out Monroe." She leaned back on her elbows and stared at the sky. "I really thought we were working toward the same goal--to put that bastard Lyle behind bars, but it seems his only agenda is to make a name for himself by bringing me in."

"Would you like me to take care of this prick of a federal agent for you?"

Jackie suddenly straightened and eyed Zach with surprise and possible horror. "What do you mean 'take care of him'?" she suddenly gasped and felt her entire body tense.

Zach fidgeted slightly then responded with, "You know, hold him at bay for a few days. I could lead him on a wild goose chase." He suddenly grinned and added a humored chuckle. "You didn't think I meant *eliminate* him, did you? I mean, he's a federal agent. That kind of heat I don't need."

Jackie was relieved and managed a smile. Zach was known for being wildly unpredictable, and she didn't need him doing anything stupid, particularly on her behalf. She finally took a deep breath and sighed.

"No, I think I've shaken him for now," she replied. "By the time he realizes I'm not going to some airport and thinks to look here, Monroe will have me hidden away." She hesitated and looked at the man massaging her feet. "He's constantly messing with my head. Just when I think I have him figured out, he's someone else."

She suddenly couldn't help the overwhelming feeling of anger surging through her. "I've been betrayed by people before, but I seriously wanted to hurt him last night. I guess I wanted to trust him so badly, that I couldn't handle it when he proved he couldn't be trusted."

"Did you sleep with him?" Zach asked casually.

She felt her cheeks immediately redden and pulled her feet from him. "My God, no!"

Zach appeared curious but showed little emotion. "Old, fat, and ugly with a bad rug and body odor?"

She suddenly hesitated. "Well, not exactly."

Zach's eyes suddenly lit up along with his grin. "Do you *want* to sleep with him?"

Now he was just interrogating her for his own amusement. "No, certainly not," she firmly insisted.

"There you have it," he replied casually.

"There I have what?" Jackie demanded and wondered why she was even having this conversation with him. Talking with Zach was enough to make her head spin.

"It's pretty obvious. You're sexually attracted to him and he's not taking the bait."

She groaned with annoyance. "I told you I didn't want to sleep with him."

"Yeah, so you've said, but that's not what you were thinking," Zach casually informed her. "Your pheromones are betraying you, my dear."

"I'm not attracted to him," she snarled then took a moment to consider the lie. "Sure, he's cute, but he's so ungodly straight. No sense of humor whatsoever. He's like some sort of FBI lab experiment gone astray."

"Yeah, I know the type," Zach replied with a sigh. "Ass could be on fire but nary a flinch."

"Oh, so you've met him."

Zach eyed her and chuckled. She sank into thought then looked at her strange friend.

"Maybe I should call him, you know, just to make sure he got out of those handcuffs."

"Yes, I'll bet he's in a good mood," he remarked. "Nothing burns a man's ass more than being cuffed to a bed in his own handcuffs."

"I put on pay-per-view porn for him, but somehow I think that's only going to increase his bitchiness."

Zach eyed her with surprise, smiled, and laughed softly. "And you were counting on his backup to release him?" he suddenly asked then laughed again while shaking his head. "Oh, that's so embarrassing. You are a devil, Jackie." He gave her a quick, lustful once over. "It's a tragedy that some men just don't appreciate you the way I do."

She grimaced slightly. "I was pretty mean. Think I should call him?"

"Yeah, I'm sure he'd appreciate that," Zach remarked. "Rub it in a little deeper while you're at it."

"I guess that's a negative on calling him."

"Yes, that's a negative on calling him," he replied. "See, that's the sort of thing I would do, and I wouldn't want you turning into me."

She eyed him sharply. "I think we're safe, Zach."

He stared at her with his mouth hanging open, slowly shook his head, and appeared offended. "You've never appreciated me or my work."

"Your work?" she questioned and nearly choked. "Your *work* scares the shit out of me."

"You're turning into such a girl."

Chapter Twenty-three

*D*ark Water Island was home to a small town with a slightly booming population. A few years ago, everyone knew everyone else, but there had been an influx of wealthy people attempting to make the secluded island their home. New homes were being built in the island's interior by the dozens. It was nearly impossible to find a beach house on the beautiful island. Locals refused to sell to non-locals in silent protest to big city attitudes attempting to change their simpler way of life. The Dark Water Island fairground was alive with activity as its annual fair continued into the weekend. The extensive fairground was filled with attractions, rides, games, and food vendors of all types from all across the country. As the sun was setting, the lights from rides and attractions lit up the fairground, giving it a romantic glow. Jackie walked through the massive crowds with Zach, who ate pink cotton candy. He looked so much like the innocent fatherly type; it almost caused her to laugh. Looks were so deceiving!

"You didn't have to come along, Zach," she informed him as they maneuvered through the crowd. "I'm meeting Monroe in half an hour."

"People don't travel alone to fairs," he casually informed her in a slightly mocking tone. His eyes suddenly lit up as they neared one of the game stands. "Oh, a stuffed elephant," he exclaimed with childlike glee. "I've got to have one of those!"

Jackie began to wonder if he was just messing with her for fun or if he really wanted the pink, stuffed elephant. Something was obviously off in his mind. Once, while on shore leave at her house, she caught him watching cartoons at two in the morning while smoking Cuban cigars. Sadly, he wasn't even drunk at the time. As he dragged her toward the game stand, she saw Holden standing in the crowd fifty yards from them. Jackie felt her heart leap into her throat. She suddenly yanked on Zach's hand, nearly pulling him off his feet, and pulled him alongside the vendor's booth. Without warning, she kissed him passionately. Zach tossed his cotton candy aside, pulled her against him, and returned the kiss. Despite Zach's passionate and aggressive kiss, Jackie watched Holden pass them. Once he was past, she broke off the kiss, despite Zach's efforts to prolong it.

"That's him," she gasped softly.

Zach paid little attention to her concern or comment and began affectionately kissing her neck, completely preoccupied with his own sexual desires.

"Him who?" he groaned softly.

Jackie suddenly realized he was kissing her neck, stopped him, and nodded across the crowd. "The guy who looks suspiciously like an FBI agent at the popcorn counter," she remarked then shook her head. "How did he find me?"

Zach zeroed in on Holden. Before her very eyes, he suddenly morphed into the highly trained soldier she remembered. "I've got this. You meet Monroe," he firmly ordered. "Don't bother waiting for me."

Before he could take off, Jackie grabbed his arm to stop him, forcing him to face her. "Don't hurt him," she threatened with a serious look.

He grinned boyishly. "Relax, Jackie, I'm just going to have a little fun."

"Yeah, but your idea of fun is disturbing."

"Trust me--" he said while grinning.

Those were famous last words that always frightened Jackie, especially coming from Zach. Men from her father's old platoon always said 'trust me' before they did something frightening or wildly inappropriate. Zach kissed her quickly on the lips, groaned while grinning lustfully, and then hurried behind several gaming booths to get ahead of Holden. He merged into the crowd, removed his cell phone, placed it to his ear, and kept his head down while looking around nervously as he walked a few feet in front of Holden.

"Where are you?" Zach said into the phone while maintaining mild suspicion. "I'm getting worried."

Zach continued walking and didn't bother looking back. Holden suddenly looked through the crowd, noticed Zach, and followed him from a distance. Zach shifted his eyes in every direction, increasing suspicion upon him.

"Okay, I'll meet you at the pier in thirty minutes," he announced into the phone.

Zach disconnected his fake phone call, replaced the cell phone to his pocket, and moved quickly through the crowd. Holden followed him at a safe distance and made his own call.

"Pier--thirty minutes," Holden said into the phone. "Send two of your best men."

Holden replaced his phone to his jacket and watched as Zach headed in the direction of the pier. Holden remained a safe distance behind him.

Just across the fairground, Jackie approached the Ferris wheel area and scanned the crowd of people with anticipation. A suave looking man in his mid-thirties, Monroe, stood not far from the Ferris wheel. He wore expensive clothes and had a commanding presence despite his lanky stature. Monroe looked more like a rich playboy than a scheming mastermind. A feeling of relief swept over her to the familiar man.

"Monroe--" she whispered softly with relief and visually took him in with a sweeping gaze.

Jackie quickly maneuvered through the crowd and suddenly ran into Dexter. Their eyes met, startling her. He grabbed her arms before she had a chance to react. She appeared momentarily horrified to see the governor's hitman standing directly in front of her. It was the first time she'd seen him since that night, and she was surprised by the feelings of fear shooting through her. Her leg seemed to throb in response.

"Miss Remus, imagine finding you here?" Dexter said with a devious grin on his face.

It didn't seem possible. How did he know where to look for her? Jackie instinctively thrust her knee for his groin. He deflected it with anticipation, but she had struck him hard enough on the thigh to force him to release her. Jackie turned and ran. Monroe appeared oblivious to her situation while casually looking around the crowd. Jackie ran through the crowd and saw another tough and sinister looking man making his way toward her. She'd never seen Oscar before, but the way he stared at her told her he was to be avoided. She turned and continued through the crowd in the opposite direction of Monroe with both men closing in fast.

✝

Dark Water Island harbor was filled with boats tied to the dock as well as anchored in the bay. Tourists traveled great distances to enjoy the town's well-publicized fair. Since hotels on the island were scarce, most had to bring their own place to sleep, which usually involved a boat of some sort. Zach walked along the dock while eyeing several boats crowding the dock and slips. Holden and two officers pursued him from a distance, attempting to remain inconspicuous. Zach seemed to find what he was looking for, jumped the railing onto one of the boats, and disappeared from their sight. Holden motioned for the officers to take either side. Holden jumped onto the boat and approached the cabin. A woman's laughter was clearly heard. He drew his gun and kicked in the door. Holden and the officers entered the cabin with their guns aimed at the couple beneath the covers on the bed.

"FBI! Hands up!"

A naked man and woman jumped up in the bed. The man put his hands in the air, the horror showing on his face, while the woman held the sheet over her naked body. The unfamiliar woman screamed in response. Holden groaned, rolled his eyes, and lowered his gun.

"Sorry, there's been a mistake," he announced gently in an embarrassed tone.

Holden left as the officers attempted to smooth things over with the irate man and panicking woman. Holden jumped off the boat and saw Zach walking along the pier. He caught sight of Holden and immediately bolted.

"Stop! FBI!"

Holden ran after Zach, gained ground on him, and tackled him to the dock. It was a hard tackle, but Zach didn't appear harmed. Holden flipped Zach onto his back and held him by his shirt collar. Zach stared back at him and appeared genuinely frightened.

"Where is she?" Holden demanded.

"Are you Sherry's husband?" he suddenly cried out while trembling. "I don't know where she is, I swear! Sherry and I are just friends!"

133

The police officers hurried toward them with their guns drawn. Zach saw them and attempted to point at Holden while his hands trembled.

"Officers, thank God! This man tried to kill me!" Zach yelled to both officers. "He thinks I slept with his wife, but we're just friends!"

Holden stood with a look of distrust and pulled Zach to his feet. "Let's see some ID."

Zach fumbled in his pocket, removed his wallet, and handed it to Holden with trembling hands. His look of distress was frighteningly convincing. Holden looked at the ID then tossed Zach's wallet to him.

"Go on. Get out of here," Holden growled with disgust while looking moderately embarrassed and mostly defeated.

Zach hurried away then slowed his pace, smiled deviously to himself, and removed his cell phone. He pressed a button and waited for the response.

"Hey, do you have her?" Zach asked. There was a pause as Monroe responded from the other end. Zach suddenly stopped and appeared alarmed. "What do you mean? I left her there." He hesitated then sank into thought while listening to the response. "I'll be there just as soon as I divert her FBI stalker."

Zach disconnected the call and pushed another button. Holden's cell phone rang as Zach walked away.

Holden answered his phone with annoyance. "Falcone--"

"I have some urgent information regarding that young woman," Zach whispered into his cell phone.

Holden immediately straightened and appeared interested by the call. "Yes?"

His voice became bold. "When a beautiful, sexy, young woman handcuffs you to a bed, enjoy it, you lucky bastard," he announced into the phone while grinning.

Holden looked across the dock and met Zach's gaze from fifty yards away. Zach flashed a mocking smile and took off across the pier toward nearby buildings.

"Son-of-a-bitch," Holden exclaimed. "That's him!"

Holden and both officers ran after Zach, who already had a healthy head start. He seemed to vanish mysteriously near the buildings. Holden suddenly stopped the two officers.

"Whoa, wait," Holden announced and looked around. "He wants us to follow him. He's a diversion. Get everyone back to the fairground. She's there."

All three hurried back toward the fairground. Zach sat on a nearby roof while watching them with a look of disgust. He placed his cell phone to his ear and headed for the fire escape.

"They're heading back to you, Monroe," Zach grumbled. "Find her and get the hell out of there. I have one more card to play." There was a brief pause as he stopped before the fire escape. "Which card?" he repeated the question with surprise. "Joker's wild, which else?"

Chapter Twenty-four

Jackie ran through the crowd toward the farm machinery display with Dexter and Oscar chasing her. They were quickly closing in on her, since neither man seemed to care who they shoved from their path while Jackie relied more on ducking and dodging fairgoers. When she hit the clearing surrounding the farm machinery display, she was able to pick up speed and her goal was in sight. Beyond the farm machinery sat a news helicopter! Both men appeared to come to the same conclusion about the direction she was heading. They knew if she reached it, she would be gone. She knew better then to look back, since it would only shave precious seconds off her speed. A man suddenly turned unexpectedly into her path. She collided with him, nearly knocking him down. Although she didn't fall, it slowed her momentum.

Before she could continue her sprint for the helicopter, Dexter tackled her to the ground. He barely had her on the ground when her body reacted subconsciously to the tackle. Jackie threw herself into a roll, taking him with her. She continued through with the roll and was on her feet like a cat falling from a tree. As Dexter scrambled to his feet, she kicked him in the chest, bowling him over.

Oscar suddenly grabbed her from behind in an attempt to subdue her. As she struggled to break free, Dexter made it to his feet and approached to help Oscar. His twisted, confident smile infuriated her. Jackie used Oscar's body as leverage to brace herself as she kicked Dexter in the chest with both feet, sending him backwards and into a tractor. A crowd began to gather at the otherwise empty, boring exhibit. As Jackie's feet hit the ground, she used her forward momentum and threw herself to her knee, flipping Oscar over her shoulder and roughly to the ground. Despite the hard hit, he immediately sprang to his feet.

Jackie spun into a roundhouse kick and nailed him in the chest. He was thrown violently to the ground. Dexter had recovered from his hard hit to the tractor and lunged for her, throwing a punch. She blocked his punch and rammed her knee into his side, winding him slightly. She spun into a high roundhouse kick and struck him in the face. He was thrown roughly to the ground, writhing in agony. Oscar stumbled to his feet and took a step toward her. Despite the cheering from the growing crowd of men to the beating she was giving her attackers, several men stepped forward to aid her and shoved Oscar back.

"Leave the lady alone!"

Her rescuers were met with booing from the men enjoying watching a woman beat two grown men. More men soon joined in. Oscar was quickly surrounded by fired up local boys looking to find a new source of entertainment. As they pushed and shoved Oscar while yelling profanities at him, Jackie turned and ran back toward the Ferris wheel. She removed her cell phone while jogging and darting through the crowd. The phone was immediately answered by a concerned Monroe.

"Jackie! Where are you?"

"On my way to you with some bad company," she quickly informed him. "I have a thirty second head start. Get ready to move."

"I'm heading to the rendezvous now," Monroe responded from the other end. "Zach says your boyfriend is on his way too. He's attempting a joker's wild, so be prepared."

Her look shattered. "God, help us!"

"Yeah, I know," came the response.

Jackie replaced her phone and picked up speed through the crowd. As she approached the Ferris wheel, she could see several officers in the crowd. Just as she'd seen them, they saw her and pointed. Several policemen were heading in her direction. Jackie felt cornered and looked for an escape. Zach suddenly appeared out of nowhere and took on the first policeman with high roundhouse kicks. The remaining three officers assailed upon him. He skillfully handled all four with little effort and amazing skill. Watching Zach take on several men with martial arts moves was almost like watching a graceful dance. Had he actually intended to harm any of them, none would be returning to their feet. Jackie turned for the Ferris wheel to keep her date with Monroe. As she turned, she came face-to-face with Holden, who had an unpredictably calm look about him. Jackie suddenly stepped back into a fighting stance. Their eyes locked as he anticipated her move. She knew she had to go through him. Since he would be prepared for her karate moves, that meant she'd have to hurt him seriously. She considered a plan of attack that would take him down with minimal injury. She hesitated while staring at him and felt her body twitch. Jackie relaxed her fighting stance and lowered her fists. She couldn't do it! She wasn't willing to hurt him to go through him! Holden removed his handcuffs, swiftly grabbed her wrist, and forcibly cast her forward over one of the game stand counters to cuff her.

"You're under arrest," he growled lowly.

He roughly kicked her legs apart with his foot and cuffed her other wrist behind her back. He aggressively moved against her from behind, leaned over her shoulder, and spoke gruffly in her ear so no one else could hear.

"Anything you say will give me just cause to shoot you," he scoffed and scanned the prying eyes around them. "Do you understand these rights?"

"Yeah, go fuck yourself," she snapped in response.

Holden pulled her up from the counter by her arm. She looked several feet away at Zach, who was now subdued and on the ground with his hands cuffed behind his back. He met her sympathetic gaze from where he lie and gave her a baffled look. With the way he was looking at her; she knew he'd witnessed her inability to fight Agent Falcone. She couldn't bear to face him. She then glanced to her right and saw a concerned Monroe standing in the crowd, watching the entire scene with his hand to his temple. Apparently, he too witnessed her surprising surrender without a fight. She'd successfully betrayed the two men who'd laid their lives on the line for her. Jackie then saw Dexter and Oscar standing several yards away, watching the capture of *their* trophy.

"Dexter three o'clock," she muttered to Holden.

Holden looked to their right. The two men slipped into the crowd and successfully vanished before he could identify either. She glared at Holden but was more disappointed in herself.

"I hope you're happy," she scoffed. "We'll both be dead before morning."

The officers brought the unusually cooperative Zach to Holden. He gave the appearance of a man with no fight left in him, but Jackie knew better. Zach scolded Jackie with a stern look. She could almost hear him mentally cursing at her. She frowned and looked away with disgrace. She didn't want to involve Monroe, but now she'd made things worse by inadvertently handing Zach to the authorities. Considering he was supposed to be dead, she'd put him in a grave predicament, which could land him in an actual grave this time. Holden indicated Zach with a slight nod to the arresting officer alongside him.

"Find out who the hell he really is," Holden remarked then indicated Jackie. "I'll need somewhere to secure her. Think Alcatraz secure."

The remaining three officers joined Holden in boxing around her, shielding her with their bodies, as they hurried her through the crowd of onlookers. She kept her head down to keep from having it unexpectedly blown off and also out of shame for disappointing her friends.

†

*T*wo unmarked police cars pulled up to an average looking house on a residential road. Holden got out of the backseat from one of the cars and pulled the still handcuffed Jackie out behind him. She gave him a scathing, dirty look.

"Police brutality--"

"Shut up," he growled at her then looked at the officer who got out of the driver's side. Holden glared at Jonas with astonishment. "This is it? This is your safe house?"

Despite being a small town cop, Jonas didn't appear offended by Holden's criticism. "I know it doesn't look like much, but it's built with steel and concrete," Jonas informed him.

"Hmm, sort of like a tomb," Jackie remarked and eyed both men. "How fitting."

Jonas glared at Jackie then looked back at Holden. "Are you sure you wouldn't prefer keeping her in a jail cell?"

"No offense, but that place is a cardboard box," Holden remarked. "Any gunfire would shred through it."

"The cells are in the basement," he insisted. "That's cement, and it's underground."

"With one way in and one way out," Holden reminded him sternly. "If those were the governor's hitmen hanging out at the fair, we're not safe anywhere. At least here, we have a sporting chance of survival."

"We have four officers, including myself," Jonas informed him. "One will take the front, one the back, and two outside in patrol cars."

"I don't want to tell you how to do your job, Officer," Holden announced then gave him a firm look, "but allow me to tell you how to do your job. Position one of your men on the roof with an assault rifle with a night scope. The other three should remain inside and keep watch from alongside the windows." Holden had successfully offended Jonas, but he didn't seem to care. "These men are professional killers. If you leave your men alone in patrol cars, they'll be sitting ducks. I'd take her back tonight, if I could, but the fair traffic on the water puts us at risk for an ambush at sea. Then there's that hurricane off the coast causing air transportation problems for my men, so my backup won't be here until morning."

"Then you'll want to get her out first thing tomorrow morning, because I heard that hurricane is picking up speed and intensity. It intends to hit the island head-on tomorrow evening," Jonas informed him. "If we survive tonight, we may get wiped off the island tomorrow."

"We intend to be out of here long before that storm hits," Holden assured him.

Jonas cast a stern glare at one of his men, Frederick, and indicated the house. "Show our guests to the Presidential Suite," he announced.

Frederick nodded and escorted Holden and Jackie inside. Jonas nodded one of the officers to the roof.

"Care to take the crow's nest?" Jonas asked the officer.

He nodded in response.

"Grab one of the assault rifles from the weapon's safe in the house," he informed him.

The officer hurried for the house to secure his weapon and take his crow's nest position. Jonas stood alongside the last officer, Dan, and shook his head with disgust while staring after Holden and Jackie as they entered the house.

"Let's make sure we don't screw this up," Jonas remarked. "Damned feds with their superior attitudes. Acting like we don't know how to handle a few bad asses."

"Bad asses we can handle," Dan replied. "Hired assassins? We may be in over our heads a little."

He glared his disapproval to his deputy's lack of confidence. "We're holding her inside a fort," he announced. "No one's getting inside without a written invitation. Did you bring along that bag Frederick found?"

"Yeah, I've got it in the trunk," Dan replied. "Want me to take it inside?"

"After I've checked it out," Jonas informed him. "I'll meet you inside."

✝

*H*olden forced Jackie into the bland, prison cell like second floor bedroom. He locked and bolted the door behind them. The only window within the drab room had bars and steel shutters, giving the illusion of safe. He pushed Jackie onto the bed and approached a small room in the back. He peered into the small, concrete room and nodded his approval.

"Panic room," Holden remarked. "Nice touch."

Jackie sat on the bed with her hands still cuffed behind her back and watched him with little expression. He checked the bathroom then approached her with the handcuff keys, motioning for her to stand. Jackie showed little expression and did as he indicated, allowing him to remove the handcuffs. She moved away from him and gingerly rubbed her wrists. He glared at her in an unusually threatening manner.

"I'm warning you, Jackie," he growled. "Fuck with me again, and I'll shoot you myself."

She was oddly silent but didn't take her eyes off him. "Can I use the bathroom?"

"Sure," he replied a little too quickly. "There's no window and no lock. Take as long as you like."

Jackie sneered at him, headed into the bathroom, and slammed the door with added vigor. Holden didn't even flinch. There was a knock on the bedroom door. Holden looked out the peek hole then unlocked and opened the door to reveal Dan, who handed him Jackie's duffle bag.

"We found her bag in a locker at the fairground," Dan informed him. "She had two guns, phony ID's, and over twenty thousand in cash."

Holden took the bag from the officer. "Did you remove the guns?"

"Yeah, we locked them in the squad car," he replied. "We left the cash in the bag. No one wants to be responsible for it, so I guess it's your responsibility now."

"Thanks," Holden grumbled, lacking enthusiasm for that sort of responsibility. "I'll take a change of clothes for her, but I'd prefer if you kept the bag downstairs. There's no telling what gismos she has hiding in there."

Dan snorted a laugh, mocking Holden. "You think she's that resourceful?"

Holden gave the officer a serious look and nodded. "Yeah, I do. She's Houdini with a black belt."

Chapter Twenty-five

*H*olden sat on a chair alongside the door with his feet propped on the nightstand and flipped through an old magazine. He glanced at his watch and frowned. Jackie finally emerged from the bathroom, having been in there over an hour. She was freshly showered and changed into in a pair of clean shorts and a tank top. With the way Holden looked at her above his magazine; she knew she had succeeded in making him squirm with the length of time she'd spent in the bathroom. If he wanted to play her keeper, she was going to make him earn the title. Jackie glared at him then climbed onto the bed. She sat against the headboard, hugged her knees to her chest, and stared at the blank television screen. She had no interest in watching television or holding a conversation with the insufferable man.

If she was honest with herself, she was actually angry at her own actions more than Holden's. She'd betrayed her friends. Zach would undoubtedly be punished severely for current and past crimes. She wasn't even sure what those were, but it couldn't be good. Monroe, with his hero complex, would undoubtedly do something stupid and she no longer had the means to tell him not to risk it. She didn't even want to think about what he was plotting at that moment. Holden glanced at her over his magazine.

"Is that your helpless caged animal act?"

She didn't bother looking at him. "I didn't realize we were talking."

"We're not," he scoffed and tossed his magazine aside. "Try to get some sleep."

"Thanks, but I prefer to be awake when they come to kill me," she remarked lowly. "If you think you can sleep, I'll be sure to wake you when they get here."

"No offense, but I'm never shutting my eyes around you again," Holden announced sternly.

Jackie continued to stare at the television in silence. Holden eyed the bruises on her wrists from the handcuffs. He frowned and moved to the edge of the bed facing her.

"I'm sorry for being so rough with you tonight."

"Yeah?" she asked without looking at him or lifting her head from her knees. "Well, I'm sorry I didn't kick the crap out of you when I had the chance."

He stared at her a long moment in silent question. "So why didn't you?"

Jackie lifted her head and glared at him. "Momentary lapse in judgment. I thought about Harris and lost my nerve," she remarked then replaced her head to her knees. "Of course, two minutes later, I regretted that decision."

Holden again eyed the bruises on her wrists. He hesitated and then reached for her wrists. Jackie yanked her hands away from him and shot him a venomous glare.

"Touch me and die."

Holden sighed while frowning. He turned on the bed alongside her and positioned his back to the headboard. He leaned his head back and stared at the ceiling.

"I had no right to be so rough with you," he said gently. "I was still pissed about this morning. I don't normally allow my emotions to surface like that."

"I suppose if it made you feel better--"

He cast a sharp look at her even if she didn't look back at him. "No, it didn't make me feel better."

She suddenly glared at him. "Oh, that's a lie and you know it. You know damned well it wasn't necessary to throw me over that stand." Jackie sharply raised her brows. "And you know exactly why you did it."

"Of course I do," he replied sternly. "I did it because I was angry."

"No, you did it to establish sexual dominance."

Holden stared at her and appeared stunned by the comment. "I did no such thing."

"Oh, please! You already had me subdued, but you threw me over that stand and gave me a good bump and grind for added measure. That's the definition of sexual dominance."

Holden stared at her with complete surprise and shook his head. "I know I didn't do that."

"I'm not going to argue with you about it. I know what you did. I was there," she snapped. "Honestly, I was a bit surprised by your behavior too. You probably felt emasculated when you were found that way in the motel room, so you felt the need to 'put me in my place' so to speak."

Holden appeared to consider the comment and looked across the room while deep in thought. He glanced back at her and raised his brows.

"I'm sure I didn't do that, but you don't exactly bring out the best in me," he replied.

"Yeah, well, I don't mix well with cold and unfeeling people," she muttered.

"You think I'm cold and unfeeling?"

"Yeah, pretty much," she snapped while glaring at him. "I've tried dragging emotions out of you several times with little success. I suppose I should be happy with sexual dominance. At least it's something."

"That's not really a fair assumption, you know. I'm here to protect you, not entertain you," Holden informed her. "Although, you seem to think I'm your personal lackey."

Jackie groaned softly and allowed her head to fall back against the headboard. A thousand thoughts raced through her mind as she searched for some excuse to why she didn't stomp on him when she had the chance. A little bruising to his ego and she would have been home free with Monroe. She just didn't understand why she stopped herself. Why did she give in to that handsome face? The realization that she'd answered her own question hit hard. How could Zach have been right about her feelings for Agent Falcone? What the hell did Zach know about women and emotions? She felt sorry for herself a moment longer then looked at him.

"Harris and I would have gotten along a hell of a lot better," she remarked.

"Would you have left him handcuffed to a bed?" Holden suddenly demanded.

Jackie tilted her head with arrogance and raised her brows. "If I had, he would have enjoyed it."

He seemed momentarily set back by her comment. If he was uncomfortable, he didn't show it. "You've fucked me twice already, and I can't say I enjoyed it either time."

Jackie sharply glared at him in response. Had that comment come from one of her father's military buddies, she would have found it amusing. Hearing it coming from him just added to her growing annoyance with him.

†

*T*he Dark Water Island police officer sat quietly on the roof and scanned the dimly lit neighborhood surrounding the safe house through the night scope on his rifle. Despite the earlier storm clouds, the night was clear and quiet. In the distance, faint sounds from the fair could be heard. It was getting late, close to ten o'clock, and the Friday night fireworks would soon be displayed. The officer would have a perfect view of the fireworks from his position perched on the second story roof. He again scanned the surrounding area through the night scope of his rifle. Something moved just beyond his line of sight. He scanned further into the development to catch a glimpse of what he had possibly seen. The tail end of an unfamiliar vehicle was seen partially exposed beyond a newly built garage. The vehicle hadn't been there earlier.

He scanned the area near the newly arrived vehicle for signs of life. There was always the possibility the vehicle just belonged to some kids looking for somewhere quiet to get drunk or make out. He caught a glimpse of a man with what appeared to be an assault rifle. The officer zeroed in on the man just before he darted behind the nearby house. The man again appeared at the edge of the house with what was definitely an assault rifle in his hand. The officer caught the man in the crosshairs of his night scope and aimed for his leg. A gust of parting air broke the silence. The officer's finger tightened on the trigger and the rifle fired with a loud crack. He immediately looked to his shoulder and saw blood spreading across his shirt. Before he even realized he'd been shot, there was another gust of parting air.

†

*H*olden and Jackie heard several shots being fired from the roof. Holden jumped over Jackie and off the bed to the side closest to the window. He hurried for the window and peered out from the side. The police officer positioned on the roof plummeted past the window and to the ground below. Holden quickly closed and latched the interior steel shutters. Jackie jumped off the bed with alarm and slipped into her shoes. Holden ran for the bedroom door with Jackie directly behind him. He turned and stopped her. His look was stern.

"Lock yourself in the panic room," he informed her. "Don't come out for anyone but me."

"Holden--"

"Do it, Jackie!"

Holden unlocked the door, hesitated, and then removed the revolver from his belt holster. He turned toward her and handed her the gun.

"Use it if you have to."

Jackie uncertainly accepted the gun. Holden turned back for the door. She grabbed his hand, forcing him to look back at her concerned face.

"I don't want anyone else's blood on my hands," she whispered softly.

Holden offered a sympathetic smile and caressed her hand clinging to his. "You're not responsible, the governor is," he said gently. "Do as I say. It's going to be okay."

"Please don't die," she said softly while staring into his eyes with concern.

He stared back into her eyes and smiled warmly. "I haven't failed a mission yet."

Her expression suddenly shattered. Thoughts of her father crept into her mind. He'd never failed a mission; not even the day he died. Holden slipped out of the room. Jackie felt paralyzed with fear. She hesitated only a moment then shut and locked the door behind him. She cast her back against the door, drew a deep breath, then eyed the gun and looked at the panic room just across the room. She shut her eyes and softly released her breath. She couldn't handle any more loss. People were dying all around her, and there wasn't a damned thing she could do about it. There would be no escape, and she knew they would all soon be dead.

"I haven't failed a mission yet," her father's voice echoed through her mind.

"I'm sorry I couldn't save you," she whispered softly. "Please forgive me for what I'm about to do."

She pinched her eyes shut and sank back into a different day that felt awkwardly similar.

✝

*T*hree years earlier. Jackie felt a tremendous stinging sensation throughout her entire body. She wanted to open her eyes, but she couldn't seem to wake. Something warm and sticky ran past her eyelid. She soon tasted a horrible, familiar liquid. It was blood! She desperately tried to open her eyes. The light hurt at first. She didn't know where she was but something was wrong. Jackie slowly lifted her head. It pounded in response. Blood ran freely from a gash on her scalp and streaked down her face. She was in the wreckage of 'old Marge'. At first, she didn't know what had happened or how she even got there. She remembered the dreadful alarm sounding and several lights on the control panel flashing but very little after that. All she knew for certain was she crashed 'old Marge'. Jackie looked to the co-pilot's seat. Her father was reclined back in the seat with blood streaking the side of his face. For a moment, she could only stare at him. He wasn't breathing! She removed her harness and slid closer to him.

"Dad," she gasped softly and touched his face.

His skin was already excessively cool to the touch. He'd been dead too long for any hopes of bringing him back. As reality set in, she found herself staring at the blood saturating his abdomen. There was so much blood! His hands were covered in dried blood as well as the controls before him. He'd attempted to help her land the plane as she went down. Once again, he'd completed his mission, but it was his last. He died a hero, as he always wanted to die. He died *her* hero.

Chapter Twenty-six

*H*olden hurried down the stairs from the second floor and entered the dimly lit living room with the three remaining officers. Jonas had turned the lights down to keep the shooters from seeing their position beyond the bulletproof windows. Jonas was perched alongside the front window, and Frederick was near the back window. Holden joined Dan by the side window. All three officers were silent while clinging to their weapons and looking for signs of the shooter. It was obvious the governor's men had weapons with silencers. The only reason they had been alerted to his hired killers lurking around was that the officer on the roof got off a few rounds before being fatally shot.

"They got your man on the roof," Holden announced while keeping his voice down in case the hired killers outside had ears on them.

"There are at least two shooters, as far as I can tell," Dan informed him while keeping watch out the window. "Reinforcements should be here in ten minutes. The glass is bulletproof and the doors have floor and ceiling bolts. Nothing short of a tank is getting inside this place."

"They have to know we've called for backup," Frederick remarked. "Why would they hang around?"

"Because they want her that badly," Holden replied.

"They must have a man in the Bureau," Jonas announced then looked at Holden across the room. "It's the only way they could know where we were."

"This guy is corrupt and powerful," Holden informed them. "There's no shortage of men in his hip pocket. Men like that have a long reach."

"I see one of them," Dan suddenly announced and became alert. "He's heading for the back door."

"I'm on it," Holden replied and darted for the back door to cover it.

The front door was suddenly broken open with unusual ease, startling everyone. Oscar dove into the dimly lit room and was out of their sight before they barely saw him. Frederick fired at Oscar as he rolled across the floor before losing sight of him. Jonas saw the hired gun from his vantage point and was about to squeeze the trigger when Dan suddenly turned and aimed his gun at Jonas from behind. Holden witnessed the double-cross and shot Dan, hitting him in the shoulder rather than the chest. Dan's gun fired simultaneously but being shot threw his aim off and the bullet hit Jonas in the arm instead of the head, which was his intended target. Everyone leaped to the floor except Frederick, who appeared shocked by his fellow man's double-cross. Oscar shot Frederick twice in the chest. His body jerked from the shots and fell to the floor.

Holden dived behind the sofa with Jonas, who didn't have time to worry about his bleeding arm. Dexter stormed into the living room and joined Oscar and Dan. All three fired their handguns at the two men behind the sofa. Holden and Jonas took cover to the barrage of nearly silent gunfire. The sofa seemed to absorb the bullets better than anticipated. They were boxed down and the last line of defense before the stairs leading to the second floor and Jackie's safe room.

"Last stand, huh?" Jonas said to Holden while both remained hidden behind the sofa.

"And they know they have to go straight through us," Holden informed him while frowning.

"I'm sure we have them shaking in their shoes," Jonas teased and indicated the stairs near them. "Think you can make it up the stairs if I draw their fire?"

"Three on two," Holden replied. "Together we stand a chance. Even if I make it up the stairs, they'll swarm you for sure. You don't stand a chance."

"Got a better idea?"

"Give me a second."

"We haven't got a second," Jonas informed him. "Get ready to run."

Before Holden could protest, Jonas took advantage of one of them reloading and poked his head out, returning their fire. Oscar fired back at him, hitting Jonas in the head. Jonas immediately dropped to the floor, having died instantly. Holden stared at Jonas' blood spilling across the floor from the large hole in his head. Holden's look conveyed his hostility. He looked to the grandfather clock near the stairs on his right. Dan's reflection could be seen through the glass of the large clock, giving his exact location. Holden aimed his gun around the sofa, using the image in the mirror to line his shot, and fired several rounds. The first shot hit Dan in the chest and the second hit him directly through his eye. As Dan collapsed to the floor, there would be one less dirty cop in the world. Another bullet pierced the sofa, found its way through, and struck Holden in the arm. He clutched his bleeding arm but didn't allow his minor injury to stop him from returning fire.

"Find her! Check upstairs!" Dexter cried out.

Dexter fired wildly at Holden, who had little choice to take cover behind the sofa, giving Oscar a chance to run up the stairs. Holden attempted to fire at the running man, but Dexter continued with heavy gunfire. Holden never got a shot off at Oscar. Thumping and thudding was heard from the second floor above the sound of their guns firing.

"She's in the panic room," Oscar was heard shouting down to Dexter.

Holden looked at the grandfather clock and saw Dexter's attention fixed on the stairs. He was obviously frustrated that the woman they'd come for had locked herself in a panic room. Retrieving her would cause a significant problem for them. The only way they'd get her out of there is if she opened the door willingly; and there wouldn't be any reason for her to do that. Holden had one chance at a clear shot at Dexter while he was momentarily distracted. Holden aimed his weapon, again using the image in the mirror to aim and squeezed the trigger. His gun clicked empty. Although the sound wasn't excessively loud, to Dexter, it was loud enough and the only sound he needed to hear. Holden hastily popped out the empty clip and quickly replaced it with a full one. Dexter suddenly stood over him with his gun aimed at his head. Holden froze and stared at the gun pointed at him. Dexter grinned, pleased with himself.

151

"You're going to call her out," Dexter boldly announced to Holden.

"No, I'm not."

Dexter struck Holden in the head with his gun, dropping him to the floor alongside Jonas' body.

Chapter Twenty-seven

The safe house bedroom appeared unusually quiet. There was no sound and nothing moved. The panic room door was shut with no way of entering without a writing invitation. Dexter and Oscar dragged Holden's nearly unconscious body into the room and dropped him to the hardwood floor. Holden fell to the floor as blood streaked his face after being pistol whipped by Dexter. Dexter pulled Holden to his knees and aimed the gun at his head. His look was cold and serious.

"Call her!" Dexter ordered.

"Reinforcements are on their way," Holden gasped with some disorientation.

"Now why would reinforcements arrive?" Dexter mocked. "Dan never made that call and the houses around here are empty." He gave Holden a sinister, creepy grin. "No one's coming." He then looked toward the panic room. "Jackie! Come out now or I pop the fed!"

"Nice try, but she hates me," Holden muttered.

Oscar pounded on the panic room door. "Come on out or the fed dies!"

"They can't get you!" Holden yelled out.

Dexter struck Holden in the head with his gun then aimed it at him where he lie motionless. He smiled deviously with his finger tight on the trigger.

"Say goodnight, Gracie," Dexter retorted.

"Goodnight, Gracie," Jackie's voice was heard hissing from behind Dexter.

Dexter suddenly spun with surprise. Jackie stood directly behind him in the bedroom doorway. She hadn't been in the panic room! Before Dexter could even react, she spun into a high roundhouse kick and struck him in the head. The gun flew from his hand as he was thrown across the bed with a bounce. Jackie immediately turned toward the panic room door and fired Holden's revolver at Oscar, hitting him in the side. Her aim had been a little off, but she wasn't exactly trained for military combat. Oscar roughly struck the panic room door. Dexter had recovered at the same time and tackled Jackie to the floor. As he landed on top of her, she was winded by his weight. Without hesitation, Dexter punched her in the face. Jackie appeared momentarily stunned by the hard hit. He was about to hit her again when something snapped inside her. She suddenly grabbed his crotch with her left hand and gave it a hard squeeze and a violent twist.

Dexter gasped with surprise and instant agony, half-collapsing on top of her. Jackie barely released his crotch with her left hand as she punched him in the throat with her right. Dexter fell off her while gasping and wheezing in agony. It was a favorite move of her father's, and she now understood why. She'd done a number on him, and he wouldn't recover nearly as quickly from the assault. Jackie slowly pulled herself to her knees and scanned the room for either of the two discarded guns. Her eyes momentarily stopped on Holden, who lie motionless while bleeding from a head laceration. She saw Dexter's gun just beyond Holden near the bed. Out of the corner of her eye, she saw Dexter scrambling to his feet. She couldn't believe he had actually recovered from her father's signature move so quickly. Jackie lunged for the gun. Rather than attempt to beat her to the weapon, Dexter ran from the room. He wasn't in any condition to fight her, and he knew it.

Jackie's hand hit the gun while she was hastily reaching for it, causing it to slide under the bed and further out of reach. She quickly sat up and looked for her revolver. Oscar was now on his feet by the panic room door and shot at her. The nearly silent shot ricocheted off the bedpost near her head. She gasped with alarm and rolled across the floor into Holden as the hardwood floor splintered from the silenced shots. She was now exposed in the center of the room and both she and Holden were clean targets for the hired killer. She looked at Oscar as he straightened while panting. He was in bad shape, but that wasn't going to stop him from pulling the trigger. He kept the gun aimed at her and suddenly grinned.

"The governor will be pleased," Oscar remarked and tightened his finger on the trigger.

Monroe suddenly appeared in the doorway behind Jackie and Holden. Oscar saw him, showed his surprise to the stranger, and aimed his gun at him. Monroe raised the Uzi in his hand and fired a barrage of bullets into Oscar. The sound of rapidly firing shots was almost deafening, but Monroe didn't even flinch. Oscar's body jerked and jolted in some macabre dance of the dead before striking the panic room door. As the firing stopped, his blood-soaked body slid down to the floor, leaving a streak of blood on the panic room door. Jackie looked back at Monroe with her mouth hanging open in silent shock.

"How's that for an entrance?" Monroe announced with a pleased grin, his cocky brow raised.

She exhaled with relief and hid her smile. She'd never been happier to see Monroe. She'd never been happier that he came prepared and with guns blazing.

"Dexter is getting away," she announced and gave a nod behind him.

"I'm on it," Monroe announced and hurried back into the hallway.

Jackie hovered over Holden's unconscious body and gently tapped his face while she visually assessed his bleeding head injury. Dexter had nailed him good with his gun.

"Holden, can you hear me?" she gasped with concern.

He slowly opened his eyes and attempted to focus on her. "I'm okay," he replied softly but seemed to have trouble focusing. There was the very real chance he didn't even know where he was. "Help me up."

Jackie attempted to pull him to his feet. His legs gave out and he fell back down, taking her to the floor with him. She couldn't deny the drop to her knees hurt with his added weight.

"You hit like a girl," he scoffed with all seriousness. He really had no idea where he was.

Monroe entered the room as Jackie stood and again attempted to help Holden to his feet. The federal agent was flopping from his knees to his backside like a drunken man.

"He got away," Monroe said with disgust then watched the display. He tilted his head and appeared curious.

"Help me," Jackie quickly announced.

"Leave him," Monroe grumbled.

"No, he could die."

"So?   He's the reason you're here in the first place," Monroe reminded her.

Jackie glared at her friend.   Her look conveyed she wasn't going to ask nicely a second time.   He groaned while rolling his eyes with disgust and helped her pick up Holden.   Holden half stumbled with them as they slowly made their way from the room.

Monroe and Jackie half-carried Holden from the 'safe house' and toward Monroe's modified Hummer.   Jackie had once again secured her duffle bag, which had been discarded in the living room.   Monroe dumped Holden onto the backseat then took Jackie's duffle bag from her and tossed it into the back with the nearly unconscious federal agent.   As the bag struck Holden's body, he cried out.   Jackie jumped into the passenger seat as Monroe hurried to the driver's side.   The Hummer pulled away from the safe house in no particular hurry. Burning out and leaving tire marks would only give forensics more evidence pointing to Monroe's presence.   Monroe was always thinking and planning.   He wasn't a genius, but he was resourceful, which was probably what had kept him alive for so long.

Chapter Twenty-eight

*M*onroe's beach house, Casa d'Monroe, was lavish with tall windows facing the ocean and a large deck surrounding it. His home was located on a pristine parcel of beachfront real estate with only a few other homes within viewing distance. Monroe's wealthy status was always a bit of a mystery to Jackie. He'd come a long way since his stint under her father's command a few years ago. Jackie could honestly say that she didn't know what he did for a living or if he even worked, yet he somehow managed to live the high life on Dark Water Island. She was sure he wasn't into anything illegal, but that didn't mean he wasn't doing something slightly shady in that questionable gray area. A little after midnight, the black Hummer pulled alongside the house just beyond the garage.

Jackie and Monroe helped Holden into the dimly lit living room. He was finally able to bear his own weight, although completely unsteady on his feet. They allowed him to collapse onto the sofa within the living room, where he lie motionless and panted from the short journey into the house. Monroe looked at Jackie and appeared irritated with her.

"This is a mistake," he announced. "We should've dumped him at the hospital when we had the chance. He's going to be a problem."

"You can help him, Monroe," she pleaded and begged with her eyes. "Please."

He maintained his disapproving glare then groaned while pointing a warning finger at her. "You owe me," he scoffed. "Take off his jacket and shirt. I'll get my field kit."

It was only twenty minutes later. Holden appeared to fade in and out while Monroe cleaned and stitched the bullet graze along his upper arm. Jackie cleaned his head and face lacerations.

"Definitely has a concussion," Monroe remarked. "You'll need to try to keep him awake."

Monroe applied plastic, surgical strips to the gash on his temple. They mimicked stitches in effect. Jackie placed her hand on Holden's and stared at him as he faded in and out of consciousness and possibly reality.

Monroe sharply glared at her. "Don't do it, Jackie," he suddenly warned. "You can't keep him."

"I don't want to keep him," she protested while casting a glance at her friend. "He's a prick, but he nearly died tonight. I'm allowed to feel sorry for him."

"Feel sorry all you want, but don't get attached," Monroe snapped hotly. "He's going back to the pound in the morning. We can't take him with us."

"I know."

Monroe straightened and collected his pile of bloodied supplies. "I need to change for my date," he remarked. "Keep an eye on him."

Jackie nodded and watched Monroe leave the room. She stared back at Holden, who remained mostly out now, and gently caressed his hand.

"Holden, can you hear me?" she asked softly.

There was no response. Jackie released his hand and gently touched his face.

"Holden?"

His eyes rolled open and closed without response. Jackie leaned over him while caressing his face. She hesitated a moment, kissed him gently on the lips, and then placed her head to his bare chest. She felt responsible for nearly getting him killed. Just one more dead man to add to her growing list. Holden placed his arm around her, startling her. Jackie lifted her head and looked at him. His eyes remained closed.

"I'm not dead yet," he muttered softly, sounding more like himself. "Where are we?"

"We're safe at a friend's house."

"Monroe?"

She suddenly felt alarm sweep through her. "How did you know his name?"

"I heard you say it right before you kissed me," he replied softly.

"I didn't kiss you," she insisted as the color rushed to her cheeks. "You're imagining things."

His eyes opened briefly, as he attempted to focus on her. "Did you call me a prick?"

She grinned in response. "Just a little one."

Holden's eyes shut and he appeared to be out again. Jackie gently tapped his face and squeezed his hand.

"Holden?"

There was no response. Monroe was heard on the stairs. He entered the living room in expensive clean clothing with his usual stylish flare. She gave him a quick once over.

"Where are you off to?" she asked.

"To bail a friend out of jail."

"You won't be able to bail him out," Holden muttered, surprising both. His eyes remained closed.

"Yeah, well, our definitions of 'bail' varies greatly," Monroe casually informed him. He then looked at Jackie. "After I bail out our friend, we're going to make arrangements for tomorrow, so I won't be home until late morning. There's a hurricane huffing and puffing just off the coast, but it's not supposed to hit the island. Will you be okay?"

"Yeah, I'll be fine."

"Help yourself to snacks, drinks, and a small arsenal of weapons in my bedroom closet."

As she stared at her friend, she could feel pangs of relief that she'd finally reached him. "Thanks, Monroe."

Monroe leaned down and kissed her quickly but warmly on the lips. He offered a pleased smile then left.

"How often do you handcuff him to the bed?" Holden asked with his eyes closed then grinned at his own comment.

"None of your business."

Holden chuckled softly then immediately groaned with discomfort. He took her hand in his and gently caressed it. Jackie stared at him as he held her hand and smiled. She hated the way she felt about Agent Falcone. She had hoped those feelings would pass like with so many other men, but this was different and she still didn't understand why. Jackie rested her head on the sofa near Holden and felt her eyes grow heavy.

✝

*T*hree years earlier. Jackie stood alongside her father at the private airfield as Abbott checked over the older plane. He eyed Jackson and appeared humored.

"Old Marge, huh?" Abbott teased. "Nothing newer? A sexier model, perhaps?"

"Not for your first time out," Jackson replied with a cheap grin on his face.

"You never did like to share your toys," Abbott remarked then indicated the plane. "Well, what are we waiting for?"

Jackie looked at her father and smiled innocently. "So is it okay?"

Her father groaned then looked back at Abbott. "Do you mind if Jackie rides along?"

"Mind? Of course I don't mind," Abbott replied. "The more witnesses to my act of valor, the better."

"I call point," Jackie cried out with delight.

Jackson rolled his eyes then looked at Abbott. "It's okay," he announced with defeat. "I'll ride in the back."

Abbott's expression dropped slightly, although he attempted to cover with a tiny smile. "Maybe I should ride in the back," he remarked, seeming a little tense. "You know, in case you need to assist Jackie."

Her father snorted a laugh. "Don't be ridiculous," Jackson replied. "Jackie's been piloting small planes since she was in diapers. Soon she'll be moving on to commercial airliners. She's more than capable of getting us out to the old airfield. Once there, we'll get you in the pilot's seat and give you a crash course in flying."

Jackie rolled her eyes. "Oh, Dad, those puns are getting old fast."

Abbott didn't appear convinced but nodded his acceptance. Only a few minutes later, they were airborne. Jackie enjoyed flying the older plane. She was loud, and she was cranky. All three wore pilot aviation headsets in order to communicate with one another above the roar of the engine. Abbott sat rigid in the co-pilot's seat, obviously nervous about his young pilot. Jackie knew it wasn't that he was

160

sexist. The men from her father's SEAL team had accepted her as one of the boys a long time ago. She was sure he was just uncertain about her flying abilities. Little did he realize she was a better pilot than her father was. They were only halfway to the deserted airfield when Abbott fidgeted and seemed oddly uncomfortable.

"You know," Abbott finally spoke after near silence the entire flight, "it's nothing personal."

Jackie glanced at him with surprise to his remark. She didn't understand what he'd meant until she saw the gun in his hand held close to his chest. It was aimed at her. She met his gaze and stared with alarm.

"Abbott--?"

Her father was alerted to the conversation, noting the look on Jackie's face. He attempted to lean forward to check out the situation. Abbott aimed the gun at him. The look on his face conveyed he was serious.

"Just sit back and relax, Commander," Abbott growled.

Jackson tensed and slowly sat back without taking his eyes off the man holding the gun.

"What's going on?" Jackson demanded.

"Just a little change of plans," Abbott informed him. "We're not going to the abandoned airfield."

"Where are we going?" her father asked, seeming unusually calm.

Jackie already knew something bad was about to go down, and it wasn't going to end well for any of them.

"I need an exit," Abbott informed him. "I need to leave the country before certain people catch up to me, and you're going to help me."

"What people?" Jackson demanded.

"Just people," Abbott replied. "That's all you need to know. Just do as I say, and you'll both live to fly another day." He handed Jackie a paper. "Here are the coordinates."

She glanced at the paper, stared a moment with surprise, and then handed the paper to her father behind them. Jackson looked at the coordinates then back at Abbott.

"This won't take you out of the country," her father announced boldly. "This will take us to Washington, D.C."

Abbott stared at him with a look of surprise. "Wow, you decoded that pretty fast."

"Yes, that's why I'm a lieutenant commander," he snarled while keeping his eyes on Abbott. "We're not flying you to Washington for some suicide mission."

"What makes you think it's a suicide mission?"

"I know my men, Abbott," Jackson replied firmly. "I know you had a difficult time with PTS. We can get you help, but I can't do that with you pointing a gun at me and certainly not at my daughter."

"I'm going to do a lot more than point this gun, Commander," Abbott announced in an icy tone. "You're going to fly to those coordinates or one of you is going to eat a bullet."

There was an awkward silence. Jackie watched the tense scene from the corner of her eye in silence. Abbott aimed the gun at Jackie, keeping it close to his chest so Jackson couldn't disarm him before he would squeeze the trigger.

"What's it going to be, Commander?" Abbott demanded.

Jackson finally looked at Jackie. His look wasn't that of defeat but that of the Navy SEAL she rarely saw.

"Jackie, take him to Washington," her father announced firmly. "Take 'old Marge' down to conserve fuel, if we intend to make it there. You'll want to bring her around in a buzz saw."

Jackie held her breath, kept her eyes locked on the countryside before her, and fiddled with a few switches.

"Yes, Commander," she replied faintly and accepted her new orders.

Jackie inhaled deeply and flipped another switch. The propeller suddenly slowed and the engine shut down. Abbott looked around with surprise then to Jackie. She sharply turned the control wheel to the right, sending the plane spiraling. Abbott cried out with surprise and attempted to hold on despite his shoulder harness. He aimed the gun at Jackie and squeezed the trigger. Jackie held her breath and kept the plane steady in a spiral. Her father leaped for Abbott from the rear and attempted to take the gun from him. The gun fired and a bullet struck the control panel. The panel smoldered. The gun fired again as the men struggled for control over the gun in the spinning plane. Jackie kept the plane spiraling until the gun flew from Abbott's hand. She corrected the spin and immediately restarted the engine. The engine sputtered as lights flashed and alarms sounded. She fought to level the plane before the engine seized altogether. Old Marge was tough, but she'd given it her all and had nothing left. Her father released his safety harness, lunged forward, and punched Abbott in the face several times.

Abbott only got in one shot, being restricted by his safety harness, but it was enough to send her father into the backseat. Abbott immediately dived on Jackie, attempting to force her to crash the plane. She managed to punch him away from her, his seatbelt

162

restraining him from getting any leverage on her. She saw the lake up ahead and feared crashing into it. Abbott released his safety harness and attempted to jump on her. Jackie sent the plane to the right, tossing him against the door. As he attempted to recover, she partially turned in her seat and kicked him in the chest, throwing him backward and against the door. The door gave and Abbott plummeted from the plane. Jackie struggled to regain control of the now rolling plane. Her father weakly climbed into the co-pilot's seat, strapped himself in, and engaged the controls on his side to assist her. They leveled the plane as the engine continued to sputter. Jackie looked at her father fighting the controls alongside her. She saw the large amount of blood on his abdomen. He'd been shot!

"Keep her steady," he shouted as they fought the controls and the failing engine. "We'll need to find a clearing and glide her in for a landing!"

"You've been shot," Jackie cried out in panic.

"I've been shot before," he launched back at her. "Land the plane!"

Jackie continued to fight the controls as the engine suddenly seized. There was an eerie silence. She saw a clearing just beyond some trees. They were going down, and that's where she was going to land.

"Up ahead," she yelled to her father.

As she fought to keep the plane in the air long enough to reach the clearing, she looked over at her father. He was slumped in the seat with the harness holding him upright. Jackie stared at her father with horror then looked back out the windshield. She needed to clear the trees. The plane struck the tops of the trees and teetered wildly. Jackie fought the controls, but she was coming in too hot. The plane struck the clearing with incredible force, tearing the wheels off the bottom. Jackie was thrown violently within her seat. She felt several contact points of pain as the sound of tearing metal echoed loudly throughout the cockpit. Jumbled images turned to darkness.

Chapter Twenty-nine

$\mathcal{I}$t was early the following morning. Jackie's dreams had been a roller coaster of never-ending, emotional sequences involving her father and, at times, Holden. Several times throughout the night, she had woken from a bad dream involving Holden's death and had to check that he was still alive. Jackie remained asleep on the floor alongside the sofa with a throw pillow under her head and a quilt over her, where she had been all night. She jerked awake from yet another nightmare and wearily looked around the dimly lit room. The sofa was empty! Jackie jumped up with alarm and hurried through the house. If Agent Falcone did something stupid, Monroe would never forgive her. She entered the kitchen and suddenly stopped before the glass deck doors. A look of horror swept over her as she stared at the black, violent skies and high, crashing waves. Water from the massive waves reached almost halfway across the sandy beach to the house.

The wind blew harshly and the rain poured down while objects violently blew across what remained of the beach. Jackie backed away from the glass doors, quickly turned, and nearly collided with Holden. He appeared fresh from the shower and wearing Monroe's clothing. His face was a little battered, but otherwise, he looked like he was ready to go a few more rounds with Dexter. Holden looked past her with the same concern on his face to the raging storm just outside.

"So much for the hurricane not reaching the island," he commented.

Jackie stared at him in Monroe's expensive clothes. That Monroe wore his clothes slightly loose was to Holden's advantage, giving him the extra room he needed so they'd fit his larger build. He noticed her gaze upon the clothes he wore. A tiny grin crossed his face.

"I'm sure your friend will be a little pissed about me borrowing his clothes, but I figured fuck him," Holden remarked and proudly gave the jacket a slight tug to straighten it. "They look better on me anyway."

Jackie wasn't sure where their current situation was about to lead, but she needed to remain casual if it became necessary to outwit him. It was best just to play along for the moment.

"He has expensive taste in clothes," she replied matter-of-fact. "He's like a girl that way." She indicated the frightening storm beyond the French doors. "Would you check the weather and see where that storm is heading? I'm going to take a shower before we lose power."

"I can tell you where that storm is heading," Holden replied with little emotion. "Right through us. You'll want to make that shower a quick one."

She again looked outside and felt panic sweeping through her. He was probably right. She'd never seen the sky look so black and threatening.

"I don't suppose this place has a basement," he remarked, lacking enthusiasm.

"It's a beach house," she casually reminded him. "A basement would be considered an indoor swimming pool. The house is on stilts."

"Then you'd better hurry," Holden remarked. "We'll need to reach higher ground within the hour."

Jackie nodded and hurried for the stairs. She ran up the steps with more on her mind than just the storm. Holden was acting too casual. He was up to something, and whatever it was, it was probably already set in motion. She knew for a fact that Monroe didn't own a landline phone, so he wasn't able to make any phone calls that way. She needed see if their cell phones were still in her duffle bag, which was in Monroe's bedroom. She entered Monroe's bedroom and shut the door behind her. She removed her duffle bag from under the large bed and unzipped it. Both cell phones were gone as well as Holden's shoulder holster. Jackie tossed her duffle bag back under the bed and hurriedly opened Monroe's closet to reveal a wardrobe of expensive clothes.

She pushed the hanging clothes aside and opened a secret back panel to reveal an extensive gun cabinet containing a range of handguns and rifles. Monroe's personal arsenal. Jackie removed a small revolver from the cabinet and placed it down the back of her pants. Whatever series of events were about to unfold were already set in motion by whomever Holden had called that morning. Now Jackie had to do some serious damage control concerning Holden. What pissed her off most was she couldn't even call Monroe to warn him, since Holden obviously had both his and her cell phones. She closed the gun cabinet, keeping it hidden, and then paced the bedroom for nearly ten minutes. She contemplated her next move while also keeping an eye on the raging storm outside. She finally left the bedroom with the worst plan in history. Direct confrontation.

Jackie took the stairs quickly but quietly, in case Holden was waiting to pounce on her as she had him so many times. From her hidden position at the bottom of the stairs, she saw him in the kitchen. He was casually leaning against the counter with his hands on either side behind him. His expression conveyed that of deep thought. She wondered if that was guilt for whatever it was he had done that morning. Jackie decided to take a more aggressive approach to catch him off guard. She stormed into the kitchen and confronted him.

"Where's your cell phone?" she suddenly demanded but didn't wait for a reply. "You called them, didn't you?"

He stared at her with a strange look, lacking reaction to her outburst. "Jackie--" he said softly then allowed his eyes to signal something not far to her right.

She looked to the alcove near the door leading beneath the house. A man in his early twenties, Sal, had a gun aimed at her. She recognized it as Holden's gun. Her expression immediately dropped.

"Oh--"

Another man also in his early twenties, Wes, and a woman about the same age, Mandy, appeared in the doorway just behind Sal. Mandy smiled, approached Jackie, and removed the revolver from the back of her pants. All three were little more than street thugs taking advantage of the approaching hurricane to loot wealthy homes. Both young men had visible tattoos, body piercings, and low-slung trousers. Mandy resembled a Goth prostitute in her short skirt, black fishnet stockings, and platform high heels. Her lip, eyebrow, and nose piercings added to the drama of her persona.

"Just take what you want. We have enough to worry about with the storm," Holden announced firmly, although remaining non-confrontational.

"Don't worry; we will," Mandy replied and giggled with delight. She flipped Holden's badge open with all seriousness. "FBI--you're under arrest."

It was obvious to Jackie that the trio of young thugs were slightly unbalanced and therefore unpredictable. Considering the fact that they were now armed made for a more frightening situation. Any sudden movements could get both of them killed.

Wes dangled Holden's handcuffs while wearing a cheap grin that conveyed his lack of empathy for human life. "Imagine what we can do with these." He then smiled lustfully at Jackie. "Wanna play good cop bad cop?"

"Don't be an idiot," Sal snapped with annoyance to his friend's lack of maturity and slapped him on the back of the head. "Cuff them to the counter. We have a house to pillage."

With both sets of handcuffs, Mandy cuffed each of their left wrists to the island counter post, which was cemented into the floor, then hurried from the kitchen. Wes winked at Jackie as he walked away. Holden glared at the young thug as he left. Jackie sneered her annoyance at Holden.

"Some FBI agent," Jackie suddenly snapped. "You let three punks get the drop on you?"

He seemed surprised by her outburst directed at him. "I didn't see you going Bruce Lee on anyone's ass," he snapped back. "What's your excuse?"

"Oh, so I'm in charge of the ass kicking department? Nice to know," she lashed out. "What happened to all that macho male dominance from last night?"

He obviously wasn't in the mood after being disarmed by three thugs. "Hey, I was shot and pistol whipped last night. I'm still not seeing straight," Holden launched back. "What's wrong with you picking up some slack?"

Jackie gave him a stunned look to the comment. She couldn't believe his nerve. "I've been picking up your slack from the first day I'd met you!"

Mandy popped into the kitchen and glared at them. "Excuse me. Can you save the domestic dispute for the marriage counselor?"

"Us--married? That'd be a cold day in hell," Jackie snarled while looking away.

"You certainly act like you're married. Just keep it down," Mandy announced almost sweetly. "You're taking the fun out of our home invasion party."

Mandy disappeared to join her friends. Both collected themselves and attempted to remain calm. Holden eyed the wooden post with which they were both cuffed then gave Jackie a curious look.

"Can you break the post?" Holden asked softly.

"They'll hear it."

"What if I created a diversion?"

Her look conveyed her concern. "What sort of diversion? They have our weapons."

"Relax, I know how to be subtle," he replied then cleared his throat and spoke louder than necessary. "It's all your fault. We wouldn't even be here if it wasn't--"

Jackie gave the post a firm kick. It cracked coinciding with his low, harsh words.

"--for that idiot friend of yours. Where the hell--"

Jackie again kicked the post with a little more vigor. It cracked but still didn't give.

"--did you find that guy!"

Jackie applied a little more force behind her third kick. The post splintered and broke. Both slipped their cuffs off the broken post. Footsteps were heard on the stairs, alerting both. They didn't have time to plan a surprise attack. Jackie and Holden moved closer together in front of the broken post with their backs to the counter, giving the appearance of still being cuffed to the post. The three street thugs entered the kitchen, each carrying a bag full of Monroe's possessions. Wes dropped his bag, smiled deviously, and approached Jackie with the handcuff keys.

"Time for you and me to have our own little party," Wes said while dangling the handcuff keys in front of her.

Jackie suddenly snapped kicked Wes in the groin and elevated him off the floor. She'd struck him so fast and hard, he never saw it coming. He hit the floor before he even had the chance to clutch himself in agony. Mandy and Sal gasped as they watched their friend hit the floor. After the initial shock, Sal became enraged and aimed his gun at Jackie. Holden knocked the gun from Sal's hand and punched him in the face. Jackie leaped for the discarded gun. Mandy kicked it away just before she reached it and aimed the revolver at Jackie's head.

"Don't make me shoot your girlfriend!" Mandy cried out to Holden.

Holden saw the gun aimed at Jackie's head, frowned, and released Sal's shirt. Sal jumped away from him looking more like a frightened kid than a tough street thug.

"What do we do with them?" Sal asked with concern while eyeing their friend, who still writhed around the floor in agony. Wes wasn't going to walk right for days.

"I know where we can put them," Mandy replied with giddy delight.

Chapter Thirty

$\mathcal{R}$ickety steps from the kitchen led beneath the house, which was a large, empty dirt pad containing the massive stilts with which the house sat. Decorative skirting enclosed the home's stilts for greater curbside appeal. Jackie and Holden bickered while walking down the creaking steps with Mandy and Sal behind them.

"My God! You two are annoying!" Mandy finally proclaimed, having had enough of their arguing.

There was nothing to see beneath the house beyond the stilts holding it up off the sandy dirt. A network of pipes and drains lined the ceiling. Monroe had a few beach items scattered about, which included a surfboard, a deflated, inflatable raft, and an old jet ski, which had been torn apart. Parts for the jet ski lie scattered about on a heavy, plastic rolling cart. Sal indicated the piping along the support stilt and ceiling. The ground was already wet from the storm and the rising surf.

"They'll never break that," Sal said.

"I have the perfect punishment for these two lovebirds," Mandy announced with enthusiasm.

Mandy handcuffed Jackie's wrists over the ceiling pipe, which also ran down the support stilt. She was positioned with her back to the sturdy stilt with her cuffed wrists above her, almost extending her arms straight up.   Mandy grinned at Holden and motioned with Jackie's revolver.

"Now give your girlfriend a big hug around the waist," she teased.

Sal grinned and motioned with Holden's gun as well.   Holden frowned and placed his arms around Jackie's waist while facing her. Mandy cuffed his wrists around the pipe against the support stilt behind Jackie.   Holden could only move his arms up and down a few inches before hitting connectors holding the pipe to the stilt.   Jackie and Holden glared at each other while only inches apart.   Mandy appeared pleased and smiled mockingly.

"Now you two kiss and make up," Mandy teased.

Mandy dropped the keys on the plastic cart ten feet away from them.   Both laughed and headed up the stairs.

"Well," Jackie huffed while staring into Holden's eyes only inches from hers.   "This sucks."

Holden pulled on his handcuffs behind Jackie's back, frowned, and then looked above him where she was cuffed to the pipe along the ceiling.

"I can't move at all," he informed her with disgust.   "You have only a foot or two forward and backward before hitting the connecting pipes."

"We'll just have to wait for Monroe to return.   It's only--" Jackie groaned lowly, "--four or five hours."

Holden looked at the dirt floor with water now collecting on it in small puddles.

"That hurricane is going to hit us head on long before Monroe gets back," Holden remarked.   "There was a mandatory evacuation of the entire Eastern half of the island.   This area will be flooded in an hour or two."

His news was the last thing she wanted to hear.   She glared at him with distaste.   "I'm developing a healthy dislike for you all over again."

"We can beat the crap out of each other later.   Is there anything behind me that you can reach with your feet?"

Jackie leaned over his shoulder to look behind him, hesitated, and smelled him.   She pulled back and looked at him with surprise.   "Are you wearing Monroe's cologne?"

"Jackie--"

"No, there's nothing behind you," she muttered.   "Do you have your cell phone?"

"No, your friend confiscated it," he remarked.   "I thought it was in your bag with my holster, but it wasn't there."

She was a little surprised to hear him say that. She had been sure he found both their cell phones, but perhaps the disappearing cell phones was Monroe's insurance policy when she decided to bring home the stray federal agent.

"Do you have anything in your pockets?" she finally asked with a defeated groan.

"I have a pocketknife in my pants pocket, but it won't do us any good. Neither of us can reach it."

She rolled her eyes and groaned softly. "No imagination, Agent Falcone."

Jackie wiggled her right foot out of her shoe. She was suddenly aware that the water was now ankle deep. The water was rising rapidly with the storm and possibly high tide as well. There was no time to waste thinking about their situation. She needed to work on a solution and remain productive. Jackie grabbed onto the pipe above her for balance, raised her foot to Holden's leg despite their closeness, and ran her toes along the outside of his pocket. She felt around for the pocketknife with her foot. Holden took a deep breath and tensed.

"Found it," she announced with relief. She worked her toes along his pants with determination. "Now I just have to work it out of your pocket."

"Jackie," he announced gently while clearing his throat, "that's not the pocketknife."

She met his stare and immediately wished she hadn't. His look was serious, but he was possibly blushing as much as she was.

"Okay then--"

Jackie moved her foot over a little further, found the actual pocketknife this time with her probing toes, and inched it up his pocket from the outside. It slipped back down. She cursed under her breath then looked at the collecting water on the floor. It was starting to spill in over her shoe on her other foot.

"This could take a while," she said while attempting to sound calm.

"Yeah, sure. No pressure," he muttered while attempting to hide his concern for their deteriorating situation. There was an awkward moment of silence before Holden finally spoke. "So what's the deal with Monroe?"

Jackie became immediately hostile by the question and glared her disapproval at him. "I'm not going to let you interrogate me about my friends."

"I already know about your father's team," he informed her. "I'm just passing time."

She was silent a moment and considered his comment then continued on her pocketknife quest. "Okay, I'll play along. What about Monroe?"

"You two seem rather *close*."

Jackie slid the knife within his pocket with her toes but kept losing it when it reached his pocket opening. "Probably because we are close," she casually informed him while keeping her eyes on her work. "I had a major crush on him when I was eight. Around the time I turned sixteen, Monroe started paying a lot of attention to me. When I graduated high school and was ready to go off to college, it was only natural that I wanted him to *educate* me before I went away."

Holden suddenly appeared tense and a little surprised by the comment. He stared at her even though she wasn't looking at him. "Are you saying he actually slept with his commander's eighteen-year-old, virgin daughter?"

She suddenly looked up and met his gaze with a dumbfounded expression. "He was a young, horny Navy man. What do you think?"

He shook his head in silent disbelief. "Did your father ever find out?"

Jackie returned to fishing for his pocketknife and sighed deeply. "Unfortunately," she replied. "Monroe became obsessive and wanted me to be his girl in port. When my father found out, he beat the crap out of him."

"So you sold out the poor bastard just because he wanted a relationship?"

She again looked at him and stared with her mouth hanging open. "Are you kidding? I'd never tell my father something like that," she gasped then turned serious. "Monroe made him suspicious. When my father confronted me, I tried to deny it, but you couldn't lie to the commander." She shook her head with disbelief. "My father actually grounded me for a month."

"He grounded you? Seriously?" he asked. "I thought you were in college."

She looked back at him with some confusion. She laughed and shook her head. "No, he *grounded* me. He took away my flying privileges. Longest month of my life," she huffed and returned to working on the knife in his pocket. "Swore me off men for nearly a year."

"I assume it was over with Monroe after that," he remarked.

"As far as I was concerned, we were only ever friends," she announced simply. "That's why I chose him for my first time.

Everyone kept saying a woman's first time should be with someone special. Well, Monroe was very knowledgeable when it came to sex, or so he bragged on many occasions. Seemed like he'd make a good teacher."

Holden was awkwardly silent a moment then finally spoke. "You're not exactly inhibited about things of a sexual nature, are you?"

She glanced at him, noted the color in his cheeks, and hid her smile. "I think it's cute that I can make you blush." She returned to working on her assignment then muttered, "You wouldn't last a day with my father's team."

"I'll admit; I'm a bit reserved," he replied.

She smiled but didn't bother looking up at him. "Yeah, you're a bit reserved," she teased.

The water rose at an accelerated pace, startling both. The hurricane had to be intensifying outside. The water was now up to their calves, rising faster than either had anticipated. Holden eyed the water and appeared uncomfortable.

"How's that pickpocket thing coming?"

"Slow," she muttered while attempting to ignore the height of the quickly rising water.

Jackie gripped the pipe above her for better stability. There was a loud creak followed by a metallic clang. She looked up with surprise. The pipe had broken at a soldered joint before the connecting pipe just beyond Holden's head. Holden looked up and saw the break as well.

"The pipe broke," Holden announced with renewed enthusiasm then looked at her. "Can you slip the handcuff chain through the opening?"

Jackie held onto the pipe and allowed her body to sink, using her weight to pull down on it. The pipe creaked again, leaving a half-inch gap.

"I can now," she announced while grinning. "It's behind your head. I won't be able to reach it without getting up and underneath it. Can you bend your knee?"

Holden did as she requested. Jackie placed her wet foot onto his thigh and attempted to pull herself up with use of her hands on the pipe. Her wet foot slipped off his thigh, and her back struck the pipe attached to the stilt behind her. She grimaced from the pain shooting through her back from the hard hit. Jackie took a deep breath, considered her options, and looked into Holden's eyes.

"Okay, plan B," she announced firmly. "Don't take this the wrong way."

"What--?"

Jackie grabbed onto the pipe with both hands, pulled herself up, and threw her legs around Holden's waist, locking them at the ankles behind him. Holden appeared slightly startled by the compromising position. Or was it how easily she got there?

"Okay, not taking it the wrong way," he gasped softly.

"Now help me balance."

"Balance? How?"

She suddenly glared down at him. "Grab a handful of ass, Agent Falcone! Come on, work with me here!"

Holden pinned Jackie between his body and the pipe behind her and held onto her buttocks, supporting her weight. Jackie moved her hands along the pipe over top of him toward the break. She continued to lean forward to reach the break, pressing her exposed cleavage into his face.

Holden suddenly tensed as his face became buried in her chest above her tank top. "Uh, how's it going up there?" he asked in a muffled voice.

"It'd be going a lot better if you weren't breathing down my shirt."

"Sorry, I'll try not to breathe."

Jackie had the handcuff chain against the break, but she needed just a little more forward momentum. "I'm going to let go of the pipe, so the chain will slip through. Hang onto me."

"Won't be a problem," he muttered into her breasts.

Jackie released the pipe. The chain roughly slipped through the break, causing her to lose her balance momentarily. She caught onto Holden's shoulders to keep from falling. She laughed with enthusiasm and pulled her chest away from his face. He stared into her cleavage almost mesmerized.

"Okay, coming down." She suddenly hesitated and eyed him sharply. "You can let go of my ass now."

Holden released her backside on command. Jackie slid down his body, since there was little room between them and the stilt to which he was cuffed. She suddenly hesitated, slowly looked down to his crotch, and then met his gaze with a look of surprise.

"Seriously?" she blurted out. "*That* turned you on?"

Holden appeared embarrassed and avoided looking her in the eyes. "Hey, I had a face full of breast and a hand full of ass. Something had to give."

Jackie hid her smile to his embarrassment and removed her cuffed hands from around his neck. She slipped out beneath his arm between him and the pipe. She ran her hand firmly along the enlarged bulge in his pants as she passed. Holden jumped with surprise and stared at her.

"Oh, but that's okay?"

Jackie snickered softly as she waded through the knee-deep water. She grabbed the keys from the nearby cart, unlocked her handcuffs, and then returned to Holden still cuffed to the pipe. She offered a teasing smile while dangling the keys.

"This is becoming a little too familiar."

"Don't you dare!"

The look on his face was priceless. "I would, but we're pressed for time."

She unlocked his handcuffs, releasing him from the pipe. He grabbed her hand and pulled her through the water toward the steps. Judging by the aggressively rising water, they *were* truly pressed for time. Getting out was more urgent now than before.

Chapter Thirty-one

*J*ackie and Holden hurried across the kitchen, his hand firmly gripping hers as they ran. Both immediately stopped when they saw a large piece of driftwood had shattered one of the heavy glass doors to the deck. Rain poured through the broken glass and into the house from the gusting winds, nearly flooding the floor. The area beyond the broken glass door was completely black. They couldn't even see the beach anymore. It was part of the ocean now. Jackie felt alarm spread through her entire body to the seriousness of the hurricane just outside their door.

"This house is going to be in the Atlantic in less than an hour," Holden announced and looked at Jackie. "Does Monroe have another car?"

"Yes, but I don't think he'd--"

"I don't really care what he thinks. Where are the keys?" Holden demanded.

"On his dresser."

Holden yanked firmly on her hand and pulled her up the stairs behind him. His grip on her hand was so tight; she felt it cut off her circulation. Holden entered Monroe's bedroom with Jackie only an arm's length behind him. The bedroom window facing the ocean was shattered as well. Wind blew rain into the bedroom, leaving standing water on the floor.

"Where are the guns?" Holden demanded while turning to face her and finally released her hand.

"In a hidden cabinet inside his closet," she replied.

Jackie opened the closet and showed him the gun cabinet hidden in the wall. Holden removed two semiautomatics and additional clips for each. Jackie hurried past him, grabbed the car keys from the dresser, and removed her duffle bag from under the bed. Thankfully, it had been hidden or their street thug friends would have taken it. As she approached, Holden handed her one of the guns in a shoulder holster. She slipped into the shoulder holster as he placed the other gun into his empty holster. He removed a leather jacket from the closet and tossed it to her.

"I don't think we need to worry about Dexter right now," Jackie informed him. "That hurricane might do us in long before he does."

"People become irrational and sometimes violent when confronted by disaster--like our friends who left us to die," Holden remarked. "We need to be prepared for anything, and I don't mind the added insurance."

Holden again grabbed her hand and hurried her from the bedroom. As they ran down the stairs, they could hear the wind ripping at the house, creating a strange thumping sound. Neither commented, but Jackie was certain they were both thinking the same thing. They paused at the bottom of the stairs and looked at the storm beyond the glass doors. The deck was already gone, having been torn away from the house. Both stared with alarm as water from the ocean greeted them in the kitchen, partially flooding the floor. It was Jackie's turn to pull Holden behind her. They ran from the kitchen for the front door and higher elevation.

Upon stepping outside, the day appeared as dark as night. Jackie had never before seen nature look so unfriendly. The wind blew objects and rain in every direction. Palm trees were bending unnaturally, and the entire beach was now part of the ocean. Jackie and Holden hurried through the pouring rain for the detached garage, which, thankfully, was built higher up than the house, so it wasn't yet underwater. Holden opened the garage door and stared at the red Ferrari. Despite the violent storm, he grinned with the appearance of a schoolboy.

"Well, if you're going to die, you may as well do it in style," he announced with a little too much enthusiasm then looked at her. "I'm driving."

Jackie groaned and gave him the keys. "Just try not to get us killed."

"It's not me you have to worry about," he muttered while looking back at the rising water.

✝

*T*ree branches were scattered across mild to moderately flooded roadways with several abandoned cars stranded within the deep, standing water off to the sides of the road. The Ferrari avoided several larger branches across the road then slowed as it approached a fallen tree on top of a car, which was now blocking the main road leading away from the rising ocean. Beyond the fallen tree was the severely flooded bridge. There appeared to be people still within the smashed car. Judging by the damage to the car, the condition of the passengers was easily assumed. Holden and Jackie got out of the sports car, ran through the pouring rain, and approached the mangled car beneath the massive tree. The rain continued to drench them as they paused before the driver's side to check on the passengers. Sal, Wes, and Mandy were crushed within the car. It was difficult to tell the mangled metal and fiberglass from their mutilated bodies. Blood covered the entire mess. Jackie grimaced at the sight and turned away. Holden reached into the car through the broken window and removed his badge and gun from what was left of Mandy's body.

The pouring rain easily cleaned his badge of the young woman's blood. Despite the pouring rain, both took a moment to assess the road ahead of them. Water from the river ran over the bridge and was at least two feet deep. The bridge was now part of the raging river of murky discolored water containing debris, some of it being fairly large. They watched a small car being swept away in the rushing water. Thankfully, it had no passengers. Even if there had been, there was nothing they could have done to help. The bridge was impassable, assuming the bridge was still intact beneath the raging water. They exchanged looks as the rain drenched them. The storm was closing in on them, and with how bad the conditions were surrounding them, they still weren't seeing the worst of the hurricane. Holden hurried Jackie back to the sports car. Their options were limited and time was running out. They had to find suitable shelter as far from the coast as they could safely get before the storm was directly upon them.

†

*S*everal new, expensive homes were lined along the streets of the recently built development further inland. All the homes appeared abandoned, or in some instances, were still under construction. Everyone had been evacuated despite being a few miles inland and at a higher elevation, possibly due more to the high, damaging winds than flooding waters. The Ferrari pulled up to the first stately home and parked in front of the garage. Jackie and Holden ran through the rain to the large, covered porch. Holden knocked on the door, not expecting an answer. When there was no response, he kicked in the door. The lock gave more easily than an expensive home should.

"They just don't make locks like they used to," he remarked with disgust.

Jackie cast a look at him. "That's breaking and entering, Agent Falcone."

"I prefer the term 'commandeer'."

He hurried her inside and shut the door behind them. Thankfully, the deadbolt still worked after his assault on the door; otherwise, the door wouldn't stay closed. Jackie looked around the new home and marveled at its grandeur while Holden checked the hall phone for a dial tone. Not surprising, there wasn't one. He frowned and replaced the phone.

"I think we'll be safe here until the hurricane passes," he informed her. "Make yourself comfortable. We're going to be here until morning."

Jackie flipped the light switch. Nothing happened. "No power," she informed him with a dreary sigh and looked around. "We should probably find some flashlights or candles before it gets dark. I'd rather not spend the entire evening in darkness." She then glanced at him. "I'd like to get my bag from the car and change into some dry clothes."

"I'll bring the car into the garage and get your bag," Holden replied. "You look for flashlights and see if there's any bottled water."

She folded her arms across her chest and glared at him. "You still don't trust me, do you? There's no place to go, yet you think I'm going to steal my friend's car and make the great escape to who the hell knows where."

"Why should I trust you?" he asked with surprise. "You've used every trick in the book to evade protective custody."

"No," she replied firmly, "I didn't want to see anyone else killed because the governor has a hard on for me."

"We have all night to debate it," he remarked, attempting to avoid another argument with her that he couldn't possibly hope to win. "I need to get the car into the garage or it may not be there after the hurricane hits."

Holden headed into the kitchen and left the house through the garage. A few seconds later, Jackie heard the garage door being manually opened. She sank into thought and considered her next move. There was a clunk from upstairs. She looked up the steps, wondering what she had heard, and then headed cautiously up the massive, spiral staircase.

Chapter Thirty-two

*H*olden pulled the sports car into the empty garage that apparently hadn't been used for anything since being built. The garage was nearly spotless, indicating the people living there had recently moved into the brand new home in the influential neighborhood. Holden got out of the car, manually shut the garage door, and retrieved Jackie's bag from the small storage area behind the car's seat. Holden entered the house through the kitchen and headed into the rapidly darkening grand hallway. He set Jackie's bag near the stairs and looked around. She wasn't anywhere to be found. Everything was eerily quiet.

"Jackie, bell service." There was no response or sound except for the howling wind and rain pounding against the roof and sides of the house. Holden approached the living room and looked around. "Jackie?"

Holden looked toward the stairs, appeared curious, and cautiously headed up them. The second floor was even darker than the first floor. There was a loud clunk from one of the nearby bedrooms. He hesitated, removed his gun, and slowly pushed on the partially open bedroom door. The generous sized master bedroom was dimly lit by a flashlight lying on the floor. Holden stepped into the doorway with his gun in his hand.

"No games, Jackie."

Across the massive room, Jackie lie limp on the bed with a nylon curtain cord around her neck. The bed was slightly rumpled and several objects within the room were overturned. Holden appeared alarmed, hurried for the bed, and removed the cord from around her neck. Jackie grabbed his wrist and used her leg to toss him over her and onto the bed. As if anticipating her actions, Holden counter flipped her onto her back and pinned her to the bed by her wrists while on top of her. She was startled by the swiftness of his counterattack.

"Nice try," he mocked.

Jackie attempted to get leverage with her free leg, so she'd be able to kick him. Holden pinned her leg with his and held her immobile with nearly every part of his body. Jackie made another attempt to free her wrists. Holden appeared humored and chuckled softly.

"Well, this is a pleasant change," he announced cheerfully. "I have no idea what game we're playing, but I think I'm winning for a change."

"Fine, you won," she scoffed. "Get off me!"

"No, I don't think so," he snapped in response and turned serious. "I know you hate me, but can we get through one crisis at a time?"

Jackie finally stopped struggling, frowned, and avoided looking at him.

"And back to the silent treatment," he muttered with a defeated sigh.

There was a long silence between them. The only sound came from the raging storm outside just waiting to tear the house from its concrete pad. Neither moved. Jackie remained completely relaxed and non-threatening beneath him. Holden remained tense and distrustful of her peaceful nature. She knew her actions caused him concern. Jackie learned that sometimes the most threatening words were the ones not spoken. Her silence and lack of aggression was causing him stress, she could tell. She reflected on his earlier words and lost enthusiasm to fight him.

"I don't hate you, Agent Falcone," she finally replied in a soft tone without looking at him then carefully considered her next comment. "I don't even dislike you."

Holden appeared curious by her comment but dismissed it. "If I get off of you, are you going to behave?" he asked as he stared at her profile.

"No."

"At least you're honest," he groaned with defeat. "So we're going to stay like this all night?"

"I'm quite comfortable."

"Fine, then I'll just make myself comfortable too," he remarked sternly.

Holden maneuvered his legs between hers, placing them in a compromising position. She was startled by his actions. There was no denying he was attempting to make a point, but his motive was puzzling to her. What did he hope to achieve? What was the purpose of trying to beat her at her own game? He had to know she could feel the enthusiasm rising in his pants. Apart from her quickening pulse, his actions made no sense.

"Asserting that male dominance?" she asked and finally met his gaze.

She attempted to remain cool despite his body pressed against hers. She felt embarrassed by her flushed cheeks, although, it wasn't as if he could see them in the dim lighting.

"It gets your attention," he replied while staring back at her.

She raised her brows in a slightly seductive manner while staring at him through the dim lighting from the flashlight. Jackie then said with all seriousness, "Try asserting it a little to the left."

Holden stared at her a moment with a strange look then uncertainly moved his hips slightly to the left.

Jackie groaned softly to the sensation of his arousal pressed against her. She smiled lustfully while staring at him. "Assert away, Agent Falcone."

Holden was clearly surprised by her reaction. He suddenly groaned and kissed her passionately yet aggressively on the mouth while pressing his hips eagerly against her. Jackie gasped softly from his body pressing into hers and wasted little time returning the aggressive kiss. His passionate kiss sent shockwaves through her entire body, and she ached for him. It had been a long time since she wanted a man this badly. Holden appeared hesitant to release her wrists; although, it was obvious he wanted to. She could feel his conflict about her intentions, since she'd tricked him several times before, but she needed him to release her if this was going to work. Jackie broke off the aggressive kiss and immediately kissed his neck while breathing heavily.

She cooed softly in his ear, "You've got me where I want me. I'm not going anywhere."

Holden hesitated only a moment to consider his next move and possibly her sincerity then released her wrists. His mouth again sought hers as his right hand firmly caressed her breast and traveled along her side to her thigh and buttocks. She clung to him and attempted to keep up with his aggressive kiss and rising passion. He moved to his knees and wasted little time removing his jacket, shoulder holster, and shirt. She couldn't deny that the way he hastily shed his clothing was an instant turn on. She could only compare it to the Navy's thirteen-button salute. As Jackie sat up, she felt Holden tense to her sudden movement. It was cute that he feared her intentions yet was brave enough to want her anyway. She grinned in response as she removed her tank top. He appeared relieved when she tossed her shirt to the floor. Jackie immediately reached for his belt buckle and worked on opening it with one hand while caressing his hard bulge with the other. Holden groaned softly, gathered her in his arms, and tackled her to the bed.

†

*A*n hour later, Holden and Jackie lie naked in each other's arms beneath the covers while panting heavily. Both appeared exhausted while listening to the raging storm outside. It almost sounded as if the house was about to lift off from its concrete pad. The banging sound continued from outside, which was undoubtedly siding being torn away from the house. The devastation outside was furthest from their minds. It certainly hadn't interfered with their wild sexual fling. The boyish grin on Holden's face conveyed he hadn't a care in the world. Jackie rested her head on his chest and listened to his pounding heart while she weaved her fingers through his chest hair.

"I have a newly found appreciation for your aggression," he announced with a soft chuckle.

"That was all you, Agent Falcone," she announced teasingly while attempting to control her own elevated heart rate. "I suspect all that pent up sexual frustration finally exploded." As she thought about her comment, she was aware she could have easily been describing herself.

"It may have been awhile, but I don't remember it *ever* being like that."

Jackie couldn't help feeling a little proud of his comment. Although she'd never admit it aloud, she had good training in that department. Navy SEALs weren't just highly skilled in combat. They tended to overachieve at *everything*. She lifted her head from his chest, met his gaze, and smiled lustfully.

"That was a pretty good warm-up exercise," she announced playfully while running her fingers along his chest. "Let me know when you're ready to get serious."

He looked back at her with surprise then immediately grinned. "Okay, *that* game I will play."

"Good, because I'm good to go all night," she teased and allowed her hand to slide firmly down his abdomen and beneath the covers.

Holden groaned, half rolled on top of her, and kissed her warmly. He then hesitated, looked into her eyes, and smiled with some embarrassment.

"You know, I wanted to have my way with you from the moment I met you."

Jackie was surprised by his comment. She certainly didn't get any sexual vibes from him in their early confrontations. She wished she had known. It may not have changed much, but they would have had more fun getting there.

"Really?" she asked with a cleverly raised brow. "What stopped you? Because I know it wasn't me."

He shrugged and hid his embarrassed smile. "A conflict of interest, I suppose." He hesitated then laughed at himself. "--and I *can* be a bit of a Boy Scout." His glanced at her as his look turned serious. "The thought of being found naked and handcuffed to a bed certainly didn't help either."

She smiled sweetly, ran her leg along his bare hip beneath the covers, and caressed his body. "I would've dressed you before I left."

"I'm beginning to think you were serious with your little seduction scenes."

Jackie caressed his shoulders and smiled lustfully. "Oh, I was serious. I don't know if it's the Boy Scout or the badge, but I like the way you walk into a room. Very commanding and sexually dominant."

"Is that how you see it?"

"Hmm, definitely," she cooed. "And when you handcuffed me at the fair, I was a little turned on."

Holden stared at her a moment, appeared to consider his response carefully, and then sighed softly with defeat. "I'm a little ashamed to admit it, but I did sort of bump and grind you just a little."

She attempted to hide her knowing smile as she brushed her lips past his. "Want to arrest me again and show me what you really wanted to do?"

"You don't have to ask twice," he moaned softly and playfully tackled her to the bed.

Chapter Thirty-three

Brilliant sunlight flooded into the bedroom through a part in the curtains. With the sun shining so brightly, it didn't seem possible that a major hurricane attempted to take the island off the map just last night. Jackie slowly woke beneath the covers on the massive bed as Holden snuggled against her from behind. Jackie, wearing Holden's shirt, stretched onto her back to reveal her left wrist was cuffed to his left wrist. She turned over and into him with a playful grin on her face. He woke, smiled warmly, and nuzzled her face with his face.

"How's my prisoner this morning?" he teased.

"Pleasantly sore."

He hid his disappointed look. "Does that mean you're closed for business?"

"Pretty much," she replied while caressing his bare chest. "But that doesn't mean we can't have some good, clean fun in the shower." She warmly kissed his neck and down his chest then looked up at him from her lowered position near his abdomen. "I'm sure I could find some way to satisfy you."

Jackie kissed her way under the covers. Holden chuckled softly to the comment then suddenly groaned with intense pleasure.

✝

*H*olden searched the kitchen cupboards with a mission but seemed unsuccessful. He was wearing a pair of shorts clearly too big for him, indicating he borrowed them from the absent homeowner. Jackie entered the kitchen in fresh clothing from her bag, hoisted herself onto the counter, and watched as he routed through the cupboards with disgust.

"Who lives here?" he suddenly demanded while throwing his hands in the air. "There's no coffee."

"Maybe they're tea drinkers," she offered.

He cast a glance at her. "Do you see the size of these shorts I'm wearing? This guy doesn't drink tea. There has to be coffee around here somewhere."

She secretly hid her smile. "Your clothes are dry." Jackie considered the comment. "I mean, the clothes you stole from Monroe are dry."

"That's a relief," Holden replied with a sigh. "I don't think I'd make a good impression in this guy's clothing. He must be a former linebacker."

He finally gave up his quest for coffee and leaned on the counter, a frown permanently on his face. She stared at him a moment and shifted uncomfortably.

"Holden," she said gently, "do you intend to take me back into protective custody?"

He looked at her and seemed unusually silent. Holden took a deep breath, straightened, and gently touched her face. "You know I have to."

Jackie frowned her disapproval. Holden moved between her legs, slid her hips across the counter against him, and caressed her back. He stared into her eyes with a serious look.

"Monroe's protective custody," he announced gently.

Her eyes suddenly lit up. "Really?"

Holden brushed the stray lock of hair from her face then touched her cheek. "Until we find out who at the Bureau is on the governor's payroll, you won't be safe," he informed her. "You saved my life the other night. It was supposed to be the other way around." He drew a deep breath as he stared into her eyes. "I won't jeopardize your safety by getting in your way. You know what you're doing, and I trust you."

She placed her arms around his neck and clung to him. "Thank you, Holden."

"But," he announced firmly, causing her to pull back and meet his gaze, "you'll have to call me daily."

She brushed her lips past his. "I'm really going to miss you chasing me." She grinned slyly. "I kind of enjoyed it."

He groaned softly. "I enjoyed catching you."

They kissed warmly then held each other in a tight embrace. His caressing hands traveled her body and pulled her hips against him. She groaned in response and ran her hands along his bare chest toward his shorts. He stopped her traveling hands and chuckled softly.

"You're a bad influence, and we definitely don't have time for that," he announced then turned serious. "We need to find Monroe and get you away from here. From what I've seen out the window, it's going to be rough traveling out there, so we'd better get going." He stared into her eyes and gently caressed her face. "I won't leave you until you're safely with Monroe."

Jackie smiled timidly and nodded. "And I think I know where we might find him."

t

*T*he red Ferrari drove along the slightly flooded back road while avoiding fallen tree branches and debris. Cars were abandoned along the sides of the road, trees were uprooted, and power lines were down. The destruction was catastrophic. There appeared to be no signs of life anywhere. Holden and Jackie stared out the windshield with complete amazement at the destruction surrounding them. What few homes they passed had some degree of damage ranging from broken windows to torn gutters and ripped siding. Roof shingles were strewn miles from any homes, revealing the magnitude of the hurricane.

"I've never seen anything like this," Jackie said while staring at the devastation. "It's kind of creepy."

What amazed her the most was how a tourist island could become a ghost town overnight. The Ferrari was the only car traveling on the road since they set out from the abandoned development nearly forty minutes ago. Driving, particularly in a sports car, was challenging. There were many obstacles scattered along the road, and the sports car's low frame made driving over even the smallest debris difficult. Thankfully, they hadn't come across any more bodies since they found the three home invaders dead last night.

"How far is this airfield?"

"On this road somewhere," she informed him. "I'm sure this is where he was going after bailing out Zach."

"Maybe he was arrested while 'bailing out' your friend," Holden mocked.

"Oh, please," she groaned while rolling her eyes for effect. "Monroe is smarter than he looks, and Zach is a genius. They don't get caught."

He snorted a laugh and cast a glance at her while concentrating on driving the disastrous road in front of them. "Oh, really? Your little Kung Fu friend looked pretty incapacitated the last time I saw him."

She eyed him sharply. "He sacrificed himself for me," Jackie firmly replied. "For Zach, being captured is only ever temporary--" she then muttered, "--sort of like being dead."

Holden appeared bewildered by the comment then quickly brushed it off. She had to admit, she enjoyed the look of confusion on his face.

"Are you sure you'll be okay with those two for several months or longer?" Holden asked, appearing concerned about the company she'd be keeping for the first time.

"They'll keep me safe," she replied without hesitation. "Monroe's lustful nature will be my biggest worry."

Holden was unusually silent and suddenly avoided looking at her. Jackie glanced at him, noticed his solemn attitude, and smiled.

"Are you jealous?"

He still didn't look at her. "No, of course not," he said firmly, although his clenching jaw told a different story. "Several months alone with your old boyfriend, Captain Flash," Holden muttered under his breath. "Why would I be jealous?"

She half turned in the seat and stared at him with her mouth hanging open. "You are jealous!" Jackie found it humorous, although Holden didn't share her humor. "You want me all to yourself. Just admit it," she teased.

There was a long silence. "Okay, yes," he suddenly scoffed. "I want you all to myself."

She stared at him a moment while enjoying the warm feeling sweeping through her body. She no longer found his jealousy humorous either.

"Was that so hard?" she announced almost timidly then grinned. "Fine. I'm exclusively yours."

Holden attempted to hide his surprise then smiled more to himself. He stared out the window to avoid looking at her, but she could tell he was pleased.

"Of course, that's a two-way street, Agent Falcone," she announced slyly.

Holden appeared humored and chuckled. "Abstaining has never been a problem."

"The Boy Scout, I forgot." She was silent a moment as several thoughts raced through her mind. She cast a look at him and suddenly felt uncomfortable. "Do you really think it'll be around six months until the trial?"

"Six months minimum. We have Dexter dead bang in the murder of three police officers, but, apart from your testimony, we still have nothing to link the governor to the murders or ordering the hits," he replied. "If we only knew why Harris went there."

"The library used to be the governor's mansion," she informed him. "Harris may have seen something that required his immediate silence. I'm sure the governor didn't anticipate killing a federal agent after the fundraiser. After all, he knew I was coming to meet him." She sank into thought and recalled the events of that night. "I just can't believe you didn't find their bodies in the fruit cellar. I mean, where else would he have taken them. You didn't find any blood in the car he used either, so he couldn't have moved their bodies. It's just not possible."

"You were there, Jackie," Holden replied. "We didn't find any bodies in the fruit cellar."

Jackie looked out the window and stared at the ruins of an old, stone building. It looked almost medieval. She then remembered something Vicki had said that night, and how she had gone on about the fruit cellar being medieval.

"Odd," she suddenly remarked, catching his attention.

"What?"

"Vicki bragged about the fruit cellar, but it just looked like an old basement to me," Jackie said while deep in thought. "What if that room wasn't the room she was taking me to see? What if there was more to it?"

Holden glanced at her several times and appeared deep in thought by the comment. "You mean a hidden room within the hidden room?"

"Maybe."

"I think we need to go back in there with cadaver dogs, and see what they turn up," he insisted. "It's worth looking into. I mean, we wouldn't even have known there was a room there if you hadn't shown us. It's possible there's more to that room than what we'd found."

"Something was going down in that fruit cellar," Jackie replied sternly. "Harris saw something and it got him killed. I don't know what he saw, but I didn't see drugs or guns or anything like that. I mean, I wasn't exactly looking, but I would notice something like that lying around. There hadn't even been a briefcase or bag in that room. So what did he see or hear that got him killed?"

"Secret compartment with drugs, perhaps," Holden announced. "Something you wouldn't have noticed or that he closed before you arrived. Being the library was the governor's mansion from years past, he'd probably know of any hidden rooms."

"Their bodies are there," she said firmly. "I'm convinced of it. If you find their bodies, you'll probably also find your motive for murder."

"I think you're right," Holden replied. "If we can find something to link the governor to criminal activity within the library and a motive for murder, we might have enough evidence to go to trial sooner."

"You'll have no complaints from me," she remarked.

Chapter Thirty-four

The private airfield had been hit particularly hard by the severe hurricane. Several planes were overturned and the roof from one of the hangers had collapsed onto a larger plane. The large-scale destruction gave the airfield an eeriness about it. There appeared to be no movement or signs of life anywhere. The Ferrari slowly drove across the abandoned airfield past several demolished planes. The sports car stopped near one of the destroyed planes, keeping their distance from the larger, undamaged hanger. Jackie and Holden got out and looked at Monroe's Hummer near the intact hanger in the distance.

"That's Monroe's," she informed him then looked around. "I don't like how quiet it is."

"I agree," Holden responded. "I think we should approach with caution, just to be safe."

Both removed their weapons and walked nearly thirty yards to the parked Hummer. Voices were heard from within the hanger. At first, it was a welcomed sound, but once Jackie recognized the voice, it sent chills down her spine. She looked at Holden and mouthed the name 'Dexter'. Holden grabbed Jackie and pulled her alongside the hanger door. Both peered inside through the partially open bay door.

A badly beaten Monroe was tied to a chair in a clearing near the center of the hanger. The hanger contained an old jeep, a small, private plane, machinery, and large gang boxes. Dexter paced in front of Monroe and flexed his hand. His bleeding knuckles matched Monroe's bleeding face.

"You had better hope your friend knows where she is or you're both dead," Dexter remarked lowly. "My men won't hesitate to slit his throat."

"If he says she's on his boat, she's on his boat," Monroe informed him then shrugged. "If his boat is still there, well, that's another story."

Dexter punched Monroe in the face, momentarily stunning him. Dexter again flexed his hand. It was unclear who was in more pain. Monroe spit out blood and looked up at Dexter with a twisted smile on his battered face.

"Is that the best you've got?" Monroe asked while snorting a laugh. "Because I can do this all day."

Dexter appeared to consider striking him again, but he flexed his sore hand and thought better of it. There were two more armed men standing nearby while guarding both entrances. The entrance to the back was only open a foot or more for cross ventilation. Holden pulled Jackie away from the hanger and both crouched behind Monroe's Hummer.

"There are three armed men inside," Holden informed her. "It sounds like two others took your friend, Zach, to the docks. The phones are down, so we have no back up."

"Zach wouldn't leave Monroe here without a plan," she informed Holden. "He always has a plan." She then considered her comment and grimaced. "--however devious and twisted it might be."

"Monroe may not have much time. We need to act now," Holden warned. "I'm not thrilled with my plan, but we don't have much choice."

"Or we could just do it my way," Zach announced softly from behind them.

Jackie and Holden spun with surprise to see Zach casually crouched alongside them behind the Hummer. His sudden and silent appearance was alarming to both. Despite his shirt being covered in blood, he appeared unusually calm. Jackie didn't know why she was surprised to find him alongside them. Zach had a bad habit of sneaking up on people. She swore he was part ninja.

"Were you injured?" Holden asked with surprise.

"No, why do you ask?" Zach suddenly asked with an innocent look on his face.

Holden eyed his shirt and indicated the large amount of mostly fresh blood. Zach casually glanced at the blood and appeared disinterested.

"Oh, that. Just a little disagreement with two thugs," he announced simply then smiled most sinister. "They eventually saw it my way."

"What--?" Holden started to ask but Jackie was quick to cut him off mid-sentence.

"Don't ever ask Zach what he does," she said firmly as her eyes widened. "Trust me; it'll just give you nightmares."

Holden glanced at her with moderate concern, took a deep breath, and then looked at the creepy man alongside him. "What's *your* way?"

Zach grinned deviously.

†

*W*ithin the hanger, Dexter stood near Monroe while the two gunmen guarded the front and back entrance to the hanger. Dexter appeared to be losing his patience. Monroe, on the other hand, seemed relaxed and in no particular hurry. It seemed only a matter of time before Dexter just decided to shoot Monroe out of sheer boredom. Zach suddenly appeared in the main entrance to the hanger and bowled with a grenade. The men saw him and then the rolling object.

"Grenade!" Dexter shouted.

All three scattered and dove for shelter from the rolling grenade. Zach gave the signal for a strike and disappeared before detonation. Monroe remained quietly seated in his chair and appeared less than impressed. The grenade emitted a large cloud of smoke. Zach slipped in through the front entrance and Holden appeared through the back with his gun drawn. Dexter and the two gunmen realized the grenade was a decoy, saw the ambush, and immediately fired at Zach and Holden on opposite ends. Monroe casually straightened, smashed the chair with his foot, and rolled out of the ropes that were once around him. Monroe dove behind the nearby gang box with Zach and easily found the spare semiautomatic down the back of his friend's pants. They'd obviously played this game before. Holden took cover behind a generator not far from the back entrance. Dexter and the two gunmen moved behind the old jeep and fired at the intruders. Zach leaned his back to the gang box and casually lit a cigar. He took several puffs from it, eyed Monroe, and grinned. Monroe offered no comment or question; instead, he fired back at Dexter and the two other hired killers. Zach casually lit a stick of dynamite from his cigar. Monroe met Zach's nearly psychotic gaze with little reaction.

"I love this part," Zach chirped cheerfully.

Monroe took his silent cue and rapidly fired at the three men, allowing Zach enough cover to stand and throw the dynamite at them. The cheap grin on his face was frightening.

"Fire in the hole!" Zach shouted with enthusiasm.

Holden saw the dynamite, gasped, and ducked behind the generator. The dynamite landed just before the jeep. Dexter and the first gunman saw the sizzling fuse attached to the explosive and dove out of the way. The dynamite exploded, flipping the jeep over and onto the second gunman, who didn't have time to get out of the way. Dexter and the first gunman were catapulted through the air and landed roughly on the ground behind the overturned jeep. Dexter rolled several times but quickly recovered, reclaimed his gun, and fired while running out the main entrance, not caring that he had abandoned the other gunman. Holden ran after Dexter. The remaining gunman recovered more slowly from the impact and his unplanned flight.

Zach and Monroe charged him while he was down. The gunman recovered and fired at Monroe and Zach from behind the overturned jeep. Monroe leaped for cover to the sound of the first shot. Zach never slowed, scaled the overturned jeep, and kicked the gun upward from the gunman's hand. The gun flew straight up into the air. The gunman caught the falling object as Zach leaped off the jeep, but what he caught was a grenade instead of the gun. Zach and Monroe ran for the back entrance as the grenade exploded, taking the last gunman with it, raining down chunks of his singed flesh.

Chapter Thirty-five

$\mathcal{D}$exter ran for Monroe's Hummer not far from the hanger with Holden just behind him. He stopped alongside the Hummer and fired back at Holden. Holden leaped to the ground behind an overturned drum for safety. The wording on the drum read 'gasoline'. Holden saw the warning, appeared alarmed, and shot at Dexter as he made a run for the side of the hanger instead. A stray shot hit the drum. There was a tremendous explosion and a fiery ball of flame. Holden was partially projected through the air as he dove for safety. He hit the ground alongside the hanger a little harder than anticipated. Dexter ran for the Hummer's driver side door and threw it open. Jackie was crouched on the driver's seat. She clutched the seat and steering wheel to brace herself as she kicked him in the chest with both feet.

Dexter was thrown roughly to the ground and the gun flew from his hand. Jackie gracefully jumped out of the Hummer and approached him where he lie on the ground. Her expression was cold and hard. Dexter scrambled for his gun. Jackie kicked it out of the way and stared down at him as he looked up at her, now on his backside. Dexter slowly moved to his knees and watched her, obviously contemplating his next move and hers. She removed her semiautomatic then casually tossed it aside.

"You want me?" she growled lowly. "I'm right here. Let's end this."

Dexter hesitated only a moment then sprang to his feet and lunged for her. Jackie spun into a roundhouse kick and struck him in the chest. He stumbled back with surprise and rubbed his chest. She went for a second kick, but he was anticipating it and grabbed her ankle, twisting her leg. Jackie used the momentum from the twist to flip her entire body and struck him in the face with her free foot. He flew backward onto the ground, striking it harshly. Jackie rolled across the ground and immediately sprang to her feet facing him. Holden was about to move in from alongside the hanger when Monroe suddenly stood alongside him and placed a hand on his shoulder.

"Let her go," Monroe announced. "Therapy, man. It's good for her."

Zach mysteriously appeared near the fight in progress and casually sat on the Hummer's hood while puffing on his cigar. He watched the fight with a pleased smirk on his face. Dexter only got in one good shot while Jackie dominated the fight with high kicks and defensive blocks. She kicked Dexter in the face with a final blow, throwing him against the Hummer's hood not far from Zach. Zach eyed him from only a few feet away and grinned through the cigar clenched in his teeth. When it appeared as if the battle had ended, Holden and Monroe approached them and the Hummer. Monroe grinned and slapped Holden on the back while raising his brows and indicating Jackie.

"Pretty hot, huh?"

Holden eyed Monroe without response. He obviously didn't care for his version of 'hot'. As Dexter weakly clung to the Hummer hood for support, Jackie grabbed him by the throat and stared into his eyes.

"Give Lyle a message from me," Jackie snarled through gritted teeth.

Jackie rammed her knee into Dexter's groin and released him as he dropped to his knees while clutching himself. Monroe and Holden suddenly stopped and grimaced. Zach grinned lustfully while watching Jackie.

"God, you are sexy," Zach groaned softly.

Jackie eyed Zach, hid her smile to the comment, and then walked toward Holden and Monroe as they continued their approach. Dexter suddenly removed a small semiautomatic from a hidden ankle holster and aimed it at Jackie's back from where he knelt on the ground near the vehicle. Holden saw the gun and immediately raised his weapon.

"Gun!" Holden shouted.

Jackie only had to hear the word and threw herself into a roll across the ground, giving Holden a clear line of fire. Holden shot Dexter twice in the chest. His body jolted before striking the Hummer then falling to the ground. Zach remained casually seated on the Hummer's hood and watched Dexter collapse lifelessly. Zach loosened his finger on the trigger of his carefully hidden gun. No one needed to know that he had the situation under control if Holden had failed to take out Dexter in time. Jackie looked back at the dead man on the ground then allowed Holden to assist her to her feet and gather her in his arms. She smiled as he held her.

"Nice shot," Jackie announced cheerfully.

Monroe's expression suddenly dropped. "Oh, God," he groaned and rolled his eyes. "She's keeping him."

Holden released Jackie and holstered his weapon. Monroe approached Dexter, kicked his shoe, and then looked at Jackie while giving a nod at the dead man.

"Was this the ringleader?" Monroe asked.

"Yeah, that's Dexter, the governor's second in command," Jackie replied.

Monroe searched the dead man's pockets, removed Dexter's cell phone from his jacket, and tossed it to Zach. Zach caught the cell phone and pressed a button while casually puffing on his cigar. Thankfully, cell service seemed to be working.

As the phone was almost immediately answered, the governor's familiar voice spoke hastily. "Is it done?"

"Yes, Governor," Zach said in a creepy tone. "It's done."

"Who is this?" came the governor's confused response from the other end.

"You should have sent more men," Zach said low and evilly. "I don't appreciate my talent being wasted on mere play dates." He hesitated then grinned. "We should arrange for our own *play date*. It'll be *fun*."

Zach disconnected the call, smiled deviously, and wiped his prints from the phone. Monroe hid his smile, sharing in Zach's twisted and devious nature.

"You're sick, man," Monroe remarked.

Zach tossed the cell phone over his shoulder and maintained his devious smile through the cigar. Monroe eyed Jackie and indicated Holden with a nod.

"So what are we doing with the fed?"

"He's relinquishing me into your custody," Jackie informed him cheerfully.

Monroe appeared slightly surprised then smiled proudly. "Oh, well, in that case, I may not kill him after all." He glared at Holden as his look turned serious. "--for taking my clothes." Monroe then looked across the airfield and appeared horrified while pointing at the sports car. "--and my Ferrari?" He looked at Jackie and appeared to pout like a child. "You let him take my Ferrari?"

"We didn't have much choice," Jackie protested. "Your house is somewhere in the Atlantic."

Monroe groaned and shook his head. Zach looked at his watch then to the sky and stared with more than a passing interest, catching everyone's attention. Holden looked to the sky as well and listened. A helicopter was heard approaching. As the large helicopter came into view, Holden straightened with concern.

"Is that--?"

Monroe smirked and nodded. "Oh, yeah."

The helicopter gracefully lowered to the ground several yards away from them. Three intimidating looking men with assault rifles jumped out before the helicopter had completely landed, flanked them, and immediately aimed their weapons at Holden. It was unclear if they intended to shoot first and ask questions later. Jackie gasped and jumped in front of Holden. She didn't want to find out the answer after the fact.

"It's okay! At ease!" Monroe ordered.

The three men lowered their weapons on command. As the helicopter shut down, a fourth man appeared and joined them. The men smiled deviously at Jackie and swarmed her. Jackie playfully screamed as the first man, Ross, lifted her up and kissed her quickly on the lips. She was tossed from one man to the next for their official greeting. Holden watched with concern then appeared suddenly aware of Zach standing alongside him with a disapproving look on his slightly psychotic face.

"Pitiful display of male dominance, don't you think?" Zach remarked.

Holden eyed Zach, who had once again mysterious appeared alongside him. Jackie approached Holden, took him by the hand, and led him toward the four intimidating looking men.

"This is Special Agent Holden Falcone," Jackie announced then glanced at Holden and indicated the serious looking men. Despite being mostly middle-aged men, they still retained their muscle mass and stature. "Holden, this is the rest of my father's old SEAL team. Ross, Beck, Gil, and Kirk."

They eyed him with moderate distrust. Holden gave Jackie's hand an oddly firm squeeze. Ross finally smiled and extended his hand.

"Pleasure to meet you, Agent Falcone," Ross announced cheerfully.

Holden accepted his hand and appeared relieved that the men were friendly--ish. The other men quickly joined in to greet him, their moods immediately turning jovial and less intimidating. They finally looked around at the destruction and at Dexter's blood-soaked body on the ground near the Hummer.

"This looks familiar," Kirk muttered. "Someone certainly screwed the pooch."

Gil puffed on his cigar and grinned at his comrade. "Now, see, this is what happens when you leave Monroe in charge of shit. Momma's boy can't coordinate anything but his wardrobe."

There was a round of laughter from the men. Monroe sneered at Gil and didn't appear amused. Kirk eyed Monroe's battered and bleeding face.

"Using your face to pound on someone's fist again?" Kirk teased his friend.

Beck removed a cigar from his jacket and indicated the charred ground and smoke billowing from the nearby hanger. "You can tell Zach was here," he remarked while lighting his cigar and eyed Zach. "Did you ever meet anyone you didn't blow to bits?"

"That's classified," Zach teased.

"What a cluster fuck," Ross scoffed while shaking his head. "Who's cleaning this shit?"

Everyone pointed at Holden. Holden eyed them, groaned, and conceded. Monroe looked at Ross, tapped his watch, and gestured with his hand. Ross took his cue and looked at the other retired SEALs.

"Okay, men, stand by to stand by," Ross bellowed. "We're bugging out in fifteen!" Ross then looked at Monroe while aggressively chewing on his cigar. "You're meeting us at the rendezvous, right?"

"I'll be a few hours behind you, as planned." Monroe turned to Holden, placed his hand on his shoulder, and gave him a stern, serious look. "If you and Jackie want to sneak in a quick one, you'd better do it fast."

Holden seemed surprised by the suggestion, hid his embarrassed smile, and shook his head in response. Without hesitation, Jackie grabbed his hand and pulled him toward the smoldering hanger, startling him.

"Oh, okay--" he gasped and hurried to keep up with her as they disappeared inside the hanger.

Ten minutes later, Jackie and Holden emerged from the hanger, the stench of smoke lingering on them. Jackie was all smiles. Holden attempted to tuck in his shirt while hiding his boyish grin to their unplanned sexual romp. All six men leaned against the helicopter with their arms folded across their chests, cigars in their mouths, and looks of disapproval on their hard Navy SEAL faces. Holden stopped smiling when he saw their looks and immediately fidgeted. After successfully intimidating him, they straightened and Ross began shouting orders to the men.

"I want every swinging dick on station, now!" Ross cried out while gesturing with his hand.

The men sprang into action. Jackie kissed Holden quickly but passionately and smiled her goodbye.

"Call me as soon as you're settled," Holden reminded firmly without taking his eyes off her.

Jackie smiled and nodded, fighting her own tears. She didn't want to show weakness in front of her father's team. They'd never let her live it down, and it would be a long enough flight as they would undoubtedly torment her endlessly about her escapades with Holden in the hanger. She didn't want to think about how much she'd miss Holden, and if he'd still feel the same about her when they finally met again. She'd never been in a relationship, so she had no idea what to expect. Ross jolted her out of her self-pity daze while yelling to the men.

"Drinks are on Jackie!" Ross yelled excitedly.

The men cheered in response and began piling into the helicopter. Beck stopped before Holden and handed him a business card.

"If you're ever in Colorado and need a quality used car, give me a call," he announced while grinning then joined the others in the helicopter.

Monroe remained behind with Holden. Both watched as Jackie and Zach joined the others in the helicopter. Jackie waved to them as the helicopter lifted off.

One of the men exclaimed, "Alpha Mike Foxtrot!" It was followed by a round of laughter as the helicopter flew away from the private airfield and the men left behind.

Holden glanced at Monroe and appeared bewildered. "Is that code for something?"

"Yeah, it means goodbye," Monroe remarked then offered a slight shrug. "In not so polite terms."

Monroe turned toward him, extended the Hummer keys to Holden, and glared while snapping his fingers. Holden frowned and handed him the Ferrari keys. Monroe snatched the Ferrari keys and shook his head with disgust.

"You can steal my woman, but don't you *ever* touch my car," Monroe growled.

Holden looked to the sky and the helicopter fading into the distance. He placed his hands in his pockets and frowned. Monroe noted his look and snorted a soft laugh.

"Relax," he announced. "She'll be safe. She's in the best hands possible. Every single one of those men would kill for that girl."

"I don't doubt it," Holden replied while lacking enthusiasm.

Monroe studied him a moment then appeared humored by what he saw in Holden's distant look. "Don't worry; she'll still want you when this is all over. If she wasn't serious about you, she wouldn't have gone into the hanger with you. No way would she open herself up to that sort of ribbing if she didn't have strong feelings for you."

Holden finally looked at Monroe and hid his pleased smile. "Thanks--for everything."

"Remember that," Monroe announced while grinning slyly. "I may ask for a *favor* one day."

Chapter Thirty-six

*F*our months had passed and Governor Lyle Kempton was scheduled to go on trial for his role in the murders of Agent Harris Benton, and Vicki, the librarian. A crowd of reporters had gathered outside the courthouse as the governor approached the steps with his assistant and an entourage of lawyers. Television and newspaper reporters swarmed him with cameras flashing and questions about the murders. His lawyers kept them at bay and hurried him inside, away from the chaos outside the building. Police officers attempted to bring other prisoners in and out of the building through the crowd of onlookers and media. Even the streets were bumper-to-bumper with passersby attempting to get a look at the infamous governor about to be tried for homicide.

Within the safety of the crowded courthouse, Lyle appeared repulsed as gang members and prostitutes brushed past him in the tight quarters of the main hallway. Lyle walked with his assistant past several prisoners awaiting their trials. Gang members shouted profanities at one another from across the corridor while prostitutes appeared calm and collected. Lyle's lawyers busily talked to the prosecuting attorney as they waited for the trial to begin. Lyle moved closer to his assistant and spoke softly with him while looking around the crowded corridor.

"Any news?"

"I heard they're flying her in by helicopter," his assistant announced in a hushed tone.

"Tell me something I don't know," Lyle groused. "Who's *they*?"

"No one knows," his assistant replied. "They don't even know where she's been the last four months. It's like she fell into a black hole."

"So as far as we know, she still intends to show up for the trial." His expression turned serious as he nervously looked around. "She can't make it into that courtroom," the governor muttered firmly then cast a look at Agent Falcone across the crowded corridor from them. The governor indicated Holden to his assistant. "He's looking a little nervous himself. Did you talk to our guy at the Bureau?"

"I'm afraid he didn't know anything either," his assistant gently informed him.

"How the hell could she disappear like that?" he demanded more to himself. "What about our welcome party?"

"Already on the roof."

"That's good," Lyle replied and attempted to look calm, but it was obvious he was worried Jackie would make it to the courthouse alive.

Holden stood in the crowded corridor off to the side and glanced at his partner across the hall. Agent Fields talked with the prosecuting attorney, who seemed uptight about the start of the trial without his primary witness. Holden appeared calm but repeatedly checked his watch every thirty seconds. His star witness was running late without so much as a phone call. A seated prostitute rubbed her stiletto foot against his leg. Holden eyed the bleached blonde prostitute with some annoyance then moved away from her. Lyle checked his own watch, nudged his assistant, indicating the time, and grinned his approval. He noticed Holden across the corridor and approached him with a smug look on his face.

"Well, Agent Falcone," Lyle announced cheerfully. "Where's this star witness of yours? Running late?"

"She'll be here, don't worry," Holden replied. "There's plenty of time before the trial starts."

"I'd say you're cutting it close. She should have reported by now." He appeared pleased with himself as the scheduled trial time was rapidly approaching. Things may have been looking up for the former governor, particularly if Jackie was a no show. "When I'm found not guilty, I'm going to have your badge," Lyle announced cheerfully.

Holden wasn't impressed and didn't give him the satisfaction of a reaction. He remained unusually calm even if he wasn't. "I think you're forgetting a very important detail. We found the bodies of one of our agents and the librarian that your thug killed and dumped in that dungeon death pit," Holden stated firmly and stared down the governor. "The case against you looks pretty good even without our witness."

"I don't know anything about a dungeon or a death pit," Lyle insisted with little sincerity. "I don't think the prosecutor can prove that I did."

"I'm sure you didn't know anything about it," Holden scoffed. "I know you didn't count on us finding either the secret room or the dungeon beyond that. If you had, you would have done a better job at cleaning up all the blood leading us right to the death pit in the dungeon floor." He shook his head with disgust. "Had that poor librarian known what she discovered was actually a dungeon and not a fruit cellar, she may have reported it to her supervisors. Your dirty little secret would have been exposed years ago."

"This whole trial is ridiculous," Lyle announced boldly as his frustration surfaced. "Even if Dexter did kill those people you say he did, that doesn't mean I had anything to do with it. I'm not responsible for his shortcomings."

"Shortcomings? We're talking murder, Kempton. I'd hardly call that a shortcoming," Holden announced. "You're going to have a hard time proving you weren't involved."

"I believe it's the prosecutor's job to prove I *was* involved," Lyle replied and attempted to regain his superior attitude. "Not the other way around."

"What really astonishes me are all the decomposing bodies we found within that death pit," Holden remarked while continuing his attempt at tripping up the governor. "Forensics is still trying to identify all the bodies. At last count, I think we were up to ten." He studied the governor and raised his brow. "Amazing that the estimated time of death for each of the bodies was around the time the library was your governor's mansion. Pretty suspicious, don't you think?"

"You can't prove I was involved in any of that," the governor retorted, although the comment seemed to strike a nerve, causing him to perspire.

"Our witness will confirm you ordered the hit on a federal agent and watched while it was carried out," Holden informed him. "Once we implicate you in his death, proving you knew about the bodies in the death pit will be fairly easy."

"It's that girl's word against mine. And the word of a girl like that--"

"That *girl* nearly killed your guard dog with her bare hands," Holden snarled defensively while staring down the governor. "You may want to show some respect."

Lyle glared his annoyance to the comment, collected his assistant, and continued past him without further conversation. Both prostitutes, who had been sitting on the bench, were now standing and attempted to cozy up to the governor with their cuffed hands as he passed. He brushed them off as if they were dirt beneath his shoes. Their arresting officer quickly reeled them in. A helicopter was heard approaching. Holden looked to the ceiling and appeared tense. It was a long anticipated sound. It was the sound of justice. It was also a reminder that the woman he loved was returning to him. The same blonde prostitute placed her hand on Holden's lower arm and cozied up to him. Holden eyed her with some annoyance. She had long blonde hair, a thick layer of carefully applied make-up, and an outfit that revealed too much cleavage and most of her legs. Holden brushed her hand off his arm and took a step away. He began pacing the crowded hallway while awaiting confirmation of Jackie's arrival.

†

*S*everal officers stood on the roof of the courthouse by the helicopter landing pad. The large, familiar helicopter approached, suspiciously hoovered a moment, and then gracefully landed on its mark. Several buildings away, a sharpshooter was positioned behind the ledge of the building with a high-powered rifle and scope trained on the courthouse roof. The closed helicopter door was visible through the scope. The sharpshooter tapped the wireless transmitter device in his ear.

"The chopper has landed."

"Confirm it's her," a soft male voice announced through the shooter's wireless ear transmitter. "When you have a clean shot, take it. Do not hesitate."

"Roger."

Once the helicopter shut down, the side door boldly opened. Ross, Beck, Kirk, and Gil jumped onto the roof and fanned out alongside the helicopter door. The intimidating men stood by the open door and scanned the area with an official air about them. The shooter steadied his rifle and watched through the scope with his finger on the trigger. He had a clear shot of the helicopter doorway and awaited the star witness' arrival. When no one else got out, he appeared bewildered and tapped his ear transmitter.

"Sir--?"

"What is it?" came the same male voice.

A shadow loomed over the shooter, startling him. He quickly spun from where he was crouched before the wall. Zach stood over him with a devious, twisted smile and kicked him in the face. The shooter was thrown backwards with force and writhed on the roof floor in agony. Zach removed the transmitter device from the shooter's ear, grinned while studying it, and then discharged a foghorn into it.

At the same time, within the courthouse, Agent Fields suddenly clutched his ear and tossed his earpiece across the floor. He could barely stand straight while holding his ear. Holden suddenly looked at Fields with surprise and immediately pulled his gun, aiming it at his partner.

"You're under arrest," Holden shouted.

Agent Fields looked at him and appeared stunned as he released his ear. "What are you talking about?"

Several officers approached Fields with their weapons trained on him.

Holden picked up the discarded transmitter and placed it to his ear. "Hey, you there?" he asked as the officer's handcuffed his partner.

"Did you get him?" Zach's voice was heard through the ear transmitter.

"Yeah, we got him. Good job."

On the nearby building roof, Zach stood by the roof ledge with his foot casually propped on it and the transmitter to his ear. He seemed to be enjoying the spectacular view of his Navy SEAL comrades standing at attention before the helicopter.

"Hey, Holden, would you be terribly upset if your shooter had a little accident?" Zach asked and appeared curious.

"You just cuff him and leave him for us," Holden screamed through the wireless transmitter. "We want him alive!"

He held the wireless transmitter away from his ear to Holden's raised voice. "Kill joy--" Zach muttered.

Zach casually looked over the ledge to the screaming shooter dangling by a rope attached to his ankle. "Honestly, that man lacks imagination."

†

*T*he prosecuting attorney hurried toward Holden in the crowded courthouse corridor as the officers removed Agent Fields in handcuffs.

"Where is she, Agent Falcone?" the attorney demanded in a state near panic.

"What do you mean?" Holden suddenly asked as his expression shattered. "She was supposed to be on the helicopter. That was the plan."

"Well, she wasn't there," the excitable prosecutor fired back. "Find her!"

The prosecuting attorney hurried away. Holden removed his cell phone and pressed a single button. Monroe's voicemail picked up before the phone even rang.

"This is you know who," Monroe's jovial voice said from the voicemail on the other end. "Leave a you know what--you know when."

"Damn it, Monroe, where is she?" Holden growled lowly into the phone. "Call me back!"

Holden disconnected his call with disgust and possible concern. The same blonde prostitute stood beside him and touched his arm with her cuffed hand.

"Looking for me?" the prostitute cooed seductively.

"Aren't you in enough trouble already?" he demanded and finally looked at the hooker clinging to his arm.

As he looked into her eyes, Jackie smiled lustfully at him beyond the wig and make-up. Holden stared a moment before realizing it was Jackie. She smiled and ran her hands along his chest while lustfully raising her brows.

"Play your cards right, Agent Falcone, and I'll be cuffing you tonight."

The police officer escorting the prostitutes grinned and pulled Jackie away from Holden. "Sorry, you'll have to forgive this one," Monroe suddenly announced from beneath the police officer's uniform. "She hasn't gotten laid in four months."

Jackie smiled at Holden as Monroe pulled her away and collected the second prostitute.

Monroe looked back at Holden and grinned slyly. "Pretty hot, huh?"

Holden watched them walk down the crowded corridor. Jackie waved with her cuffed hands and blew him a kiss. Holden hid his smile while watching her posterior in the slinky, tight dress as she walked away. He groaned softly then hurried for the prosecuting attorney.

Chapter Thirty-seven

*H*olden and Jackie sat alongside each other on the secluded tropical beach while sipping champagne from decorative crystal flutes. A picnic basket set nearby but remained untouched. The trial had finally ended, not taking nearly as long as originally anticipated. Forensics discovered that the nearly one dozen decomposing bodies within the death pit were all known acquaintances of the governor. All had been shot to death and tossed into the pit during the time Lyle had been living at the mansion. Jackie stared beyond the beach to the peaceful ocean. She had been silent for a long time while Holden watched her where she sat. She drew a deep breath and finally looked at him.

"For a long time, I blamed myself for my father's death," she said gently while playing with her champagne glass. "I often thought there was something I should have done differently, but I don't know what that would have been."

"You know it wasn't your fault, right?"

She nodded. "Yeah, I do now," Jackie replied. "It took some time to come to terms with what happened to him." She snorted a soft laugh and offered a tiny grin. "And a lot of help from some very dear friends."

Holden stared at his champagne glass a moment then looked at her as she stared back at the ocean. "You don't think the guy survived falling from the plane, do you?" He shifted uncomfortably. "I mean, you were over a lake, but he couldn't have survived a fall like that, right?"

Jackie shrugged and remained uncertain. "He may have had mental issues, but he was still a former Navy SEAL. My father's team dropped many times from those distances on missions," she replied. "I'd like to believe he's dead." She finally looked at him. "It's kind of strange. I went back to my father's grave a week or so after the funeral, and I found a ring that looked a lot like the one he'd worn that day. I kept it for a while, thinking it belonged to someone who attended the funeral. When no one claimed it after a few months, I finally tossed it."

"Let's be honest," Holden announced simply and leaned back on his elbows. "If he had survived falling from the plane, he certainly wouldn't have left that sort of memento at your father's grave. I sincerely doubt he would have been feeling guilty about what he'd done."

"I sort of thought the same thing," she replied then lowered herself on the blanket alongside him. She leaned on her elbow facing him while looking into his eyes and smiled warmly. "But enough of that. I'm finally free from the governor's clutches, and I'd like to spend some time living for a change."

"I think I can accommodate you there," Holden replied with enthusiasm.

They leaned closer and kissed passionately. Further behind them, the helicopter was seen on the beach not far from where they lie. Even further back, it became obvious that the helicopter was sitting on the secluded beach of a tiny island no bigger than an acre in the middle of the ocean with nothing surrounding them.

t

*T*hree years earlier. The cemetery was peaceful in the early morning hours. The sun had barely risen and the grass was still wet with morning dew. The elaborate marble headstone of Lieutenant Commander Jackson Remus and his wife, Beverly Remus, sat stately on the immaculate cemetery grounds. Several flower arrangements remained from the burial just two days earlier, giving the grave a bright, cheerful look. A shadow was cast over the headstone. Zach stood proudly before the grave wearing his best suit and perfectly shined shoes. He had a solemn look on his face and kept his hands clasped firmly in front of him.

"I'm sorry I didn't make the funeral, Commander," Zach said gently. "I know you understand, considering the trouble you and the guys went through so I could go dark." He inhaled a deep, shaken breath. "My premeditated death aside, I did have other business that required my immediate attention. I know you'd understand how important this particular mission was." He offered a tiny, devious smile. "And, maybe one day, we'll swap war stories again, if they'll let me in wherever it is you've gone." His look again turned solemn. Zach saluted the headstone and fought the tears in his eyes. He laid something at the base of the headstone and straightened. "*Now* you may rest in peace, my friend."

Zach turned and walked away. At the base of the headstone lie a severed finger wearing the decorative Purple Heart ring.

✝

*P*resent day. Former Governor Lyle Kempton, now dressed in his official orange, prison jumpsuit, was led in handcuffs by a guard past a long row of cells. Prisoners yelled profanities and whistled at him as they did with all 'fresh meat'. The trial had just ended, and he'd been assigned his new home at the infamous penitentiary. He would never again leave the prison grounds, pending an appeal. Lyle sneered his distaste toward the other prisoners and their juvenile behavior.

"I won't be here long," Lyle announced to the guard in a gruff tone while glaring at his dark profile beneath his cap. "You'll see. I'll be out of here by the end of the week."

The guard pushed him into an empty cell and shut the cell door. It made a distinctive metallic clang. Lyle turned and placed his cuffed hands through the opening, allowing the guard to remove the handcuffs.

"I have friends in high places," Lyle remarked gruffly.

The guard replaced his handcuffs to their rightful place and stood just outside the cell door. He studied the former governor but didn't seem impressed by his words.

"Yeah?" the guard remarked while staring at him and finally lifted his cap to reveal Zach. "Well, that girl you tried to kill has friends in *low* places."

Lyle glared at the guard and appeared puzzled by the unusual comment. Zach gave the governor the most sinister grin and added a throaty chuckle.

"I hope you haven't forgotten our play date, Governor," Zach teased beyond his macabre smile.

The governor's expression suddenly dropped to the familiar voice and chilling words as horror showed in his eyes. "Guards! Guards!" he frantically cried out while looking around for signs of any other guards, but there were none to be found.

Zach chuckled evilly then casually walked away while whistling Chopin's "Funeral March".

Fade Out

Other books by Holly Copella!
Reviews left on Amazon are appreciated!

"The Battle for Andrea Maria"

A cruise ship attack turns six survivors into overnight celebrities after they take credit for the heroic act of a stowaway who died saving them.

The cruise is just what Jess needed--a bit of harmless fun far from her daily grind. But what begins as a relaxing vacation turns into a desperate fight for her life when terrorists take over the ship and start piling up bodies. Teaming up with a mysterious stowaway, Jess attempts to send out a distress call but knows they cannot wait for help to come. If she or the few remaining passengers have any hope for survival, Jess must act now. The papers dub it "The Battle for *Andrea Maria*," but to Jess it is the moment she fought side-by-side with her enigmatic Romeo, saving the ship--and losing him. She thinks the story ends there, but really, the nightmare is just beginning...

"Insanely Deadly"

When the dead return to life, it's up to an admiral's daughter and a mildly insane, former war hero to save their small town.

Jetta Cross, a Navy Admiral's daughter, is tasked with keeping her father's comrade, a former war hero turned town crazy, grounded in the real world. Capt. John Hunter is still fighting the war in his head, where imaginary dead people are part of his world. When a viral outbreak brings about a zombie uprising, Hunter is left to his own devices. He must resume his role as a one-man commando unit in order to destroy the ravenous undead. With Hunter still fighting his own inner demons as well as the undead, the townspeople fear their zombie neighbors may not be the only threat. Stranded at the island's luxurious resort with a handful of workers, Jetta is forced to live up to her father's reputation and take charge of the deteriorating situation at the hotel. She must wage her own war against the infected before the government declares her hometown a total loss.

"Deadly Institution"

A town recluse suspected of killing his wife teams up with a young woman in order to stop a killer.

After being accused of murdering his wife, Konrad Asher turns his back on the town that once adored him. Ten years later, he still holds his grudge and the title of the most feared man in town. With the reopening of the burned mental institution, where his wife had died, former employees are now murdered one-by-one, throwing suspicion back on Asher. A young local reporter, Jacey, is forced to reveal her long-time friendship with the infamous recluse in order to clear his name not only in the recent murders but to exonerate him in the death of his wife as well. Will Jacey's relationship with Asher invite the killer closer to her? Or is the killer already in her life?

"Screenplays: The Island Collection"
"Jungle Princess", "A.L.F. Resort", "Brighton Island"

Discover how romance and fun in the sun can be downright *chilling*!

"Jungle Princess" is a romantic/thriller that leaves a teenage girl stranded on an island with two male shipmates and a creature of "unknown" origin. She soon discovers the island is home to an abandoned prison with several prisoners roaming free. What really killed over one hundred prisoners? And is it still out there--?

"A.L.F. Resort" is a romantic/thriller set on an island resort with Artificial Life Forms as the main draw. At this resort, all your fantasies come true...until a malfunction removes safety inhibitors on the A.L.F.'s. Zombies, biker gangs, and mobsters run amuck, turning fantasies into nightmares. A young reporter gets more of a story than she anticipates, but will she survive long enough to write the story?

"Brighton Island" is a romantic/thriller set on a private island. When the owner's niece brings her psychic friend to the mansion, his presence awakens the spirits' tortured souls. As the psychic attempts to solve the old murders, the niece is confronted with the possibility that she's next to join the mansion ghosts. Stranded on the island with a crazed killer, her uncle wages his own war to save them. Will his "shock and awe" tactics actually save them or get them killed?

"Reaper of Souls" A fantasy short story

A young woman must outwit an evil sorcerer in order to save her brother or become one of his minions forever.

Unwilling to believe her brother is dead, Reggie discovers an underhanded deal made with Kahn, a less than ethical sorcerer, who collects humans to serve as slaves in his kingdom. In order to rescue her brother from his horrible fate, she must complete his failed task or be forced to serve Kahn forever. After being transported to his world, Reggie realizes that even if she beats Kahn at his own game, she's at his mercy for him to uphold his end of the deal. All seems lost until Kahn's discontented, self-serving brother, Helsing, arrives. Can Reggie convince Helsing to help her? And at what cost?

"Death Displacement"

A grief-stricken man travels back in time to seek revenge on the woman who murdered his girlfriend but inadvertently falls in love with her.

Kane is about to marry the woman he loves. His life is perfect. A few weeks before the wedding, a vindictive woman from his girlfriend's past mysteriously arrives and kills her. He learns of a traumatic accident that happened five years earlier, which triggers Riley's hatred for his girlfriend. Distraught over his girlfriend's death, Kane uses an antique time machine to travel into the past in order to find and destroy the woman responsible. When he runs into Riley's younger self, he realizes she's not the monster she later becomes, and he can't bring himself to destroy her. With a little help from his oddball friend from the past, they formulate a plan to prevent the accident that sends Riley down her destructive path. Kane's plan backfires when he falls for the younger Riley. His new tortured existence is further complicated when future Riley, his girlfriend's killer, shows up with her own devious agenda that doesn't include him. Will he be able to stop the time ripple, which ultimately ends with his girlfriend's death? Or will future Riley take him out of the timeline forever--

"Town Darling"

After surviving a brutal attack that claims the lives of those she loves, a young woman seeks revenge on a corrupt town.

Going back home is never easy, but for Casey, it means returning to her corrupt hometown where she barely survived a brutal attack. Accompanied by two *family friends*, she seeks justice for the night that destroyed her life. Her physical scars are nothing compared to her emotional ones, forcing the local sheriff to believe that the town darling is back for revenge. As the conspiracy for her revenge appears to be leading up to the coveted town fair, the sheriff is determined to stop her from fulfilling her vengeful scheme...but guilt over his role on that fateful night continues to haunt him. His desperate need for Casey's forgiveness could be his undoing.

"Dead Village"

After strange happenings isolate a small resort town from the rest of the world, nearly one hundred residents seek refuge at the closed hotel. Only eight survive the night. And that's just the beginning...

One day after the entire population of Fox Ridge Village disappears, a car wreck forces several unsuspecting crash victims to seek help at the closed summer hotel. Within the hotel, they discover the grisly aftermath of a brutal slaughter. Crash victims Vander and Devon, a reluctant clairvoyant, team up to solve the riddle of the "haunted hotel" and the mass hysteria plaguing the remaining survivors. By the time they discover the hotel's secret, they're already drawn into the hysteria. As the body count continues to climb, it's a race to isolate the source and bring everyone back to reality before they kill one another. Will Devon be able to communicate with the traumatized spirits before their fate becomes her own?

"Basement Dwellers"

A viral outbreak at a hospital leaves a mortician, sheriff, and coroner fighting for their lives against a horde of undead and the CDC.

After a massive car wreck leaves several survivors in critical condition at the local hospital, a surgeon uses experimental drugs on his critical patients and accidentally causes a zombie outbreak. When local mortician, Lexx, receives an infected corpse as her client, she becomes stranded in the hospital basement during CDC quarantine along with the local sheriff and the coroner. The infamous surgeon struggles to find a cure for his infectious blunder by using the other survivors as test subjects. Meanwhile, Lexx and the sheriff attempt to locate his missing sister, who's stranded somewhere in the battle zone that once was the emergency room. It's a race against time and the ravenous undead. Can they survive the undead before CDC sanitizes the hospital of all infection?

Coming Soon!
"Misfits, Inc."

A seemingly ordinary, young woman meets four misfits who claim she has given them supernatural powers.

While on a business trip to a remote island paradise, a bored secretary, Hailey, has her world turned upside down when her path collides with a psychic freak, Skyler. He attempts to convince her that they had met in his dreams, and she had chosen him as one of her four mystic warriors. After Skyler foresees a woman's death, they discover an unidentified creature has killed one of the guests. They are joined by a lounge pianist and a rich playboy, who also claim they had met her in their dreams. If Skyler's prophecies are genuine, the evil entity controlling the ravenous creatures needs to destroy Hailey to ensure its survival. Reluctantly accepting her fate, Hailey has to locate the last and most powerful of her chosen warriors, The Guardian. Their fate is in doubt when The Guardian turns out to be a self-absorbed, former cat burglar with a bad attitude. Can Hailey turn her company of misfits into an elite team of mystic warriors? Or will The Guardian's secret agenda destroy them all?

Coming Soon!
"Unconditional"

A young woman puts her life on hold to care for an unstable, highly skilled combat soldier, who believes someone is trying to kill him.

A botched military coup leaves a team of elite fighters injured with one clinging to life in a coma. When Harlan wakes from his coma, he's left with no memory of his past life. His commander's daughter, Indy, takes it upon herself to care for the fallen war hero. She's challenged with more than just his physical care as she combats with not only his memory loss but also his newly found desire for her. His infatuation with her becomes the least of her worries when he sinks back into his role of a combat soldier. Believing his life is in danger, his fighting skills surface, turning him into an unpredictable and dangerous man. Will his memory return to him before Indy is forced to commit him? Or will he finally find his nemesis, "the coyote", and claim the life of an innocent person?

ABOUT THE AUTHOR

Holly Copella has been writing since the age of twelve when her frustration at a book's poor plot drove her to author her own story. Over the last decade, she's written a number of screenplays, some of which she's now adapting into novels. Her fascination with zombies and other darker material lends an edge to her writing, which tends to lean toward horror. As a fan of Agatha Christie, she appreciates the craft of a good plot and the importance of creating significant characters.

Hailing from Pennsylvania, Copella lives in the Endless Mountains on a farm with her rescue horses and other animals. In addition to writing and reading fiction, she enjoys riding horses and traveling to Las Vegas and Disney World.

www.ingramcontent.com/pod-product-compliance
Lightning Source LLC
Chambersburg PA
CBHW060918180626
46817CB00004B/1311